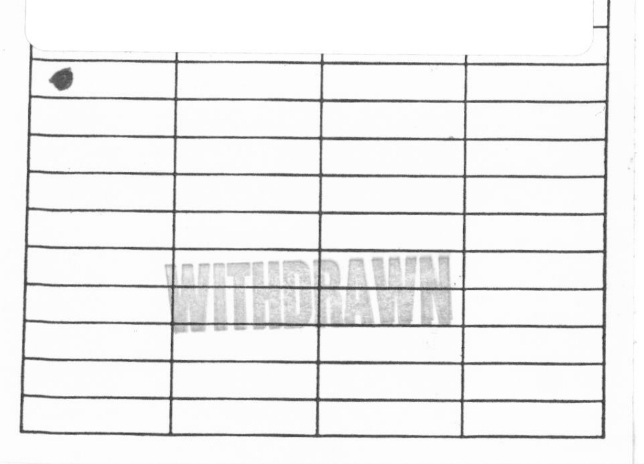
WITHDRAWN

THE TELLING

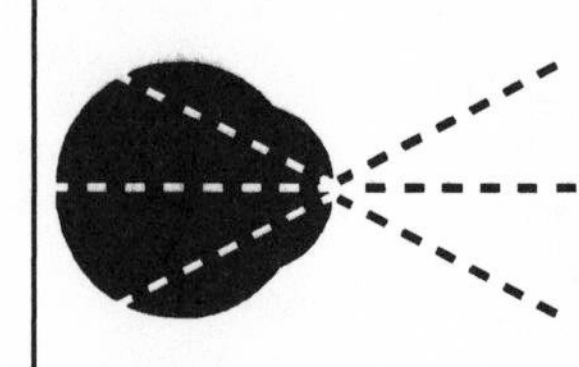

This Large Print Book carries the Seal of Approval of N.A.V.H.

The Telling

Beverly Lewis

THORNDIKE PRESS

A part of Gale, Cengage Learning

GALE
CENGAGE Learning™

Detroit • New York • San Francisco • New Haven, Conn • Waterville, Maine • London

GALE
CENGAGE Learning™

Seasons of Grace Series #3.
Thorndike Press, a part of Gale, Cengage Learning.

Thorndike Press® Large Print Christian Fiction.
The text of this Large Print edition is unabridged.
Other aspects of the book may vary from the original edition.
Set in 16 pt. Plantin.

LIBRARY OF CONGRESS CATALOGING-IN-PUBLICATION DATA

Lewis, Beverly, 1949–
The telling / by Beverly Lewis.
p. cm. — (Thorndike Press large print Christian fiction)
(Seasons of grace series ; no. 3)
ISBN-13: 978-1-4104-2259-0 (alk. paper)
ISBN-10: 1-4104-2259-3 (alk. paper)
1. Amish—Fiction. 2. Mothers and daughters—Fiction.
3. Large type books. I. Title.
PS3562.E9383T45 2010b
813'.54—dc22 2010004975

Published in 2010 by arrangement with Bethany House Publishers.

Printed in the United States of America
1 2 3 4 5 6 7 14 13 12 11 10

With love to Barbara,
my amazing sister.
One of the best storytellers I know.

A pity beyond all telling
Is hid in the heart of love . . .
— from *The Pity of Love,* Yeats

All we like sheep have gone astray . . .
— Isaiah 53:6a, KJV

Prologue

If the tables were turned, and *I* was the fancy young woman walking into a truck stop with my Amish friend this morning, I'd be choosing the table set back against the wall. *Away from curious eyes.* But Heather Nelson was the one deciding where we would sit. Wearing a loud pink short-sleeved blouse and pencil-thin blue jeans, she never once blinked an eye as she pulled out a chair and sat down . . . smack-dab in the midst of so many *Englischers.* Nearly all men, too.

Maybe she was oblivious to them — I can't really say. After all, this was a familiar world to her. As for me, my neck was mighty warm as I lowered myself into my chair, painfully conscious of the stares. I could just imagine what they were thinking about the two of us — *different as rosemary and sage.*

I reached for the menu right quick and

hid behind a long list of sandwiches, soups, and milk shakes. But my appetite was diminishing all the while my uneasiness was increasing. I lowered the menu and peered over the top at Heather. She leaned her ivory cheek into her fisted hand, her bare elbows on the table as she looked over the options. "See anything good?" she asked, her pretty blue eyes twinkling.

My mind was hardly on food. The upcoming reunion with my mother weighed heavily on me. We had driven for more than four hours and had just crossed into Ohio. *Only about an hour and a half till I see Mamma again.* My heart pounded at the thought. "I'll have something light to eat, if anything."

"A sweet roll?"

"Uh, prob'ly not." In a place like this, the sticky buns most likely came out of a box.

Heather glanced at her wristwatch. "Do you still want to arrive in Baltic by early afternoon?"

I nodded and turned to look out the window at the parking lot. I dreaded the thought of getting back in the car, nice as it was. With a sigh, I faced Heather again and was aware of two men looking our way. *"Truck drivers,"* Heather had told me when first we stopped to fill up the car.

"Grace?" She was frowning now, and the waitress was hurrying toward us. "What if we just ordered something for the road?"

I agreed as the waitress looked sideways at me before jotting down my order, her blond hair all *schtruwwlich* about her round face. "You two . . . um, together?"

Heather nodded, eyeing my prayer cap. She ordered some coffee and a cinnamon roll, then stopped, shook her head, and quickly asked if there was any fresh fruit. "Strawberries . . . an apple or two?"

After the waitress scurried off, I noticed the same two men still staring at us, their sleeves rolled up to their muscular shoulders. There were markings up and down their arms — a set of tiny baby footprints and a red rose with a black, thorny vine trailing clear down to one man's elbow. I'd never seen anything like it, and now I, too, was staring — at them. Had Mamma encountered similar worldly sights during her recent travels?

Heather squeezed my arm, tilting her head. "You all right, Grace?"

One of the men looked away, while the other seemed to be sneering.

"Frankly, I'm feelin' all in." I excused myself to the washroom to splash cold water on my face. I reached for the paper towels, which were not secured to the dispenser but stood on the ledge of the grimy sink. Quickly I tore off a piece and dried my face and hands, my fears rising. *How will Mamma react to seeing me?*

I raised my face to peer into the streaky mirror. At home our mirrors were mostly handheld ones . . . almost too small to allow me to see the whole of my head, let alone the upper bodice of my dress. Even my bureau had only a modest-sized mirror, not at all like the dressers at the home of our English neighbors, the Spanglers.

I felt momentarily ashamed. Mamma had always taught my sister, Mandy, and me not to be swayed by the temptation toward vanity. And we'd always heeded the warning. Well, nearly always.

Glancing again at my reflection, I didn't focus on my honey-blond hair peeking out from beneath my *Kapp,* nor the shape of my features. What I noticed caught me off guard as I studied my tired, even terrified, expression. I saw clearly now the uncertainty in my own blue eyes. Placing my hands on my cheeks, I breathed in ever so slowly. *Is this trip such a good idea, really?*

Sighing, I knew in my heart I was willing to put up with any awkwardness — even fear — if it meant bringing Mamma home.

No matter the gawking eyes or the inconvenience, I ought to cherish the trip for what it meant: a chance for Mamma to start over with a clean slate.

I turned on the water once again, washing my hands a second time — as if peering too long in the mirror had somehow tainted me. Surely by now Mamma understood that leaving without an explanation was a blight on us all. Besides, didn't she feel estranged, even cut off? Wouldn't she like to begin anew . . . if she could?

A chill ran down my back and I longed for my shawl as a comfort, if for no other reason. Then, reaching for the washroom doorknob, I left the small, dingy room. Shyly I moved back toward Heather's and my very public table, where Heather sat fiddling with her fancy little phone to check her email, as she'd done earlier while waiting to get gas for the car. I was grateful the two men now seemed more interested in their food than me.

I spotted our order already sitting on the table. "Did we get the bill?" I asked, reaching for the sack.

"Beat you to it." Heather smiled and clicked off her phone. She slung her purse over her shoulder.

I offered to treat next time. Then I squared

my shoulders and said, “Let’s be goin’,” and led the way to the door.

Little Lamb, who made thee?
Dost thou know who made thee?
Gave thee life, and bid thee feed
By the stream and o'er the mead;
Gave thee clothing of delight,
Softest clothing, woolly, bright;
Gave thee such a tender voice,
Making all the vales rejoice?
Little Lamb, who made thee?
Dost thou know who made thee?

Little Lamb, I'll tell thee,
Little Lamb, I'll tell thee:
He is called by thy name,
For He calls Himself a Lamb,
He is meek and He is mild;
He became a little child.
I a child, and thou a lamb,
We are called by His name.
Little Lamb, God bless thee!
Little Lamb, God bless thee!

— *The Lamb,* William Blake

Chapter One

There were days when Heather Nelson awakened in the silence, in that obscure first awareness of early morning, and believed she was back in Virginia. *Before Mom died of cancer.*

This had been one of those mornings. Yet in less than a minute, she'd remembered precisely where she was: upstairs in her cozy room in Andy and Marian Riehl's farmhouse, a real-life Amish tourist home. She was still too distracted by her own cancer diagnosis — and the recent visit from her father — to work more on her master's thesis, as she'd hoped. Her father was completely caught up in his plan to build a house in the middle of this Amish community. His revelation yesterday that she had Plain roots had jolted her, but she certainly understood a little better his reasons for relocating. And now here she was on this spontaneous trip she'd volunteered for, driving Grace Byler, the young Amishwoman in the seat next to her, to visit her runaway mother in the small Ohio town of Baltic. *Like the sea,* Heather thought, glancing at Grace, who looked so hopeful. And very healthy.

Will I die like Mom? I'm only twenty-four!

It was impossible to forget how deliberately her oncologist, Dr. O'Connor, had turned his solemn gaze away for a moment, giving Heather a chance to absorb the bad news — she had non-Hodgkin's lymphoma. There in his office, she'd stared at the back of his dark head as he looked toward the window, a frame for the parklike setting across the street. The sun, half covered by wispy cirrus clouds, had filtered its rays through the fragrantly blossoming crab apple trees below — some profusely pink, others delicately white.

That was five weeks ago. Today there were no such flowering trees near I-76, beyond the frontage road where Heather presently steered her car. The midmorning sun beat hard against a cluster of buildings, transforming the gleaming reflection of rows of windows into individual blinding darts of light.

Heather looked in the rearview mirror to check for traffic, then over her shoulder at the crowded truck stop where they'd stopped for gas and what had passed for healthy snacks. Cautiously now, she eased onto the ramp leading to the highway, feeling surprisingly invigorated in spite of the long drive.

They traveled without speaking as the car moved over the newly paved highway. Once they were situated in the right lane, Heather fumbled with opening the banana she'd purchased at the truck stop. There'd been no apples or strawberries — *"only bananas,"* according to the waitress.

Grace reached over and peeled Heather's banana halfway, then handed it back. She also opened Heather's bottled water and placed it in the holder on the console. "There," Grace said, offering a smile that almost concealed her obvious anxiety.

"Thanks." Heather glanced at the GPS on her iPhone, checking the directions ahead. As far as she could tell, they were making good time . . . right on schedule to pull up to Susan Kempf's house in less than two hours. And yet she wondered if Grace might be getting cold feet about seeing her mother. If so, who could blame her?

Heather ventured small talk. "Is the woman your mom's staying with a family friend?" They had been dancing around several issues during the trip, not delving into anything too personal. Heather actually preferred it that way, but Grace was typically much more talkative, although she seemed nervous today, if not on edge.

Grace shook her head. "I've never heard of Susan Kempf. I even asked *Dat,* and he said the name didn't ring a bell for him, either."

"What about Yonnie . . . you were talking with him yesterday. Wouldn't he know?" Heather had already admitted to having overheard Grace's conversation with the handsome young Amishman — even his suggestion that the two court.

Grace blushed. "No . . . I'm quite sure he doesn't know her."

"Did you ask him?"

"Wasn't time, really." Grace unfolded her hands and rested them against her black apron. "Yonnie's not originally from Ohio, anyways . . . he grew up in Indiana." She paused as if she was going to say more, then closed her mouth.

Heather took a small bite of the banana, waiting.

At last, Grace said, "I wondered what you thought, back at that truck stop. Truly unsettling, all those gawkers."

"We did draw some looks, didn't we?"

Heather laughed. "No doubt people are surprised to see us together. I mean, take a good look at us. . . ."

"We do appear to have little in common, *jah.* But there's *one* thing we share, though no one would know from just watchin' us." She turned to look at Heather, eyes solemn. "Both our mothers are gone."

Heather nodded slowly. "Mine passed away, and yours disappeared." *We have a Plain heritage in common, too,* she thought and contemplated telling Grace. *Would she even believe such an improbable thing?*

Grace touched her throat and her hand lingered there. "I know Mamma's leaving is not nearly the same as losin' someone to death."

"The loss has been tougher than I ever imagined," Heather conceded. She checked her rearview mirror again. "And . . . you know, I actually feel — oh, I don't know — ticked off when I think of your mom abandoning you and your family when she had a choice." She caught herself. Rarely was she so open about her emotions.

"Doesn't surprise me." Grace's face was suddenly drawn. "You must've had a close bond with your mother."

"Incredibly close," she whispered. She hadn't wanted to upset Grace, who continually exuded the gracious quality her name represented. The young woman was easily one of the most thoughtful people Heather had ever encountered. "I didn't mean to criticize your mother," she quickly apologized.

"I know you didn't," Grace replied. "I hope ya know how thankful I am, Heather . . . you drivin' me and all."

"Hey, I'm always up for a road trip."

Grace was still for a time. Then she said softly, "I don't blame ya for being aggravated 'bout my mother's behavior. I'm embarrassed by it, too."

Heather could see why. This sort of thing typically didn't happen without cause, even among non-Amish couples. Could it be possible there was something more to Lettie's escape into the night than even Grace had considered? "I wonder what your mom will say when she sees you," she said.

Grace sighed. "Honestly, I'm worried 'bout that."

"She'll be happy, right?"

"I really don't know." Grace grimaced. "Mamma's been close-lipped ever since she left last month. *Ach,* before that, really . . ." She began to talk about her mother's aloof behavior. Pausing, she stared out the window. "It all started when she ran into the twin sister of a long-ago friend at a barn raising we were attending near Strasburg. We'd gone there to help out with food."

Now, *this* was interesting. "A friend . . . or someone closer?" Heather asked, not sure she should probe further.

"That's all I best say," Grace replied.

"Sorry, don't mean to be nosy."

"*Denki* . . . for understanding." Grace turned again toward the window.

So there *was* something more to Lettie Byler's running off than met the eye. Heather had a strange feeling she might have gotten herself into something more complicated than a daughter's wanting to see her estranged mom.

Heather dropped the banana peel into the small hanging trash bag on the console. Then she pulled down the visor and reached for her sunglasses. *Just back off,* she told herself, feeling suddenly washed out — almost limp. All this talk about Grace's mother disappearing . . . she didn't understand why it bothered her so much. She didn't even know the woman.

Breathing deeply now, she tried to conserve her emotional energy, recalling Dr. LaVyrle Marshall's advice in the brochure for the Wellness Lodge: *Make every effort to avoid stress, which can cause serious dis-*

ease. But she hoped a permanent separation wasn't in the cards for the Bylers. She'd seen what that could do to families, had heard the horror stories from classmates who'd shared their pain, even the rage stemming from their parents' midlife crises. What made people go crazy like that — so selfish they couldn't see past their proverbial noses?

Like Devon Powers. Her ex-fiancé came to mind. In light of everything, Heather felt relieved, even happy, they'd split up. *I won't have to suffer his leaving me years from now . . . with kids in tow.* No matter how old, the innocent children always got the worst of it: a ripping apart at the heart seams.

Heather realized that whatever had gone wrong with Grace's mom had the potential to harm the Byler family. Yet, despite her concern for Grace, it was best she stay out of it no matter how much she might want to help. *I'll take Grace to see her mother and that'll be it.*

She needed to stay focused. Her stint at the Wellness Lodge began in four days — this coming Monday — and she couldn't allow herself to be deterred. No longer could she mark time where her health was concerned. Especially now, with her father supporting her decision to pursue alternative treatment.

Regardless of what happened in Ohio — good or bad — Heather was committed to returning to Pennsylvania by Saturday night at the latest. With or without Grace and her mom.

Chapter Two

It had been her maternal grandmother, *Mammi* Adah, who'd taught Grace Byler to print her name, even before Grace attended the one-room schoolhouse on Gibbons Road. Back when Grace was just five, Mammi Adah had insisted she use her right hand for writing her letters. *"You'll be a much better quilter if you're right-handed,"* Mammi Adah had always said, but never in a scolding tone. No, her grandmother had a unique way of pressing her influence on her grandchildren — and others. *"A back-door approach,"* Grace's mother had once whispered to her with a pained smile.

Now, as she read the travel directions on Heather's special phone, Grace tried not to dwell on what Mammi thought of her making such a trip, and with an Englischer, too. Several times she'd looked down at her lap, her hands clasped so stiffly she had to will them to relax. All the while, she prayed silently.

Presently, Grace wondered why Yonnie was so sure Mamma was visiting a *friend* in Ohio. Especially since neither Dat nor Mammi Adah had ever heard of a Susan Kempf. If she'd had more time prior to leaving the house early this morning, Grace might've run across the sheep pasture to ask neighbor Marian Riehl if she'd ever heard Mamma speak of this Susan. For the life of her, Grace could not remember her mother talking about anyone in Baltic, friend or relative.

Heather surprised her by starting to sing along with one of the songs stored on her fancy phone, bobbing her head and tapping her hand on the steering wheel. This made Grace even more nervous than Heather's juggling between what she called her "playlists" and the GPS. As the car sped up with the music, Grace literally held her breath.

They moved into the left lane and passed one car, then another, all without slipping back into the slower right lane. Grace watched the highway go by and wondered if she should say anything. It surely seemed as if Heather was lost in her music.

Then, when she felt certain Heather had far exceeded the speed limit, the worldly song abruptly ended. As if on cue, the car slowed and they moved back into the other lane, and Grace felt her muscles relax slightly. *For goodness' sake,* she thought, not wanting to interfere, yet hoping that wouldn't happen again. *What have I done, traveling with such a fast driver?*

Knowing there would be only a short lull before Heather's next tune began to play, and hoping to get her friend's attention on something other than her music, Grace asked tentatively, "What was your mother like?"

Heather checked the GPS once again before answering. "Well, she made the best spaghetti sauce in all of Virginia — even won first prize at the state fair — and couldn't wait every summer to ride up the road in a Lancaster Amish buggy." She paused a moment. "You know, when Mom learned she had cancer, she wanted so badly to live — she really fought it. After she died, there was this huge hole in my heart." She drew in an audible breath. "One that's still impossible to fill."

"If it's too painful . . ."

Heather nodded slowly. "Yes, that, but it's also maddening." She paused. "Mom's death was the very worst thing that's happened to Dad and me."

Grace almost wished she hadn't brought

it up. “One of my mother’s sisters passed away suddenly several years ago. But that’s the closest death has come to my family.” She rubbed her nose, hesitant again. “My mother cried and cried over Aunt Naomi, just heartbroken.”

Heather placed both hands on the steering wheel, nodding without speaking.

Grace thought just then of her mother and Aunt Naomi’s shared secret, but there was no need to reveal what she suspected about her mother’s first beau and his gift of poetry books — books Naomi had harbored for Mamma for many years. Or that Mamma was disappointed in her marriage . . . maybe even wished, secretly, she’d married someone else. But none of that was necessary for an outsider’s ears. Since Mamma’s leaving, Grace had been cautious, thinking twice about what she ought to say.

“I can’t imagine having a sister, much less losing her,” Heather said softly.

Grace thought of Mandy. “My own sister and I are quite close, too. But Mandy tells me more than I ever tell her.” Yonnie unexpectedly came to mind again. “I didn’t even share with her what Yonnie asked me . . . out on the road.”

“No kidding?”

“We don’t make a practice of talking ’bout

our fellas." She thought of Mandy's contrasting openness — her sister had recently shared that she hoped to soon be engaged.

"Not even if you're dating someone seriously?"

"Not even then." Smiling now, Grace explained, "And we call it courting, which often moves quickly to goin' for steady — almost engaged." She recalled how slow her former fiancé, Henry Stahl, had been to propose, but she quickly dismissed it. Grace was relieved that was over, and now Henry was most likely seeing Grace's best friend, Becky Riehl.

Heather passed the car ahead before she spoke again. "So, romance in the Amish world sounds pretty secretive."

"Oh, plenty of pairing up goes on. But it's not till a couple is published two weeks before the wedding that everyone truly knows who's getting hitched that year."

Heather pushed her light brown hair behind one ear. "Seriously?"

"Jah, it's our way."

"So I guess that means you're not going to tell me what you think of Yonnie." Heather laughed a little. "I mean . . . I *overheard* what he was saying to you."

Grace smiled, surprised she felt comfortable enough to talk like this. Truth was, off and on all during this trip, she'd pondered Yonnie's proposing that they court. No getting around it, there were some mighty big roadblocks to that happening — Mamma's absence being one of them. And even though Yonnie seemed to be finished getting to know other girls, she still wasn't certain how fickle he might be.

"He seemed very eager for your answer," Heather added.

Grace opened her window a little and breathed in the fresh outside air. "I'll admit that sometimes there *are* a few trusted people, mostly sisters or close friends, who are taken into confidence once a girl knows she's gettin' married," she said. "And mothers . . ."

Heather's heart-shaped face was accentuated by her faint smile. "Looks like I'm out of luck, then."

Grace was surprised at her wistful tone. *Surely she has many good friends back home in Virginia.*

Heather glanced again at her playlist. "Well, if you're not going to tell me, I guess I'll just have to guess what you think of Yonnie."

"Ach, it's too soon after bein' engaged to Henry. . . ." But that was far from the truth. How could a girl not appreciate such a kind and helpful fellow? Goodness, Yonnie had basically nursed their horse Willow back to full health, and in only a few days, too. And he had a winning way of making just about anyone, Dat included, feel at ease around him. Even so, what Grace thought about Yonnie was for her own heart to know and understand.

Heather brought up her own former fiancé, saying she'd liked him immediately. "Devon and I were attracted to each other from the start." She sighed as if she was disgusted with herself. "But that's over now."

"You know, I'm not sure I even want to marry," Grace confessed.

"Hey, I'm right there with you."

A great river spilled over Grace, sentiments desperate for a voice. She had felt like this before on the night of her twenty-first birthday, after she'd read the sweet note her mother had finally written on the pretty birthday card. *I will always love you, Grace.* Yet Mamma had disappeared before the sun rose that next morning.

She inhaled slowly, then began to open up a bit. "Frankly, before I can think of marriage, things need to be resolved . . . 'tween my parents, I mean. But I'm not sure that's even possible. Truly, I hope so, but I just don't know." She gathered her thoughts, yearning to feel calm again. "I can't say if I want to be courted by Yonnie or not. My mind's locked up these days . . . need to see how things are with Mamma first." She shocked herself at this admission.

Heather loosened her grip on the wheel. "Things are obviously up in the air for you."

"In nearly every way." Oh, but now she felt self-centered. "Well, I can't complain. You . . . you're the one who has every right to be concerned." She didn't need to mention Heather's worrisome illness. "I'm ever so sorry."

Heather shrugged but said nothing more.

If only I'd kept quiet, Grace thought, wishing she'd brought along a good book or some needlework. Instead, she reminded herself of the Lord's admonishment about fretting. *We're commanded not to worry.*

She turned her thoughts away from Heather Nelson and Yonnie Bontrager — and dear Mamma — and offered a heartfelt prayer for her family back home. Especially for poor Dat.

Then, staring at the air bag warning on the visor, Grace tried to relax. She leaned her head back and soon began to doze off.

She dreamed she stood in the kitchen doorway, watching her mother bustle about to lay out a hearty meal with a smile on her pretty face. *Home at last!* Grace thought. But then she realized with a sinking feeling that the kitchen was not *their* kitchen at all.

Suddenly Mamma looked up and saw Grace standing there. Grace smiled, but Mamma did not smile back. She glared.

Oh! Grace awakened with a start.

She was filled with more dread as each mile passed, and as they moved closer and closer to the truth.

Chapter Three

Lettie Byler finished reading from the Old Testament prophet Habakkuk early that afternoon, going back to reread some of her favorite verses in chapter three: *Although the fig tree shall not blossom, neither shall fruit be in the vines; the labour of the olive shall fail, and the fields shall yield no meat; the flock shall be cut off from the fold, and there shall be no herd in the stalls: Yet I will rejoice in the Lord, I will joy in the God of my salvation.*

Closing the Bible, she moved her chair closer to the window. Sitting again, she faced the narrow country road and stared out at an ocean of cornfields. Tired of living out of her suitcase, Lettie was also becoming weary of being a guest, although at least she was amongst her own people instead of in an Englischer's motel.

With the remarkable passage lingering in her mind — *Yet I will rejoice in the Lord* — she thought of her rather unfruitful search for her firstborn. She wondered if anyone had ever suspected the truth, back when she was carrying Samuel's child and *Mamm* had taken her away to Kidron, Ohio, to have the baby there. Lettie had worried that her closest family members — especially her sisters — and Samuel himself might guess her secret. Maybe they'd seen a hint of the guilt in her eyes or in the way she carried herself, shielding her stomach and the delicate life that was part hers and part Samuel's.

Yet all the while, she had attempted to trust God for her precious unborn child . . . and for the unknown future. Especially in the wee hours before dawn, Lettie had sometimes fretted, questioning if God would supply a husband for her if she was to keep her baby, as she longed to.

She remembered lying in the sweet meadow grass after chores one evening, running her hands over the length of the dark green blades and relishing the sound of bees buzzing past her . . . the sharp scent of clover in her nostrils. With her baby residing within her, Lettie had wanted to do God's will above all things — now that she'd committed the transgression. Oh, it would've been so easy to go her own way and not do her parents' bidding even then.

Like I ended up doing all these years later, going in search of my child without telling Judah . . . or Mamm and Dat.

Recalling midwife Minnie Keim's insistence that she must eventually forgive her mother, Lettie bit her lip. For too long she'd harbored bitterness toward Mamm. Had it become too much a part of her to let go?

Lettie leaned forward to watch a car turn and drive into the lane below. "Probably someone come to buy strawberry jam," she muttered absently.

Getting up, she found her writing tablet and pen on a small table near her suitcase. For several days she'd contemplated writing a letter to Samuel. She knew now what she must tell her former beau, the father of the daughter neither had ever known — and might never meet.

Picking up the pen, she began to write.

Dear Samuel,

I hope you are well.

Several times before now I've thought of writing to you. Maybe you've been wondering about my search. I must admit that it has been ever so difficult. I'd nearly given up hope of ever finding our child when, at last, I located the midwife who assisted me. And she believes I gave birth to a baby girl — something she managed to remember despite delivering hundreds of babies. She also gave me the name of the doctor who placed our child . . . hopefully with an Amish couple. Oh, I do trust and pray that is so!

I will let you know when I find out more . . . if I do.

Until then,
Most sincerely,
Lettie Byler

Setting down the pen, Lettie had a fleeting thought of her children back home. How she longed to see them again! But she would not mention them to Samuel, not allowing herself to become too familiar . . . nor too friendly. It was bad enough she'd gone shamelessly to visit him at his home in Kidron.

No, it was best she kept her distance now. *Till I find our daughter . . . and then what?* For the life of her, she could not imagine how that awkward reunion might possibly take place, or where. And would their child — if Lettie found her — even agree to such a meeting?

Prior to setting out for Ohio, Lettie hadn't known how to handle the ins and outs of all this, although many nights she had pondered the weighty matters while walking the dark, deserted cornfield. She still felt as though she was groping her way in the depths of the unknown. And she felt guilty that she had never let Judah help her, or even told him of her great secret.

Lettie rose from the chair, going to stand beneath a pretty hand-stitched wall hanging. She'd found herself staring at it several times since coming here, as if trying to fasten the words in her own mind: *Remember not the sins of my youth, nor my transgressions: according to thy mercy remember thou me for thy goodness' sake, O Lord.*

"Amen — and may it be so, dear Jesus," Lettie prayed, clasping her hands.

It was well past noon when Grace spotted the farmhouse matching the address on the GPS. "There 'tis." She pointed, her heart in her throat.

Oh, goodness . . . we're here at last!

Heather slowed the car to turn into the driveway. "Should I park here or out on the road?"

The girls deliberated whether or not it might be more courteous to park near the mailbox or in the driveway. "Let's pull in a little ways," Grace finally said. "Just off the road, maybe."

She stared at the house and lovely yard, where profuse ground cover and an edging of pink lady slippers grew in the light shade beneath an oak tree out front. Grace remembered her vivid dream earlier and drew a deep breath. When she could no longer stand the suspense, she opened the car door. *Oh, please let Mamma be happy to see me.*

Together, she and Heather made their way up the drive. Because she was traveling, Grace had worn her black leather shoes, something she was glad of as she picked her way across the pebbled lane.

Heather commented on the amount of land surrounding the house. "It reminds me of the Riehls'." Grace agreed. A good-sized horse barn stood directly behind the farmhouse, and there was pastureland beyond that. The road running past the front yard had two lanes, just like back home, with cornfields creeping right up to the grassy ditches on either side.

Tentatively, she glanced at Heather, who looked quite calm as they walked to the porch. It seemed so peculiar to make their way toward the front door. At home, no one ever used a home's main entrance, except on a Preaching Sunday or for a funeral. "I'm ever so nervous," Grace admitted, wishing it was her best friend, Becky, standing beside her instead; she might've reached for her hand for a bit of consolation. But this was not Becky — rather, a young woman Grace had met only recently. She certainly didn't know Heather well enough to ask for any emotional support, even at such an unnerving moment.

"Let's find out where your mom is," Heather replied, her expression kind. "You ready?"

Nodding, Grace put on a smile. She didn't know why, but she almost felt the house had eyes as she stood there. *Is Mamma watching?*

Heather hung back a bit, saying she thought Grace's mother should see Grace first. "In case she answers the door."

Nodding, Grace stepped forward and raised her hand to knock.

Judah Byler had been hard at work all morning, glad to be busy. His day had included looking over the older lambs, which were in the process of being fattened up for summer's end, when they would be sorted into feeder lambs and those ready for slaughter.

Following the noon meal he'd returned to the sheep barn, keeping his mind fully occupied. Mandy had served the delicious tuna and noodle casserole in Grace's stead, dutifully reminding everyone that her sister had prepared the meal ahead of time. Lettie's former place at the table, where Grace had been sitting these past two weeks, looked especially vacant, and his father-in-law, Jakob, seemed out of sorts, even leaving most of the talking to Judah's youngest son, Joe, and Yonnie. Unusual, as Jakob had seemed to take a liking to Yonnie.

Son Adam had commented favorably on the rhubarb crunch dessert, but other than that, Judah's oldest was also strangely silent. *They're all missing Grace,* he thought now. *And Lettie, too.*

To think both his wife and daughter were off somewhere, gone so far away. *Home's where they belong.* But if things went well, perhaps Grace might be bringing Lettie back tomorrow . . . or the next day.

If Judah let himself contemplate Grace's trip . . . well, he found himself grinding his teeth from a bad case of nerves. Just where was his daughter by now? Had she found Lettie?

He thought of asking Andy Riehl to phone the young driver, Heather, on her cell phone. Momentarily Judah envied Andy's barn phone — used for the family's bed-

and-breakfast business — but the idea was a mere flicker. Besides, he had been patient about Lettie this long; couldn't he simply let things play out the way the Lord God intended?

Yonnie caught his eye as he squatted to pick up the youngest and frailest lamb, not two yards from where Judah stood. "You think they've arrived yet?" asked Yonnie over his shoulder. "Grace and the Englischer?"

"Funny," he muttered, watching Yonnie raise the little white lamb to his face and nuzzle its tiny head. "I was wonderin' the same thing."

"Sure hope you ain't put out with me, Judah."

"Fer was?"

"For tellin' Grace where your wife's staying out there in Ohio."

How could he be upset? Yonnie had merely passed along the information his sister had heard from Preacher Josiah's wife, Sally. It had been Judah's own decision to allow Grace to go to Baltic with the Riehls' worldly boarder. "No one's put out, no," he said. "It'll be nice havin' my wife and daughter both home . . . safe and sound."

Yonnie nodded and petted the lamb. "Grace was mighty anxious to get goin'."

Judah knew she'd been itching to locate

Lettie and bring her home for some time — nearly since Lettie'd gone. No one could ever accuse Grace of dillydallying. But as for his own procrastination — doing nothing at all to fetch his wife — well, he supposed not taking action had changed the entire course of his life. Frozen by indecision, plain and simple.

Yonnie wandered off with the lamb in his arms, seemingly satisfied with Judah's response. Judah could see him, heading over to the horse stable, probably to look in on Willow. The old mare had certainly surprised him, improving each day against all odds. Judah watched the tall, strong lad — who'd once flat-out admitted he had his hopes set on Grace — till Yonnie disappeared from view behind the stable door.

Judah didn't feel much like smiling as he went to check on the last of the pregnant ewes. There was no way to know what lay in store if Lettie did return. Surely she'd want to give him some explanation, and boy, would he listen this time. After all, something mighty unpleasant had caused her to run away in the first place. And in the deep of his heart, he was convinced it was mostly his doing.

But supposing Lettie doesn't come back, Judah fretted. What if the thing that had sent her away also kept her from wanting to return?

He scratched his beard and wondered unexpectedly what that might do to Yonnie's plan to court and woo Grace. And what of Adam and Joe? The whole business was bound to affect them . . . and their future as husbands. Fact was, the entire family's standing in the church was at risk.

Preacher Josiah had stopped by this morning to say that the ministerial brethren were in agreement: *"Lettie has one full week to get back home and confess before the People."*

Or else, Judah thought, mighty worried about the *Bann* being put on his wife.

Hearing Yonnie talking slowly now to Willow, he realized how fond he'd become of the young man. Sighing, he freshened the bedding straw for the ewes closest to delivery, all the while attempting to dismiss his fears.

O gracious Lord, keep Lettie in your watchcare, he prayed as he worked. *And may she return before the shun falls on her.*

Chapter Four

The sun beat hard on the back of her neck as Grace waited for someone to come to the door. She felt too warm as she turned to ask Heather, "Should I knock again?"

"Why not?"

Grace stared at the door. "Maybe they're away." She knocked once more, aware of the pounding of her heart.

Finally, a woman who looked to be close to her mother's age answered the door. Her hair bun was a bit looser and higher than Grace's and the sides were not as tightly twisted as the womenfolk's in Bird-in-Hand.

"Hullo," Grace said. "I hope this isn't a bad time." She paused and offered a smile. "Are you Susan Kempf?"

"Jah." The woman's brown eyes sparkled as she searched Grace's face. "And who are you, dear?"

"Grace Byler . . . I understand my mother's here visitin'."

"Grace, you say?" Susan's face lit up. "Ach, I've heard so much about you!" She looked quizzically at Heather now and motioned for both of them to come inside. "*Willkumm.* Make yourselves at home."

"This is Heather Nelson, a friend of mine . . . she drove us here from Lancaster County."

"Goodness' sakes, all that way?" Susan ushered them into her front room and offered them a seat on a small settee.

Grace couldn't help looking around the room, wondering if her mother was within earshot. "The time went fast, really." Then, because she felt like she might burst if she didn't ask, she said, "Is my mother here with you?"

Susan turned in her chair to face Grace. "Oh, honey-girl, your mother left yesterday afternoon . . . while I was away visitin' my sister." She paused, sitting straight up in the chair. "It surprised me no end that she should up and leave like that."

Grace frowned hard. How could this be? Her head throbbed at the temples. So they'd just missed her? Or had Mamma suspected someone might come to fetch her, what with the grapevine wending back to Bird-in-Hand?

"I'm so sorry," Susan said.

Wringing her hands, Grace stared at the polished hardwood floor. Heather leaned near and touched her back briefly. Grace managed to ask, "Where'd she go, do ya know?"

Susan's eyes reflected Grace's pain. "She talked about possibly goin' to see a cousin named Hallie. She was waiting to hear from her, in fact . . . but she never said she'd received a letter back." The older woman gazed at the ceiling. "She also mentioned wanting to see a particular doctor in Indiana." Susan stopped for a second. "I don't recall his name."

"A doctor?" *First a midwife, now a doctor?*

Susan nodded warily.

A cloud of rejection fell on Grace. *Of course, Mamma doesn't know I set out to find her.* Still, she felt simply crushed in spirit. That, and terribly frustrated.

She sat there as the afternoon sun poured through the front windows, wondering what to say next. And, bless her heart, Susan looked terribly uncomfortable, too.

"Maybe we should excuse ourselves and get going," Heather whispered.

But Grace could not abide the idea of leaving, not when they'd just arrived. The whole, long ordeal streamed over her once again, and she leaned her face into her hands. Oh, she'd wanted this to turn out so differently! How could Mamma *not* be here, waiting to be found? *Wanting to be found . . .*

She raised her head. In a whisper, she asked, "Is Mamma unwell? Is that why she needs a doctor?"

"You can rest assured your mother is not sick. Not by any means." Susan rose quickly.

Wherever she's gone now . . . is Mamma happy? Grace hoped so, yet she questioned if that was possible. *So far away from her family.*

Susan offered them something to drink. "I've got some sweetened meadow tea and homemade root beer — which would ya like?"

Grace turned toward Heather to see if she cared for anything. "What do you want to do?" she asked softly.

"It's up to you," Heather replied.

"I *am* thirsty."

Heather nodded. "I'll have the tea, thanks."

"Same for me," Grace replied. And while Susan was in the kitchen and presumably unable to hear, Grace bemoaned their situation to her new friend. "Now what? You've pushed yourself hard to get here; you need to rest."

Heather's eyes were serious. "We certainly

didn't plan on this, did we?"

"Oh," she sighed, "why didn't Mamma tell Susan where she was headed?"

She and Heather sat quietly, taking in the simple furnishings, so similar to those in Dat's farmhouse. A wood-framed needlepoint picture graced the wall over the sideboard in the smaller sitting room, only a few steps from where Grace sat. She certainly didn't care to snoop, but from her vantage point, the upholstered gray rocker looked a lot like Mammi Adah's back home, as did the pretty pink-and-cream-colored hurricane gas lamp nearby.

It crossed her mind to borrow Heather's cell phone to make a call to the Riehls' — or to Sally Smucker's boutique phone — to get word to Dat that she'd arrived here safely. But now, with Mamma already gone again, wouldn't that only upset them?

"We can't just turn around and drive back today," Grace said.

"I guess we could, but . . . I am pretty wiped out." Heather sighed. "We can talk about where to stay later, in the car."

Meanwhile, Susan was coming their way, carrying a tray of goodies — not only the iced tea, but two kinds of cookies, too: butterscotch icebox and hermits. "Here we are, girls. This should perk you up a bit . . . just till suppertime, that is."

She must think we're staying! Grace looked at Heather.

Susan nodded with a smile. "I'm sure you could use a rest, jah?"

"Denki . . . ever so kind of you." Grace reached for a glass of tea.

"Oh, take a cookie or two," Susan urged. "I doubt you stopped for a nice hot meal on the road. Did you?"

Heather smiled but didn't take a cookie. "Unfortunately, one of us is on a very strict diet."

"Ach, you girls look fit as all get-out." Susan tilted her head comically. "Please say you ain't tryin' to lose weight — neither of ya?"

Grace glanced at Heather, but it was her friend's place to bring up her illness.

"Oh, it's definitely not that; I'm trying to eat more healthfully," Heather explained.

"Well, would you prefer fresh fruit? I have some in the kitchen." Susan set the tray down on a small table near the settee.

"Yes, please," said Heather.

Quickly, Susan returned with a bowl of fresh strawberries, bananas, and sliced apples. "Here we are, dear."

"Great, thanks," Heather said, reaching for a napkin and a few berries.

"Getting back to wherever my mother went," Grace said once Susan sat again, "did she mention when — or if — she might be returning to Lancaster County?"

"Not really, no." Susan paused, a strange look on her face. It was as if she didn't trust herself to say more — as if she'd made some sort of promise to Mamma.

But Grace couldn't feel poorly toward Susan. Not as nice as she was — inviting them to stay for supper, no less.

"How do you know my mother?" Grace said more softly. "If I can be so bold to ask."

"Why, sure . . . I'm happy to say." Susan described how she'd met Grace's mother at a local restaurant. "I waitress there part-time. Your mother looked so lonely when she came in one evening, like she needed a friend."

So Susan had been a *stranger?* Such a revelation made Grace cringe. She did not understand one speck of this!

"I invited her to come and stay here with me, beings I'm a widow and alone myself. She was hesitant at first, but when she was able to get the little motel in town to refund her money, your mother came. She seemed truly anxious for company."

This didn't sound like something her mother would do. Grace shook her head.

"Are we talking 'bout Judah's Lettie from Bird-in-Hand?"

"The selfsame." Susan went on to say she'd heard from Lettie about Grace's father, Judah, and her siblings, Adam, Mandy, and Joe. "And all the new little lambs comin' on this spring."

Lambing season. Grace felt badly for having left her father at such a busy time. But she'd also promised to return quickly, and now that Mamma was clearly not here, they would be home by tomorrow evening at the latest. "Did she ever say what she was doin' here . . . in Ohio?"

Susan glanced down at her lap. "Not at first."

Heather made a little sound and rose, making a beeline to the door. "I'll let the two of you talk alone." With that, she was gone.

Susan eyed the door. "Is Heather a friend of yours?"

Grace nodded. "She's not accustomed to our ways, so she prob'ly thought you wanted privacy."

"Well, that's not the case," Susan was quick to say. "Not at all."

"I don't mean to pry." Grace was eager to know what Mamma's new friend knew but wasn't sharing.

"Heather — your English friend — looks awfully pale. Is she feelin' all right?"

"She did all the drivin', so naturally she's tired." Grace realized that she, too, was holding back.

"Well, I hope the two of you will stay the night. Your Mamma would insist, as well — if she were still here."

Would Mamma have insisted on riding home with us, too? Grace looked out the window and saw Heather leaning with her back against the car, working her thumbs on her little phone.

"Why'd Mamma leave so suddenly from here . . . do ya know?"

Susan adjusted her Kapp, then sighed. "Grace . . . can you trust me?" Her eyes glimmered. "She's goin' to be all right . . . and so are you. Your mother will be home in due time."

"But when?"

"When her search is finished." Susan brushed her tears away. "That's all I best be sayin'."

What search?

In spite of her frustration, Grace's heart went out to Susan, seeing how moved she was. *So Mamma will return home eventually.*

Grace glanced out the window again, but Heather was no longer near the car. "Well, I ought to be checkin' on my friend."

"Please feel free to rest up or do as you wish," Susan invited. "You'll each have your own room upstairs . . . if you'd like."

"That's very nice of you. I'll see if Heather wants to stay." She rose and moved toward the door. Her black shoes seemed out of place in Susan's neat and tidy front room. Then, turning, she gave the generous woman a smile. "I can see why Mamma wanted to be here . . . with you."

Susan placed a hand on her chest and nodded. "She's a dear woman. I'm just glad I could help her out during this time."

Grace felt thankful for Susan, too, but she was completely mystified by Mamma's peculiar behavior. She gathered her wits and reached for the doorknob to let herself out.

Chapter Five

The last thing Heather wanted to do was sit, whether in Susan Kempf's house or back in the car. Her back ached, her thighs were numb . . . her brain hurt. To think they'd made this trip for nothing. Like Grace had said, *now what?*

Actually, it looked as if they were being offered a night's lodging at Susan's. And because Lettie's friend was so kind, Grace would undoubtedly want to settle in for the rest of the day. *We can get up early and head out tomorrow.*

For now, though, Heather could not imagine making small talk during a long, drawn-out meal in Susan's kitchen. If she were back at Marian Riehl's place, she'd probably opt out once again and go walking beneath the trees along Mill Creek. Compelled to get some exercise here, as well, Heather grabbed her sunglasses and hurried north on the little stretch of road, wondering where it might lead.

As she went, she occasionally admired the astonishingly straight rows of corn on either side of the road. She felt literally surrounded by acres of the low cornstalks, enjoying the idyllic setting. *Like I belong here somehow,* she mused. *Dad said I was born out here . . . to an Amish girl.*

Dad's sudden revelation was still nearly incomprehensible. Not only hard to believe, but, for someone who'd grown up so incredibly modern, even mind-bending on some level.

She lifted her hair and let the air cool her neck. What she wouldn't give for a firm bed right now. That and some salty chips and chocolate ice cream.

Her phone chimed and she saw that Wannalive — or Jim, as the blogger had recently revealed his name to be — was texting her again. Of course, she'd gotten things started earlier while pumping gas at the truck stop, telling her online friend about the impulsive road trip. But she hadn't revealed she was driving her new Amish friend to visit her mom until just a few minutes ago.

Hey, I know some Amish farmers, he'd written back.

She was cautious in her reply, not saying where she and Grace had ended up: the smallest town she'd ever seen. But where had *he* encountered Plain folk? Amish farmers were buying up land from Kentucky to Montana, according to her dad, with some even settling into the southern Colorado hamlets of Westcliffe and Monte Vista.

To think my "English" dad's doing the opposite, moving into an established Amish community like he is.

Thanks to her dad's recent visit to the Bird-in-Hand area, she'd had a crash course in Amish-style home building after he lined up preacher-contractor Josiah Smucker to build his house. She laughed, even though the surprising turn of events continued to perplex her. Dad's excuse was that it had much to do with his and Mom's hope to retire someday in Lancaster County, a connection having formed to this particular part of the country during their visits there over the years.

Familiar as Heather was with the Lancaster Amish, she'd never really been to this part of Ohio before — that she knew of, anyway. Here in the place of her birth, the reality of her roots struck her, and for the life of her, she didn't understand the instant surge of raw emotion. Moved by the serenity of nature encircling her, she breathed in the air's fragrance to keep from crying. She had walked farther than she'd intended to, and she was almost relieved when her phone chimed again.

This time it was Dad. *Did you arrive in Ohio, kiddo?*

Sure — easy for a girl with a GPS, she quickly replied. She laughed, unable to help herself. Better to laugh than to weep senselessly.

Then, since she was in texting mode again, she sent one back to Jim: *Looks like I might be on a wild goose chase here.*

Quickly, Jim replied. *How are you doing?*

I'm wiped out. But my Amish friend and I haven't decided what to do yet. Doubt we'll turn around and drive right back.

Well, take it easy, he responded. *Hope things work out there.*

Thanx.

She waited, feeling a little surprised that she hoped he'd write again. But more than five minutes passed and his texts had ceased. Glancing back down the road, she estimated she'd already walked a good half mile from Susan Kempf's farmhouse. Was Grace getting caught up on her mom's whereabouts to her satisfaction? Heather hoped so . . . wanting something good to come of this trip. *For Grace's sake.*

Pushing her phone into her jeans pocket,

she reached into her shirt pocket and pulled out a hair binder. She gathered her thick hair into a ponytail and secured it, feeling nearly childlike as she relished the rolling landscape, utterly aware of the ticking of insects on all sides.

Lettie stared at the floral psalm calendar and silently counted the days till the summer solstice — June twenty-first. Oh, so many hot and humid days ahead. As a girl, summertime had always seemed long, back when June and July lingered like a tomato slow to ripen.

Now it was nearly Memorial Day, the official start of summer for most folk. And here she was in Nappanee, Indiana, at Cousin Hallie Troyer's, still far from Bird-in-Hand. She'd heard Hallie's jam or jelly customer leave by way of the wheezing screen door only a few minutes ago. Hallie's strawberries had come on much earlier than usual. *"A good thing for business,"* Hallie had told her last evening, when Lettie first arrived.

Having relaxed in her room following the noon meal, Lettie felt it was time to venture downstairs to visit some more. She stepped into the hallway, enjoying the feel of the well-worn runner against her bare feet.

There was only one more important thing to accomplish before she could locate her daughter.

One more necessary thing . . .

In her letter to Lettie inviting her to come, Cousin Hallie had seemed rather elated at the prospect of a visit. That and full of questions. It was time to fess up, though not fully; Lettie was wiser than that. She would not share with Hallie the things she'd so openly told Susan while in Baltic. As fond as she was of sweet Hallie, Lettie felt sure it was best to keep mum about her search for her lost child. A faraway stranger-turned-friend was one thing, but revealing all of this to such a close cousin? That sort of connection had a way of divulging such news against one's hopes . . . and better judgment, too.

She closed her eyes and pondered a line from the Lord's Prayer. *Forgive us our debts, as we forgive our debtors.* Indeed, Lettie had much to be forgiven for.

Creeping down the long staircase, she was careful to grip the handrail. She'd slipped before — slipped and fallen — on steps this steep back in Kidron while she and Mamm were helping her father's ailing aunt, when she was expecting her first baby. *When my pregnancy was supposedly a secret.* But her great-aunt, ill and elderly as she was, had put it together when Mamm insisted Lettie rest on the sofa, urging her to get off her feet *"right quick."* Mamm had been worried — even seemingly convinced — that Lettie would miscarry after her fall.

The secret . . . ended by a mere accident. Even Mamm had not wished for that. Sighing, Lettie dismissed the melancholy musings. She was plagued enough by nighttime worries without allowing such thoughts during the day.

Downstairs, she made her way through the kitchen and found Hallie in the front room, sitting near the widest window, embroidering a pillowcase, her reading glasses perched halfway down the bridge of her nose. A rose-shaped design was centered perfectly in the embroidery hoop.

"May I borrow your phone book?" Lettie asked.

Hallie looked up, her cheeks bright with peachy red spots. She wore a wine-colored dress and matching half apron, and a cup-shaped white Kapp with pleats that covered her tightly bound hair bun. "Not sure I've got one."

Lettie had seen one under the table near the front room sofa, though why on earth her cousin owned it, Lettie hadn't any idea.

"Actually, you do. See? Right there," she said, nodding at the small table.

Hallie looked surprised. "Well, it's prob'ly so out of date."

"That's all right." Lettie went to lift it out of its hiding spot. Needing to see with her own eyes that Dr. Joshua Hackman did indeed practice medicine in Nappanee, she opened to the *H*'s and ran her pointer finger down the page. *Hackenberg . . . Hackett . . . Hackford . . .*

"What do ya want with it?" Hallie asked, her head tilted inquisitively like a puppy's.

"Oh, just looking up someone I once knew," Lettie said absently.

Hallie whispered to herself as she sat there. Was she counting stitches?

There it is! Lettie was greatly relieved to see Dr. Hackman's office was in fact located nearby. *This should be easy.* She yearned for this to work out . . . just as she'd dreamed all these years. *I've come this far.*

"Hallie, where might I find a telephone in the neighborhood?" She felt strange asking.

"Eddie and Lana, our neighbors up the hill, have one." Hallie peered over her glasses. "They don't seem to mind folks traipsing in and out."

"You sure?"

Hallie laughed a little. "Would I lead you

astray, Lettie? We've known each other since childhood." Hallie's father and two first cousins and their families had all pulled up roots from Lancaster County to relocate here in Nappanee when Hallie was only eleven, pleased at the prospect of more available land. Yet even after she'd gone, Hallie had remained faithful in her letters through the years, sharing even her disappointing experiences with Lettie.

Lettie glanced out the window. "Where's your neighbor's house?"

"Not so far, just over yonder." Hallie waved toward the east. "Some of our young girls sneak up there and practice their typing skills on Lana's computer. Strange that they'd want to dabble in the world like that."

"Not so strange, really. Don't ya remember your own *Rumschpringe?*" Lettie cringed. Oh, but she wished she hadn't brought that up. Far as she knew, Hallie had been much more chaste than Lettie during her running-around years.

"Things can get out of hand fast when you've got Amish girls pokin' round the Web, as they call it," Hallie said.

"Hopefully it's just a passing fancy for most. What's worse is when young Plain women get educated up through high school and beyond. Why, I heard of one even wanting a job as an assistant to a lawyer."

"A paralegal?"

"Not sure I know what that is," Lettie admitted.

"Just what you said — an assistant to a lawyer" came Hallie's swift reply.

Lettie looked at her cousin. Innocent as she was, it was clear Hallie was no longer a spring chicken.

Hallie continued. "That sort of thing does annoy me." She sighed sadly and wrung her hands. "That, and hearin' one of my own granddaughters complain about the Old Ways."

"*This* is a surprise. Which granddaughter?"

"Rachel's Linda. If you stay round long enough tomorrow, you'll see her. She's comin' over for a cooking lesson in the morning."

Lettie hadn't seen little Linda in years. "That should be fun."

"You think so? Well, let me tell ya, it's like ropin' a young calf for the first time. Seems Linda likes to put up a fuss whenever her Mamma tries to work with her." Hallie looked tuckered out at the very idea. "This one doesn't know yet how to make a piecrust from scratch."

"Well, is there any other way?"

Hallie grimaced. "Linda keeps insisting

she needs a recipe. 'How can I make it if it's not written down somewhere?' Linda's always sayin'."

Lettie listened, amused.

"Rachel said Linda once wanted to know how much water to add to the dough, as if there's a certain amount that always works."

"What'd Rachel tell her?"

"She said to add water till it felt right." Hallie shook her head. "Goodness, but the poor thing complained up and down, 'Well, how am I s'posed to know what it should feel like when I've never made it before?' And ya know what? Linda's got a point."

Lettie could no longer squelch her smile.

"Finally, Rachel said right out, 'Linda Ann, if ya throw it up to the ceiling and it sticks, you've added too much water!' And that was that."

Now both Hallie and Lettie were nearly bent over, laughing. "Sounds like something my own mother said to all us girls when we were growin' up."

"Why, sure. It makes plenty *gut* sense, doesn't it?"

They were nodding and joking about this so much that Lettie forgot to write down the phone number for Dr. Hackman. "Well, for goodness' sake," she muttered, realizing it only after she'd closed the phone book.

"What's wrong?" Hallie asked.

"Just forgot the phone number, is all."

Hallie fell silent. And Lettie decided yet again that it was truly best not to involve her cousin in her highly unusual mission.

Chapter Six

Dad, you joker, thought Heather after he sent a text reminding her of the lodge program next week. *I won't forget!* She smiled as she walked past yet another farmhouse that afternoon. The road was winding — and earlier, poor, anxious Grace had been forced to keep a sharp eye out for every mailbox on their drive to Susan Kempf's. *And now to discover her mom's missing . . . again.* Heather felt terribly sorry for her.

"Something's really messed up about this," she whispered, leaning her head back so the sun could shine full on her face. She really wanted to meet Grace's mom, this woman who flitted so easily in and out of lives. Lettie Byler's behavior perturbed her, especially now, when it appeared she'd slipped away as if she'd been tipped off about Grace's coming.

Heather's mom would never have done

something that odd. But now, her father was a different story. He had certainly seemed impulsive lately in his decision to buy land in the heart of horse-and-buggy country, then construct a modern farmhouse on it. Yet other than this surprising turn of events, the only other impulsive act he — and Mom — had ever committed was adopting her. At least it seemed spontaneous to her, based on Dad's recent account of how she had come to be theirs.

She couldn't forget how he looked when he'd told her, just days ago. It was still hard to accept that she had an Amish mother somewhere. *Here in Ohio, perhaps?* Well, not a mother *per se,* but someone who'd given her life. Her father had looked almost vulnerable as he revealed the story — she'd missed his tender side since Mom passed away. Her lifelong impression of who she was before his startling news — and the way she viewed herself now — were all mixed up in her mind, crisscrossed like a pattern on one of Marian Riehl's quilts.

Her thoughts flew back to Grace, and she wondered how her friend was getting along with Susan. Had Grace ever been this far from home before? Heather seriously doubted it. As for herself, this trip would be her last for a while.

She sighed. When she attempted to view her life through the prism of the future, she hoped for an opportunity to live many more years. Besides, as Mom had said just weeks before she died, it wasn't only about living: It was about loving. *"And loving well."*

How could a girl forget something like that? And to think it had been Mom's desire to see the Lancaster naturopath Dr. LaVyrle Marshall and enroll in her Wellness Lodge — a desire her mom never got to fulfill. In a very real way, Mom was responsible for Heather's own present path. *And so is God,* her mother might add if she were still alive.

Heather breathed in the rich scents of late spring. There were other memorable things Mom had said in her final weeks. *"You've got the solitude thing down, honey. Learn to gain strength from others."*

"So . . . does what I'm doing here now qualify?" Heather was so caught up in her own thoughts, she didn't realize someone was calling to her.

"Hullo" came a Dutchy-sounding voice again.

Looking up, she saw an Amishwoman dressed in a calf-length maroon dress with a black half apron, swinging a wicker basket by its handle. For a fleeting moment, it almost seemed as if the woman recognized

Heather. Either that or she was just ultra-friendly, like most of the Amish folks Heather had met.

"Hey there," Heather replied. "Nice day."

"It certainly is," the cheerful woman said, glancing at Heather's jeans and shirt. "You aren't from around here, are you?"

Well, she was . . . and she wasn't. "I'm here with a friend who's visiting Susan Kempf." Heather pointed in the direction of her house.

"Ah, such a good neighbor, Susan. We've put up plenty of canned goods over the years — quilted some together, too." The woman looked down at her basket. "I've got quilting squares in here right now, just itchin' for stitchin'."

Heather laughed softly. "Did you make that up?"

"Well, now, I guess I did!"

Heather introduced herself. "I'm Heather."

"Awful nice to meet you. I'm Minnie Keim."

"Minnie," repeated Heather. "What a cute name."

"My friends say it suits me."

"Is it *short* for something?"

Minnie chuckled. "No, just plain Minnie." Minnie waved then, seemingly restless.

"Well, have yourself a wonderful-*gut* visit with Susan. Oh, and don't say I didn't warn ya — she likes to cook and bake. Wants her guests to eat up right hearty, ya know."

"I could use a few extra pounds," Heather replied, although she had no intention of eating fattening foods. For her, it was fresh and raw all the way . . . at least until her blood tests indicated she was cancer-free. *Like Sally Smucker . . . if all goes well.*

Heather shifted her weight from one foot to the other. *And if I survive the lodge experience.*

Lettie gripped the telephone at Hallie's neighbors'. "May I please speak to Dr. Hackman?"

"The doctor is with a patient," replied the woman on the other end. "May I be of help?"

"I have a few questions, but I'd like to talk to him directly. Sometime today?"

"The schedule is filled, miss. I'd suggest making an appointment for a consultation."

She inhaled deeply. *When will I have the nerve to use this telephone again?* "Would it be possible for *you* to check on something for me, maybe?"

"I'm the receptionist, so . . . that's not possible. I'm very sorry."

Lettie pressed on. "I've been waiting a long time for this." She took a breath. "What if I told you it was something mighty important . . . about a baby? A baby girl I gave up for adoption years ago."

"You'll have to discuss that with Dr. Hackman."

"Well, I'm only in town a very short time. . . ." It wasn't like her to argue. But, oh, Lettie could almost reach out and grasp the information she yearned for, she was so close to finding out what she'd come for.

"What is your name, please?" the receptionist asked.

"Lettie Byler."

"I'll see if we can find a time for an appointment. Please hold."

There was a lengthy silence, then soft music in her ear. *O Lord, please guide me,* Lettie prayed. *May all this come together peacefully . . . according to your will.*

While she waited she recalled her firstborn son's birth. Oh, the indescribable joy she'd felt looking into Adam's tiny, round face. She could've stared forever into those milky blue eyes. And then three more children had come along — hers and Judah's. She'd experienced the same delight when first holding each of them, welcoming sweet Grace and, later, darling Mandy, then pudgy little Joe into the world.

"Mrs. Byler?" the receptionist said as she came back on the line. "We can squeeze you in tomorrow morning at nine-thirty."

"I'll take it," Lettie agreed. "Denki ever so much." She hung up the phone and turned to also thank Lana, Hallie's English neighbor, who sat on the sofa with her small portable computer balanced on her lap. "I appreciate the use of your telephone."

"Oh, that's fine. You know where we are," Lana said, glancing up at her, then quickly back at the screen.

Lettie's thoughts raced ahead to the consultation tomorrow. "All right, then." She headed to the screen door, careful not to let it slap against the frame. Yet as she strolled back to Hallie's, she was uncomfortably aware that Lana had been sitting near enough to overhear her side of the frustrating conversation. *Ach, I hope not.*

Lettie followed the narrow path and saw a cardinal's red colors flutter past her. She hoped this trip wouldn't turn out to be a dead end. She was emotionally spent and more than sorry for what she'd done to her family — nearly too ashamed to return home, although she longed to. Truly, she had no idea how to go about returning. Judah was a meek and mild-mannered man, but she wasn't so *grossfiehlich* — bigheaded — as to think she could simply walk back into his life, and their children's. Not after her unexplained absence.

There was another matter, too. The ministerial brethren would undoubtedly ask for Lettie's repentance . . . which would likely have to be offered before the church membership. Oh, dear Judah would have to endure her confession, as would Adam and Grace and Mandy, since they'd already joined church. No, it would not be easy returning to Bird-in-Hand.

Chapter Seven

Grace sat at Susan's table with her eyes closed, waiting for the hospitable woman to finish making her strawberry slush. "It's sure to perk you up," Susan said cheerfully from across the kitchen.

While she waited for Heather to return, Grace had managed to use the remote control on the key chain Heather had left behind on the front room table. She'd carried Heather's bags, and her own, in from the trunk and upstairs to each of two guest bedrooms. It seemed so strange, as she thought of it, that Mamma had sat at this very table . . . and most likely slept in the bed where Grace would sleep tonight. And the more she considered her mother's speedy departure yesterday, the more she suspected there must have been a reason to hurry up and leave. *Like she rushed off in the wee hours from home.*

She raised her head to see Susan bringing

small glasses of the icy fruit slush to the table. "Mmm, looks delicious."

"Oh, you'll enjoy this." Susan set the glass before Grace, then pulled out a chair to the right of the head of the table. She glanced at the empty spot and mentioned how her deceased husband had always sat there. "I decided to keep it empty in his honor after he died."

Grace thought this was one of the sweetest things she'd ever heard. "Did ya tell Mamma this?"

Susan smiled and reached for her own glass. "Oh jah. I'll say your Mamma's quite tenderhearted."

"That she is." Grace sipped the strawberry slush. "Your berries must be early this year."

"They're nearly done, in fact."

"Ours back home aren't quite ready yet," she said, wondering where on earth Heather had disappeared to.

The simple kitchen was light and cheerful, reminding Grace of home in so many ways. The yellowed pine cabinets stood in a neat row above the scarred and worn counter below. Several pies were set out, cooling on the rack, their crusts crimped down evenly around the edges.

"Was Mamma sad while she was here?" Grace asked quietly.

"Mostly apprehensive, I'd say."

Grace bowed her head. "I thought she might've been sad, too . . . missing her family and all."

Susan reached across the table and touched her hand. "Oh, she *did* miss all of you . . . each and ev'ry one."

How Grace wanted to repeat her earlier question, to know why Mamma had left the family who loved her to come here. But Susan seemed lost in thought. Grace fell silent yet again, beginning to worry about Heather's absence.

As a girl, Lettie hadn't wanted to play or talk to anyone after Cousin Hallie and her family left for Indiana. She'd talked if she had to, of course, to her sisters and to Mamm. But it was Hallie who'd always been her closest friend, at least till Naomi had married and the two of them became equally close. The winters had been excruciatingly long those first few years without Hallie. Lettie had missed embroidering and sewing and baking with her dearest cousin. There were times when she would think how nice it would be to go and visit her clear out in Nappanee. *Even then I must've been a wanderer at heart,* she thought as she made her way down the long hill from Lana's house.

So, at nine and ten, Lettie had stayed put at home, except to attend school, helping Mamm with cooking and cleaning afternoons and Saturdays. She wasn't much for gazing at the sky on a moonlit night and wondering if Cousin Hallie was looking up at the same black sky. She was more practical than that. Still, she'd never stopped thinking about how much more fun Hallie was having — more than she was. *"The grass ain't any greener out yonder,"* Mamm had sometimes told her when she'd catch Lettie daydreaming or moping about losing her best cousin. Lettie had used up plenty of ballpoint pens, writing long letters and sending them to faraway Hallie.

It's nice to be able to spend some time with her, even given the circumstances, Lettie thought presently. She entered Hallie's kitchen to find her cousin stirring a kettle of homemade vegetable beef soup. Hallie's husband hadn't minded one bit when the ministerial brethren there had agreed to let their women have gas ranges and ovens. Lettie smiled, remembering her own church's lively debate on that issue some years ago.

Hallie looked up from the stove. "You must've found the house?"

She nodded. "You were right . . . Lana let

me use the phone."

"Mighty nice folk."

"I hope you won't mind if I need to stay around till tomorrow afternoon," Lettie ventured, embarrassed despite their close relationship. "If I can get ahold of a driver to take me home then, that is."

Hallie laughed. "Stay as long as ya like. I'll just put you to work cookin' and what-not."

"Denki, Hallie . . . if you're sure ya don't mind."

"Well, now, I just said I didn't." Hallie stepped back from the stove to fan herself with the hem of her apron. "Ain't like I see ya very often, jah?"

Lettie smiled and nodded, glad Hallie hadn't pressed to know why she needed a telephone. *Maybe she thinks I was trying to call a driver.*

"Ben'll be in from the field shortly." Hallie glanced her way. "But there's a bit more time in case ya need to rest again."

"No need," she replied, wondering if Hallie thought she was all in due to illness. "I'll give you a hand with supper." Since Susan had been a stickler for cooking her meals alone, Lettie had a hankering to cook.

"Why don't you make the salad." Hallie reached up to open the cupboard and brought down a big wooden bowl. "And don't be shy — make plenty. We'll have extra mouths to feed tonight. Most of the field hands will be in for the meal."

"Neighbors?" Lettie knew that Hallie and Ben's sons were married.

" 'Least three that I know of."

She set to work chopping lettuce and cucumbers, peeled the skin off several tomatoes, then diced those. All the while she thought of Grace and Mandy, wondering if they helped each other in the kitchen or if Grace and Mamm were managing the meals. Lettie felt pained to think of her girls doing all the cooking without her.

When she finished chopping carrots, she sprinkled them into the salad and asked Hallie, "How old were you when you married Ben?"

Hallie's smile was priceless. "Seems like we've been together my whole life, really."

"Were you twenty yet?" Lettie honestly didn't remember, not having attended the wedding.

"Closer to eighteen." Again, Hallie laughed softly. "We knew we were meant to be together . . . so we tied the knot right quick. Better to marry than to burn with passion."

Lettie kept her attention on the salad

dressing she was making — vinegar and oil, garlic cloves and onions, salt and pepper to taste — avoiding Hallie's eyes.

"Lettie, I've been meaning to ask what you were doin' over in Ohio," Hallie said as she went to the refrigerator and pulled out her lime Jell-O salad.

"Oh, visiting."

"Without Judah?"

"Jah," she said softly, worried at the turn their conversation was taking. "Lambing season, ya know."

Hallie nodded. "And, too, our menfolk aren't usually much for traveling, ain't so?"

" 'Tis true." She felt somewhat relieved. "I'll set the table. How many places?"

"Twelve or so. Not sure. We'll have plenty of plates and glasses ready, just in case."

She moved about, hoping Hallie wouldn't bring up Ohio again. Lettie certainly didn't want to lie. *And I won't, either.*

At last, Ben and the others came tramping in and all lined up out in the mud room to wash. When Ben finished, Lettie was surprised to see him make a beeline to Hallie and plant a kiss on her cheek, then whisper something that made her cousin both blush and grin. He turned to say "hullo" to Lettie before sitting at the head of the table. Quiet as Ben was, he wasn't shy about glancing toward Hallie as she dished up generous helpings of the thick, stewlike soup. Once she finally sat down, he reached over and put his big, callused hand on top of hers for the meal blessing, then kept it there for a moment even as he reached for his water glass with the other.

All through the meal, Lettie was taken by her cousins' fondness for each other, their way of referring to each other as "love" and "dear," so rare in the Amish community she knew. Was their ongoing closeness due to having grown up together? Or were they just very good friends, like she'd read of some fictional husbands and wives?

Whatever the reason, she could hardly keep from watching them.

Lettie felt drowsy and ready to head upstairs to bed as she sat in the kitchen with Hallie. They were having a second piece of peanut butter pie, although a much smaller slice than the first helping. Hallie had a talk on, and suddenly she was saying she had "something ever so important" to ask Lettie. "It's something I heard from our neighbor Lana, up the way." Hallie's brown eyes were solemn. "Ach, I'm not even sure where to start."

Lettie's heart skidded to a halt. "Why not

say it right out?"

"Well, 'cause I can't see how it could be true." Hallie lowered her head and shook it back and forth. "*Puh* . . . feel so odd mentioning it."

"Hallie, what are ya talking 'bout?"

Her cousin raised her head and looked at her with worry-filled eyes. "Lana's concerned for you, Lettie."

"For me?"

Hallie drew a long breath. "Lana tried to be discreet, but when she stopped here to buy some eggs after supper, she mentioned something about your long-ago baby."

Lettie's toes curled against the linoleum beneath the table. *So Lana did overhear my conversation with Dr. Hackman's receptionist.*

"I'm ever so sorry to put that out there." Hallie patted her chest lightly, as if she was having trouble getting enough air.

"No . . . no, you're not to blame." Lettie was ever so weary of the secret. She felt it was long past time to get it out in the open — every last bit.

Hallie's face knit up into an awful frown. "I . . . I'm ever so confused."

"Sure you are." Lettie rose and walked the whole length of the kitchen, then turned slowly back to the table, where Hallie still sat. "I came here for this very purpose . . .

to find the child I gave away as a young girl."

"Ach, Lettie!" Hallie gasped, her eyes wide. "You can't mean it!"

"It's quite true." She pulled out the bench and sat again.

This won't be easy. . . .

Pulling a hankie from out of her sleeve, Hallie wiped her cheeks and brow. "Oh, goodness . . . oh, for pity's sake," she muttered.

"Goodness and pity have nothin' to do with it."

Hallie continued to lament. Then she surprised Lettie by saying, "Ach, and the father . . . it wasn't that fella Samuel, was it? We heard plenty of things 'bout him."

Lettie made no reply; she wanted to keep Samuel out of this conversation.

Hallie leaned forward into her hankie. "You poor, dear girl." Now she was rocking back and forth so quickly Lettie feared she might teeter right out of her chair.

"I'm not a poor girl, Hallie. Please, pull yourself together." She sighed. This was much harder than Lettie had ever thought. "All of this happened a long time ago, but I'm on a mission now . . . to right the wrongs of my past. To find my oldest daughter and tell her the truth 'bout me."

"And your family? Do they know?"

Lettie made no answer to that. "Right now, I'm tellin' *you,* because I need to, cousin. Tomorrow, I'm seein' the doctor who helped with my baby's adoption." She waited for Hallie to calm down before continuing. "I need to try and get this out, and keep myself in one piece, too."

"A doctor round here?"

Lettie nodded slowly. She began to share with her cousin, practicing the words as she might say them to Judah — for the coming day when she would reveal the same heart-breaking tale to him. "Now, then, you must keep everything I've told you to yourself, not even whisper a word of it to Ben. 'Least, not till I can get home and talk to my husband."

Hallie inhaled sharply. "You mean . . ."

"That's right," Lettie finally admitted. "Judah doesn't know 'bout my first child."

"How can that be?"

"Trust me, he knows *nothing* 'bout her."

Hallie blinked her eyes again and again. "A girl, you say?"

"Jah." Lettie sighed, hoping she'd done the right thing in revealing all of this. Hallie was known to be a tongue-wagger. Even so, what was the point of denying the truth?

"I wish I'd lived closer to you back then. Maybe none of this would've happened."

"You can't know that. Besides, it's time for me to move ahead and turn it all around for good." *For God,* she thought, going on to explain further. "I thought I was in love, Hallie. And I was hardheaded, too. Wanted my way, no matter what anyone thought of my beau. So I disobeyed my parents and broke their hearts." Lettie was quiet a moment. "It's no wonder Mamm made me give the baby away." The memories reeled in from the past, and she recalled every detail, regretting her sin anew. *Ah, but God used it to bring an innocent life into the world. A beautiful girl, so precious in her heavenly Father's sight.*

Hallie made a sad sound and leaned forward, her arms on the table. "Well, I hope you don't believe that — what you just said." She locked eyes with Lettie. "Because, my dear Lettie, that's not why your Mamm would've insisted on you givin' your baby away," Hallie said quietly. "Don't ya see? She made you do it out of love. For you . . . for your baby."

How could her cousin possibly know what Mamm — or Dat — was thinking all those years ago?

"Surely it was out of care for her grandbaby," Hallie repeated. "She wanted her to have the love of both a mother and a father. A home with two parents."

Lettie didn't know what to think. Minnie Keim had suggested the same thing, but Lettie saw things differently. Her parents had strongly disliked Samuel, for one, and they were also adamant about protecting her reputation and chance for marriage. *Not much concern for my baby in that . . .*

"Whatever her reasons, you must forgive your mother, Lettie, as Jesus teaches us to do. Release her, because forgiveness is required of you . . . as a child of God."

Hallie was right. Forgiving Mamm would be difficult, but Lettie must do it anyway.

CHAPTER EIGHT

Heather was grateful for the abundant fresh salad at supper, and all the trouble Susan had gone to, providing celery and carrot sticks, as well as sliced tomatoes and cucumbers. All the same, she'd still felt hungry at the end of the meal; she assumed her stomach was in the process of shrinking. She had also waited thirty minutes after eating before slowly drinking a full glass of water, per Dr. Marshall's advice.

Now she lay staring at the ceiling in the small guest room, having already showered and dressed for bed. If she had her way tomorrow, she'd be up and out of here before dawn, heading back to Pennsylvania. But the way Susan had talked at supper, it sounded as though she was urging Grace to stay around for a few hours tomorrow morning, to relax a bit.

She could hear Grace in the next room, humming a melody she didn't recognize. It would seem that her Plain friend had had her fill of socializing — either that, or she simply craved some downtime. *Like I do.*

Propping herself up with several handmade crocheted pillows, Heather realized again how very different this trip had turned out for Grace. For herself, she hadn't had many preconceived notions. The drive here was her little adventure, of sorts, before her upcoming stay at the Wellness Lodge. That, and an attempt to do something nice for a consistently thoughtful young woman.

Rolling over, Heather stared at the slender kerosene lamp on the nearby table. A Bible rested on the small shelf below, with a bookmark sticking out at the top. *"Mom read the Bible more at the end of her life than at any other time,"* Dad had told her a year ago. *"Don't people become more religious when they're dying?"* she'd asked. But Dad hadn't responded.

Heather slipped off her watch and placed it on the small table. She reached for the Bible and leaned up on her elbow. With a slow sigh, she slid her finger between the pages, near the pressed floral bookmark. There, she found a slip of paper with a list of various birds: *black-and-white warbler, lark sparrow, Baltimore oriole, scarlet tanager, bobolink, brown thrasher . . .*

She scanned the page and noted more than twenty birds, each with a description of its call after its name. At the bottom of the page, in even smaller letters, was printed: *LB, May 16.*

"LB?" she whispered. "Lettie Byler?" She looked around and realized Grace's mom must have stayed in this very room.

For a moment, she felt an overwhelming urge to go and knock on Grace's door, to offer to trade bedrooms, perhaps. *Wouldn't Grace want to sleep in the bed her mother slept in?* But Grace might be too settled in and comfortable by now. So Heather relaxed and soaked up the atmosphere of the space where the runaway Lettie had watched birds, read this Bible, and probably slept.

She wasn't sure how long she lay there with the Bible open, but when Heather awakened, she heard crying. Getting up, she placed the Bible back on the shelf. When the list of birds fluttered to the hardwood floor, she stooped to pick it up and noticed a reference for a Scripture verse on the back.

She had no idea where Psalm 42 was located in the thick Bible, so she didn't bother to search. Grace would know. With the list in her hand, she crept across the room, past the low windows covered by green shades, blocking out the moonlight.

Standing in the hallway, Heather heard Grace blowing her nose. "Are you all right in there?" she called through the door quietly, not wanting to awaken Susan.

"Come in, Heather."

She tiptoed inside and saw Grace curled up in the bed. "I heard you stirring. Anything I can do?"

Grace sat up and leaned against the headboard. "I had a bad dream," she whispered. "Sorry, I don't mean to sound like such a child."

Heather smiled. "My mom once said we're all children inside." It was perhaps a silly thing to say, but it was the first thing she thought of. "I'm not sure, but I may have found something of your mother's." She gave the list of birds to Grace. "Thought you might want this."

Grace got up and lit the lantern on her bedside table. The list trembled in her hand as she held it tenderly, almost reverently. "Ah . . . bird sightings. How Mamma loves her birds!"

Heather pointed out the reference on the back of the paper. "Is this a favorite, too?"

Grace pinched her lips together and closed her eyes. There was a softness in her expression as tears spilled down her cheeks.

" 'Yet the Lord will command his loving-kindness in the day time, and in the night his song shall be with me, and my prayer unto the God of my life.' " She brushed back tears. "Mamma wrote this very verse in my birthday card last month."

Not knowing what to say, Heather looked away. "I'm an April baby, as well," she said absently.

"Jah? Are we the same age, too?" Grace brushed away her tears.

"I'm twenty-four."

Grace had a look of touching timidity. "I'm twenty-one . . . and nearly a *Maidel.*"

"I sure hope that's not what it sounds like."

"Amongst the People, I'm considered nearly an old maid."

Heather turned to look at her again, offering a smile. "If only Yonnie could see you now . . ."

"Well, not *right* now. Our bishop frowns on bed courtship — *Bundling.* It's against our church ordinance."

Heather was stunned. "Hey, I was *kidding.*" There was so much she didn't know about the Amish culture. "I just meant, as long as Yonnie's sweet on you, I doubt you'll become whatever you called it."

"A Maidel."

"Yeah, *that.*"

Grace laughed softly, but all too soon her tears welled up again as she pressed her mother's list to her heart.

Heather was helpless to stop Grace from reaching for her and crying on her shoulder. Was she weeping for her missing mother, or for Yonnie? Whatever the reason, Heather was overwhelmed by this poor girl sobbing next to her.

Slowly she found herself opening her heart, astonished at how much she cared. "It's okay, Grace," she whispered, putting her arms around her. "You go ahead and cry."

Heather observed Grace's serious, almost dreary, expression as they loaded the car the next morning, relieved they were getting an early start. Grace carried her bags without speaking, deep shadows evident beneath her blue eyes. *She's devastated.*

There was still one more item to retrieve from the house. Heather headed back inside, going out of her way to thank Susan for inviting them to stay overnight. "It was really very kind of you," she told her.

Susan smiled. "Anytime you'd like to return for a visit, you have a place here. I do enjoy company."

"Well, you're a terrific hostess," Heather said.

Susan gave her a hug. "I'll be prayin' for you today while you travel."

Grace suddenly appeared at the front door. "Denki, Susan," she said quietly. "And for takin' care of my Mamma, too." There was a catch in her voice, and tears sprang to her eyes.

Heather excused herself and hurried upstairs to grab her last bag, a cosmetic case, which she slipped over her shoulder. She glanced around the room once more. Spying the Bible where she'd found Lettie's bird sightings, she felt an overwhelming sadness for Grace. So many unanswered questions — why had her mother run off, where had she gone, and when might she return home?

Outside again, she found Grace already sitting primly in the front passenger's seat, staring blankly through the windshield. Susan walked over and leaned on the open car window, talking softly. Soon, the three of them were saying another round of good-byes and God-bless-you's — Susan and Grace offering the latter.

Then they were on their way, winding back up the same narrow country road they'd come by, the cows grazing on all sides as Heather and Grace headed toward Sugarcreek.

"Susan was really something," Heather remarked.

"Like family . . . almost."

When they drove past the area where Heather had encountered the friendly woman with the charming name of Minnie, she glanced in the rearview mirror, recalling how relaxed she'd felt during the walk.

Grace turned to her. "I'm sorry this was such a dead end . . . that you drove me out here for nothing."

"Oh, don't worry about me, Grace."

"We just missed my mother." Grace wiped tears from her eyes and went silent, hardly breathing in the passenger's seat. She sat nearly like a rag doll, no life in her arms, with her legs stretched out and feet resting on the gravel-sprinkled floor mat below.

A fleeting thought crossed Heather's mind that if she hadn't signed up for the Wellness Lodge, she might have offered to play sleuth there in Baltic or elsewhere. But the clock was loudly ticking on her health.

Chapter Nine

Several other patients were sitting in Dr. Hackman's waiting room when Lettie arrived, some with children who eyed her curiously as she signed in and took a seat. Others sat and flipped through magazine pages, glancing up hopefully each time the nurse opened the door to call another name. Accustomed to being given sideways glances by Englischers during her travels or while tending tables at market, she wasn't troubled by the stares. Some folks were just more discreet than others.

At last, when Lettie's name was called, she followed the nurse through the doorway, rehearsing in her mind the questions for the doctor. Would this visit bring an end to her search, just as she'd prayed while waiting for the driver to arrive this morning?

Lettie felt nearly too reticent to speak when the doctor, a large man with gray-blue eyes, entered the room and leaned down to shake her hand. Feeling fuzzy-headed, she wished she'd written down her questions.

"My receptionist left a note for me. Am I correct that you're looking for an adoptee, a child you had years ago?" Dr. Hackman asked as they sat across from each other at his large desk.

Lettie confirmed that was the reason she'd come from Lancaster County to meet with him. "The adoption took place in Ohio," she added.

"Do you have access to a computer?" he said, frowning. "If so, you can easily print out the form and mail in a request to authorize the release of your identifying information."

"Sorry . . . a what?"

"There's a standard form for biological parents who are searching."

She shook her head. "I don't own a computer." *And wouldn't know how to use it if I did.*

His face softened to a cordial smile. "Well, then, you could simply write a letter and request a reply by mail, if you wish."

Lest she lose her nerve, Lettie asked if he remembered working with a midwife in Kidron, Ohio, named Minnie Keim. "She delivered my baby twenty-four years ago — April twenty-ninth."

He shifted his wide shoulders and glanced briefly toward the window, a contemplative frown on his portly face. "I do recall Mrs. Keim, yes. But it has been some years since I've worked with her in that capacity."

"My baby's adoption was handled privately — not through an agency. Or so I was told."

He shook his head, still looking rather amazed. "It was totally unnecessary for you to travel here."

Sighing, she thought of Hallie's neighbor Lana. But it had been hard enough to ask to use her phone, let alone asking to borrow Lana's little computer — and not knowing what to do first after that. "Would it be possible to have someone here help me . . . in your office?" Lettie did not want to risk making a single mistake in filling out such an important form. Just the thought of it made her feel nearly panicked.

He opened his mouth to speak, then hesitated, a brief smile playing on his lips. "Let's see what we can do." He rose and reached for the door. Quietly, he called for one of his staff from the doorway. "Could one of you come and assist Mrs. Byler, please?"

She was greatly relieved at the doctor's kindness and told him so. He nodded warmly and said he wished her well in her search. "The state department of health will file your request with the court and respond to you via mail at your home address. Assuming your child has filed a petition with the probate court, your information will be released to her."

Momentarily, Lettie wondered if having such a letter come to her home was a good idea. But, no, she would follow through, just as the good doctor was suggesting.

Before he left, she said, "I have one more question. Do you keep any records of private adoptions?"

He wore a fleeting look of regret. "Our files don't go back that far. You'll have to work directly with the office of vital statistics at the Ohio Department of Health. You can expect to hear back from them within two to three weeks."

She thanked him, and he was gone.

Soon, one of the nurses appeared in the room and went to sit in the doctor's chair, in front of the desk computer. She introduced herself as Fiona, and her accent and name made Lettie think she was from another country. Fiona printed out a form she found online with the Ohio Adoption Registry. Then she carefully went over the information, beginning with Lettie's legal name at the time of the birth, and the date and location of the birth. Lettie felt like a bundle of nerves, and a great shyness fell over her, like a large cobweb descending. But she did her utmost to print neatly, and to the best of her knowledge, she carefully answered each question, filling in every blank, except for the name of the baby on the day of birth.

"Ah, there you are, Martin," his wife said as Martin Puckett pushed open the screen door. "Hungry?"

"You know me well." He chuckled and glanced at his watch. *Twelve-thirty* — later than he preferred to sit down to lunch, but there had been many calls from Amish requesting his transportation services this morning.

Janet moved back and forth between the kitchen counter and the table in a sporadic dance of sorts. He leaned back in his chair, appreciative of her attempts to make every meal festive. *Festive* was her own description of the colorful napkins and ever-changing place settings. At last count, she owned five full sets of dishes. *"My weakness,"* she'd admitted to him last week as they enjoyed a light supper, complete with her maternal grandmother's best china — a pattern of small flowers — and crystal goblets. The goblets were making an appearance again today, although presently his was filled with ice water, a small slice of lemon floating down midway.

Janet was feminine in every way — the way she dressed, the way she carried herself, and her demeanor. And, good night, could she ever cook! To think this was the same woman who'd worked for years behind a cosmetic counter in one of the department stores over in the big Lancaster mall, on the other side of the bypass. She'd given makeovers to middle-aged women, recommended lipstick hues, and passed out free samples until she resigned after their third child was born. While she said she did not miss working full-time, Martin was fairly certain she missed the spending money. Particularly now, with things so tight. The exceptionally high cost of gas this spring had certainly done their bank account no favors.

"Here we are." Janet carried the last two food items and placed them just so in the center of the table, including a molded tuna salad with chopped hard-boiled eggs he could see through the gelatin. "No mayo for you, dear, but I think you'll like the healthy substitute."

Don't remind me. . . .

"Looks delicious." He smiled at his bride of nearly forty-one years. They had certainly been through the mill with two of their now-grown children. One daughter had surprised them recently by finally beginning to mellow. Even the younger daughter was showing steady indications of the same. Their sons, married with children of their own, had given them no trouble at all — at least that Martin could recall. Aside from his own forced early retirement due to stress-related health issues, he and Janet knew they had enjoyed more than their share of blessings.

Bowing his head, he offered a heartfelt prayer, being mindful to ask a blessing on "the hands that prepared this food" toward the end. After the amen, he leaned over and kissed Janet's soft, pink lips. "Let's dig in," he said.

His wife reached to scoop up an ample portion of the kidney bean salad, waiting for him to hold out his plate. Next the molded tuna salad — which he was not so fond of, though he would never let on — and a thick slice of hobo bread, one of Janet's own favorites.

Grateful, he looked down at his plate and picked up his fork, all the while attentive to his wife's pleasant chatter.

"How's the Virginia businessman's house

coming along?" Janet asked after she'd filled him in on the latest with their kids.

"The permit has been approved and the plot's been surveyed. Excavation will begin after Memorial Day — next Tuesday, I'd guess." He broke his bread in half and took a bite. There wasn't a lick of butter anywhere in sight, thanks to Janet's heeding his doctor's orders. *"Recommendations,"* she liked to say instead.

"So the house should go up quickly?"

"Yes. And according to the fellows I'll be driving to and from the site each day, there's an air of excitement about this particular house."

Her eyebrows rose. "Really?"

"Well, it's planned as a look-alike Amish farmhouse . . . except with every imaginable modern convenience," he said. "How about that?"

"Sounds like the owner is trying to fit in over there."

"That's my thinking, as well. But since I've yet to meet Roan Nelson, I can't tell you why that would be."

Janet reached for her own goblet of water. "Some of the girls in the neighborhood said they heard Mr. Nelson has a daughter about to get her master's degree. She's staying with the Riehls."

"Heard that, too." He shook his head and wiped his mouth with the napkin. "Andy and Marian certainly have their hands full with all they do."

"Running a tourist home would keep *me* hopping, let alone handling all the work of a dairy farm on top of it."

They traded smiles. Martin had had his share of working with cows, back when he was a boy. His father's older brother had a few he raised to slaughter. Martin shook off the memory of one particular day when he'd observed the process a little too closely for his liking. He'd almost given up eating meat after that, but only until the disgusting memory faded. And now here he was, happily married to a woman who excelled in the kitchen, cooking occasional beef dinners, along with other leaner meats, and he was the contented recipient.

"I'm curious to know why anyone from Virginia wants to build a modern-day house, sandwiched between two Amish farms," Janet said. "Any idea?"

"Roan Nelson's his own man, I'm hearing. And somewhat dogmatic about how he wants things done — the old way, he's insisted to the Amish contractor who's overseeing the whole thing — Josiah Smucker."

"Sally's husband? The preacher?" Janet's eyes lit up. "Are you sure?"

"You know her?"

"I've met her at the farmer's market several times. The first time we were both at a table of homemade facial scrubs."

He let out a guffaw. "Hard to imagine an Amishwoman wanting something like that."

"Well, now, darling" — and here she touched his wrist — "a woman's a woman, no matter the Plain clothes she wears."

He smiled. "Should've seen that coming." Martin finished eating his helping of tuna salad, trying for the life of him to remember how it had tasted *with* mayo.

Chapter Ten

Lettie kept coming up short Friday, trying to line up a long-distance driver for that afternoon — or even tomorrow. Feeling overwhelmingly homesick, she couldn't contact Sally Smucker, either. She hoped she might stay with the preacher's family once she returned, at least for the time being. *Out of respect for Judah.*

After what she'd done, it was not right for her to simply appear at the house and expect her husband to welcome her back. If she could only stay with the Smuckers, who had several empty bedrooms, she might be able to work things out with Preacher Josiah first, before revealing her past sins to Judah. And hopefully avoid a public kneeling confession.

With her husband on her mind, Lettie hurried to her room to jot down a few notes, things she must include in her revelatory confession to him and to the ministers.

A telling of sorts.

Quickly she found her pen and the writing paper in her suitcase. She sat at a small desk and began to write the thoughts that had flooded her heart just since her consultation with Dr. Hackman this morning. Thoughts she longed to share soon with Judah. *Lord willing.* Perhaps next week, once she had her wits about her and could look him square in the eye.

I saw a ruby-throated hummingbird early this morning. So tiny . . . and very busy. It flew back and forth amongst the blossoms, stopping for nectar. Its wingbeats were so fast they were a blur, and my heart beat faster, just watching. Then, effortlessly, it flew backward. I'd seen this before, but not till that moment did I realize that I, too, have flown backward, wanting to revisit my past and undo it somehow. Not to gather sweetness, but for the healing I hoped this difficult journey might bring to the people I've hurt. Samuel first, and to our child. But I failed to consider the hurt it might do to my husband, Judah . . . because I never had the courage to fess up to my sins.

I just pray I have not stirred up bitterness through my search for my first child.

Her need to right her past wrongs had been the very reason Lettie had never been able to make herself share openly with Judah. That and her concern that disclosing everything might simply make things worse between them. Yet now she knew she must reveal all. Hard as that would be, she was weary of the deceit: She should never have allowed Judah to believe she had been a virtuous bride when that was far from the truth.

But if she could warn her teenage self — the foolish, headstrong Lettie who had wanted her own way above all else — what would she say? How would she counsel her? *Would I make the same mistakes again?* In her heart, Lettie knew she would not. Something within her had changed . . . shifted for the better.

Tired now, yet feeling somehow freer, Lettie rose and placed the tablet and pen back in her suitcase. Then, leaving the room, she headed up the hill to Hallie's English neighbor to try to reach a driver once again.

What'll I tell Dat now? The question tormented Grace all during the trip through eastern Ohio. Of course she would tell him that Mamma had already left — going exactly where, no one knew. Yet how could she phrase it so as not to cause him far more concern than he already suffered? It seemed so unnecessary for Mamma to go away in the first place, but now this? It felt as if she'd abandoned them all over again.

Grace was drained; she hadn't slept well last night. The long stretch of highway and her all-too-modern surroundings only added to her displaced feeling as she sat in Heather's car.

Heather switched on her music once again, and Grace felt great appreciation for her kindness and comfort during the long, sleepless night. For her patience today, too. Grace laughed inwardly at herself; she'd gotten rather tongue-tied this morning and mistakenly referred to FaceTube instead of what Heather informed her was the actual name for a "social network," as she called it, as well as a way to share videos. *Honestly, how does she keep track of such things?*

Leaning back, Grace watched the mile markers zip by. It dawned on her that if all went well, they would arrive home sooner than originally planned. *I'll be back to doing what I'm cut out for — cooking and cleaning and gardening, too.*

In her drowsy state, she thought of Yonnie Bontrager. It seemed so long since he had asked her to be his girl, yet only two days had passed. His expression had been so appealing this past Wednesday morning on the road. *What will he think of Mamma now?* she wondered, remembering that he had believed Mamma was merely visiting in Baltic.

But, oh, Grace knew better. By the cautious look on Susan's face and her ever so guarded comments, she knew that Mamma still had her secrets. Truly, it would be ill timed to accept Yonnie's invitation to court. She folded her arms and looked at the sky. How could she agree to be his girl under these circumstances?

Grace wondered what Mamma would advise, ever so curious about such matters now that her mother was out of reach. How would Mamma handle a kindhearted fellow like Yonnie, as well as the possible obstacles to happiness that might lie ahead?

Her eyelids felt heavy as she pondered what Mamma might say if she were here and knew Grace's thoughts. She was fairly certain her mother could impart some sort of understanding, having lived long enough to understand about fellows and love and suchlike.

Oh, Mamma . . . I need your wisdom.

Judah shoved the door to the sheep barn shut, having heard tires crackle on the driveway. His pulse pounded as he spotted Heather Nelson's dark blue car drive up and stop at the back door. "Gracie's back," he whispered. Then, softer yet, "Lettie, too?"

Oh, my love . . . are you there?

The sun gleamed off the windshield, making it impossible to determine how many passengers were inside. He imagined Lettie stepping out of the car, smiling when she caught his gaze. *What will she say?* He tugged on his suspenders. *And what'll I say to* her?

The windbreak of trees just beyond the driveway looked suddenly taller as he waited for his wife and his daughter to emerge from the vehicle. He clenched his jaw and dug his boots hard against the graveled area between the sheep barn and the backyard. *Relax, old man,* he told himself.

And then he saw Gracie open the car door and get out. She followed the tall Englischer around to the trunk. But, no . . . by the look on Grace's drawn, solemn face, he knew Lettie wasn't with them. Still, he waited and hoped he might've jumped ahead of himself — perhaps his wife was simply taking her time gathering her things inside the car.

Just maybe . . .

Standing there in such anticipation gave

him a momentary woozy spell, and he reached for the side of the barn. *Hold on, Judah. . . .*

His heart smashed to the ground when Grace set her bags on the sidewalk and turned to wave to the other young woman. His daughter picked up her suitcase and hurried to the house while the shiny blue car — sunlight still bouncing off its windshield — backed up to the road and headed to Andy Riehl's.

He wiped his forehead on the back of his arm and sighed. "Lettie's not comin' home. . . ." He felt a sudden queasiness, which threw him off-balance yet again. Steadying himself, he dreaded more than anything going inside to hear what Grace might say.

His gut instincts had been right; his wife didn't care for him any longer. No matter what her letter had said about missing them.

Rejecting him was one thing, but for Lettie to reject her children was quite another. Judah ran his hand over his beard and jerked on it, knowing he ought to return to his work in the barn. But his fear and curiosity blended in a surprising jumble of energy, and he lifted his feet to trudge toward the house.

■ ■ ■ ■

The minute she had seen Judah Byler over near the barn, covertly observing them as they pulled his daughter's bags out of the trunk, Heather understood something of his pain. An instant look of disappointment had appeared on his ruddy face, and his shoulders had fallen into a miserable slump. The image of his distress stayed all too fresh in her mind as she entered the Riehls' busy kitchen and casually greeted Marian and her daughter Becky. They and the younger girls, Rachel and Sarah, were busy baking pies for "a church doin's," Marian explained quickly.

But Heather did not care to linger and reminded them politely she would be clearing out her room early Monday morning to go to the nearby Wellness Lodge.

Marian nodded and said she remembered but wondered what Heather would do following her ten-day stay there. "You're always welcome back. We'll be happy to make room for you, even if we're booked up with guests." The engaging woman smiled and glanced at Becky. "Ain't so?"

Becky grinned at her mother, then cast a broad smile Heather's way. "And we can cook you healthier meals, too, if you'd like. No gooey sweets and pastries."

Heather couldn't bring herself to say there'd be precious little cooked food in her near future. "Thanks, but I'll figure out something else, even if I stay around the area." Lately she had found herself pining for her home in Virginia, especially since her father had first laid out his plan to sell it and relocate to the house he was having built here. The very thought of relinquishing the house she had always loved made her eyes blurry with tears. Dad was changing everything, turning her life upside down.

But she knew that was nothing compared to Grace's feelings, nor those of Lettie's husband. The poor man had no idea where his wife was hiding. They weren't like modern couples, who could easily stay in touch by cell phone. Judah couldn't just email Lettie and find out what she was up to . . . or ask her to please come home so they could talk over whatever was bothering her.

Pulling out her phone, Heather texted her own dad, letting him know she was safely back in Pennsylvania. *I'm ready to dive into detox this Monday!*

She sent the text and began to unpack, dreadfully fatigued. Dad promptly replied, surprising her. *I'll see you next Tuesday . . . thought I'd give you a chance to get settled in at LaVyrle's.*

She laughed quietly. "How weird is that, Dad referring to LaVyrle by her first name?" The naturopath had insisted that *she* call her LaVyrle.

But, for some reason, her father's familiarity actually brightened her afternoon, and when Heather was finished unpacking, she fell onto the bed. Sighing deeply, her last conscious memory was not of Judah Byler looking so desperately glum earlier. It was of Yonnie, the guy she'd overheard talking to Grace. Heather had seen him peering out through a barn window when Grace returned, holding a white fluff of a lamb in his arms . . . a curious expression on his face.

"Mamma left Baltic before I ever got there," Grace told Dat when he came into the kitchen looking all forlorn. "Susan Kempf, the Amishwoman she was stayin' with, hinted that Mamma might've gone to see her cousin Hallie. No one knows for sure." Grace could hardly get the words out for the lump in her throat.

Dat nodded his head once. "Gone . . . again?"

"Jah." Sadly, she thought, *I want to say I don't care . . . but I do.* She felt horrid thinking such a thing. She looked around the empty kitchen, so tired she could hardly stand at the counter. The thought of cooking a big supper was insufferable. She hoped there was still a hotdish tucked away in the freezer, one she'd cooked ahead before leaving.

"Such a waste of time for ya, Gracie," he said so low she barely heard it.

She felt the same way now. At least the trip out there, when she and Heather had talked so pleasantly, had had its moments. The young woman and her brave approach to fighting her illness intrigued her more now than ever.

Grace continued. "Susan said she thought Mamma would come home when she's finished with her search."

"What search?"

"I don't know, but this Susan seemed ever so sure 'bout that."

"We'll pray so, then."

She glanced about the kitchen again. "Is Mandy in the barn?" she asked.

"Jah . . . out with Yonnie and Joe, givin' bottles to some newborn lambs." Dat sighed as he ran his callused hands through his hair.

"Would ya mind askin' her something for me, Dat?"

"Not a'tall."

"Will ya ask if she has food planned for supper?"

"Well" — Dat gave a half smile — "I'll do my best."

Going out and finding Mandy, especially amidst the boys, was the very last thing Grace wanted to do. Just thinking of seeing her siblings — and Yonnie — made her feel more exhausted, even though she was itching to see Willow again. "I really need a short rest." Tears pricked her eyes. "I'm all in, Dat."

Frowning with concern, her father nodded. "Of course ya are, Gracie. Glad ya said so." With that, Dat left by way of the side door, waving flies away with his straw hat as he headed down the steps.

Chapter Eleven

Adah Esh and her husband, Jakob, sat in the front room, well aware of the commotion on Judah's side of the house. They'd heard Grace arrive home with Marian Riehl's long-term boarder, who had headed back over to the Riehls' place. Yet there was no sign of Lettie.

Adah sat and strained to hear what Grace was telling Judah just across the hall. "What do you think we should do, Jakob?" she asked, leaning forward in the settee.

"Nothin'." He reached for the latest issue of *The Budget,* the weekly newspaper for the Plain community.

"How can ya say that?"

He chuckled and carefully folded the large paper in half. "Whatever Grace found out in Ohio, she'll come and tell us, sooner or later."

"Well, Lettie ain't with her; that's obvious."

He nodded his head slowly, his eyes peering over his reading glasses at her. "Prob'ly a *gut* thing, too."

Adah had been back and forth on that, imagining what would happen if Lettie finally revealed the reason for her leaving. That, and wondering what might happen if Lettie didn't return at all. Her daughter was prone to being mighty willful sometimes.

"Do ya think Lettie found the midwife she was lookin' for?" She sighed sadly. "And . . . the child?" She'd never posed this to Jakob, although she had worried about it.

Jakob's eyes were focused on something outside the window. He seemed to be lost in thought, not paying any mind to her ramble.

She tried again to get his attention. "And what about *him* . . . do ya think Lettie located the baby's father?"

"You're babblin', love."

Why's he making this hard? She reached for her tatting, the question still suspended between them. It was time to make a few more hankies for gifts. She wanted to give a couple to Marian for helping her with a pile of mending yesterday.

At last, when she could stand it no longer, Adah said, "You know who I mean, don't ya?" She disliked mentioning Samuel's name in the house, as if it might dirty the air.

"Sure, Lettie must've found him. How hard could it be?"

Adah stiffened. "I just thought . . ."

"Now, Adah, don't ya have some sewin' to do? Just leave the thinking to me, dear."

With that, Jakob gave her a pert smile, no doubt humored. Annoyed, she tatted clear around one whole edge of the hankie before noticing that her husband was evidently lost again in the paper's weekly accounts of various Amish communities. She wouldn't think of competing with that. No, she'd entertain her own quiet thoughts for now, all the while hoping her granddaughter might soon come over and talk to her, once things calmed down some. It was all Adah could do to sit there and not go ask Grace, *Was in der Welt is letz?* — What in the world's the matter?

Grace had purposely avoided Yonnie the whole rest of Friday afternoon and Saturday, too. Now it was the Lord's Day and the Preaching service was scheduled to begin in a few minutes. The People were gathered at the home of Uncle Ethan and Aunt Hannah Esh's house, Mamma's youngest brother and wife, expecting their seventh child in mid-July. Uncle Ethan had taken over the dairy operation at Dawdi and Mammi's old farm just before they moved into the *Dawdi Haus,* across the center hall from Mamma's kitchen.

Is it my kitchen now? Grace wondered as she stood in line with the other women outside her uncle's. Patiently she waited while the ordained ministers spoke quietly amongst themselves before going inside the temporary house of worship.

She saw Becky Riehl farther up the line, with her mother and younger sisters. When she caught Becky's eye, she mouthed the words, *Hullo, friend.*

Becky smiled immediately, apparently happy Grace was back from her trip. Becky craned her neck, gawking, no doubt looking for Grace's mother. Not seeing Mamma standing near Grace, Becky frowned hard, a questioning look on her pretty face.

Grace shook her head and opened her palms upward, not knowing what to say with so many womenfolk between herself and her friend.

So sorry, Becky moved her mouth, eyes sad.

Grace turned around and motioned for Mandy, who was behind her talking softly with two of their teenage cousins. "Time for

Preachin'," she whispered, and Mandy came quickly, her royal blue dress and white apron swooshing against Grace's own as they half bowed their heads and put on an attitude of utmost reverence.

Trying not to look toward the men's line, Grace knew it would be next to impossible to avoid Yonnie during the common meal, if not before. At some point, and soon, she must show him the respect he deserved and respond to his courting question.

The crush Judah felt in the long line on this Lord's Day was not caused by the proximity of the other men. The strain came from the intense scrutiny evident on nearly every man's face as he glanced at Judah. Some presumably felt sorry for him, while others looked more critically.

He stood silently alongside Jakob, who leaned on his wooden cane and cast him a knowing glint. His father-in-law had a keen eye and was clearly aware of the furtive looks coming their way. They were flanked by Adam and Joe, all of them wearing their pressed black trousers and vests with white long-sleeved shirts as they waited for the ministerial brethren to enter the house. Judah had seen their bishop, two preachers, and the deacon in the stable earlier, shaking hands and greeting one another with a holy kiss.

Squaring his shoulders, Judah faced the back of the house — his wife's childhood home. *Of all the places to hold Preaching today.* But the Esh family homestead had been selected two weeks ago. *So be it.* He reconciled his mind. What Lettie had done in evading Grace's recent Ohio visit was neither his choice nor his doing. Still, the way one's spouse behaved affected the entire family, and far beyond — like a stone tossed into a pond.

She'll come home eventually. He'd clung to this very hope all this time, and now to hear — although secondhand — that it was supposedly true gave him renewed strength.

But it was the strange word Grace had used upon her return that had Judah mighty befuddled. *Lettie's out there searching . . . but for what?*

He turned to glance across the yard at Grace and Mandy, in their for-good blue dresses, sandwiched between Lettie's older married sisters and several Esh cousins. But he didn't see Adah anywhere near her granddaughters, where she typically stood before Preaching service. Grace had gone over to see her grandparents on Friday evening after supper to offer them the same slim hope she'd given him: that the woman with whom Lettie had stayed in Baltic had said Lettie *would* return home eventually. Just when, no one knew.

Then, when Judah supposed Adah might be ill at home, she came rushing down in a flurry from the *alt Scheisshaus* — the old outhouse — the Eshes still kept for workdays, mostly for the men. Dressed all in black, Adah looked as if she were in deep mourning. And something about the tilt of her posture and the way she held her hands clenched at her sides reminded him of Lettie.

Several times as a young man, he'd walked down that very slope, especially late at night when bringing young Lettie home after Singing. They'd courted so briefly, he'd had very little time to get his bearings around the Esh farm. And Lettie, bless her heart, had been somewhat pitiful to be around — downcast and ever so quiet. At least for the first several dates.

But he'd never forgotten one particular evening, when she'd at last seemed more interested in being courted. Perhaps the full moon had had something to do with it as they walked along Mill Creek, which ran through Jakob's property. They had been out there for more than an hour, just taking their time and wandering alone. Stopping to rest, they'd found themselves standing beneath one of the larger oak trees, not far from Jakob's corncrib — Judah could see it even now in his memory. He'd gotten up his nerve and reached for her small, smooth hand for the first time . . . and, glory be, she'd let him!

He smiled now, recalling *der Schussel* — the scatterbrain — he'd been that night. How completely smitten he had been with Jakob and Adah Esh's beautiful young daughter.

Now the men began moving toward Ethan's house. Adah arrived at the tail end of the women's line, just in time. Not wanting to stare, Judah turned his attention to the reverent demeanor required of him, wanting to come to the meeting with a heartfelt sense of unity. Yet how could he, with his heart nearly in tatters?

Try as he might, he could think only of his wife. Surely Lettie was just off-kilter . . . not able to think clearly. What need did she have to search for anything . . . or anyone?

No matter what others might think, Judah refused to think unkindly of his bride — his dear, dear Lettie-girl.

Lettie was too excited to sleep, despite having been awake nearly all night. At last, she was going home! Although now that she was settled into the large van, she felt nearly wicked, riding in anything faster than a buggy on the Lord's Day. It certainly wasn't an emergency, yet she had paid a driver to take her all the way back to Pennsylvania today. And, goodness, she'd had a time of it, getting someone to drive her on a Sunday.

As for getting in touch with Sally Smucker by phone, Lettie had heard the ring go immediately to the dial tone at every attempt on Friday evening and all day Saturday, when she'd tried repeatedly. Not until a few minutes before the driver arrived at Hallie's — when the Preaching service started in Bird-in-Hand — was she able to get through to at least leave a message for her friend. *"Please forgive me for giving so little notice. I've tried to reach you many times, Sally. You see, I'm heading home today . . . but I need a place to stay. Lord willing, I'll arrive at your place around midafternoon, if that's all right with you and Preacher Josiah."*

She'd paused then, gathering herself lest she weep into the phone. *"I have much to ask forgiveness for,"* she had concluded, then hung up.

Lettie now glanced at the other Amish folk in the van, all of them talking amongst themselves. A family of six, with two sons and two daughters. *Like mine.*

But, forgetting to include her first baby, she caught herself. Would it always be like this — stumbling to embrace that first child in her awareness, yet living with the knowledge of that very real babe inscribed on her memory?

Suddenly weary, she closed her eyes against the busyness of the road. The driver rarely spoke, but presently he was talking to the husband of the family, and the sound of the familiar *Deitsch* comforted her some.

She couldn't help wondering if Sally Smucker would listen to the voice message in time. It would never do for Lettie, of all people, to make a surprise arrival there at the preacher's house. And what of Judah's and her reunion — how would he react?

Lettie could scarcely imagine such a meeting, yet she couldn't deny her longing for Judah's arms, for his welcoming embrace. More than almost anything.

Chapter Twelve

That evening, Grace respectfully declined Mandy's pleas to attend Singing with her. Grace stood barefoot in the grass near Adam's black open buggy as Mandy shrugged at her and hopped in. Adam, for his part, whistled as he hitched up his sorrel driving horse, Sassy, evidently not in any hurry.

The evening sky was still blue in places, though streaks of pink and gold appeared as the sun began to set. It was warm enough for Mandy to go without wearing her best shawl, although she'd tossed it into the buggy just in case.

As she waited for Adam to finish, Mandy remarked on Willow's steady progress toward recovery. "Such a blessing! And even if Willow's never a trotter again, we'll have her round for a *gut* long time now, jah?"

Adam peered across the back of his mare at Mandy. "You can't predict that."

"I'm just glad Dat gave Willow more time to get better," Mandy said, sitting there all chirpy in Adam's fine courting carriage. She seemed quite content this evening.

Is she relieved I'm back? Grace wondered.

"So, Mandy, do ya expect to have yourself a ride home tonight?" Adam flashed her a grin.

"I'm thinkin' so." Mandy glanced at Grace. "You'd have a ride, too, if you'd come along, sister."

Grace blushed, thinking of Yonnie. "I'm not up to it."

"Aw, Gracie . . ." Mandy rolled her eyes, then reached up and touched her hair, smoothing it down on either side of the middle part.

She seems so sure of herself, Grace thought, hoping Mandy's beau wouldn't judge her on whether Mamma was in her rightful place, back here at home — when and if he heard about Grace's trip. To her embarrassment, Grace couldn't imagine anyone *not* having heard by now.

"Well, if you do end up needin' a ride, just come back with Priscilla and me," Adam suggested, still tightening the lines.

Grace wasn't surprised at Adam's willingness to talk so freely of his fiancée. Thanks to Prissy's wagging tongue, most young people already suspected they were getting married come November.

"I guess Prissy must not be upset 'bout Mamma anymore," Mandy said.

"Hush, now," whispered Grace. She moved closer to the buggy, sending a warning message to her sister with her eyes.

Adam patted the horse's rump. "I s'pose Prissy's heard a-plenty."

"No doubt." Mandy sounded suddenly sad.

Adam gave her an understanding smile. "Prob'ly more than she cared to hear."

All those gossiping hens under one roof at Preaching today, Grace thought.

Mandy sulked. "What I want to know is, who's Mamma been searchin' for all this time?"

Grace didn't honestly know, so she kept quiet. Adam took off his straw hat, fanned his face, and put it back on. Fact was, they all felt helpless, and there was nothing a one of them could do to remedy the situation. Goodness' sakes, Grace had certainly tried.

Now all they could do was keep busy with their daily chores, hoping the Lord might nudge Mamma back to them — the sooner, the better.

■ ■ ■ ■

Due to unforeseen problems with the van, the trip to Lancaster had taken hours longer than Lettie anticipated. The other passengers were nodding off, including the adults.

The mother of the children riding in the van was cradling the youngest in her arms. The darling little girl was sound asleep, her blond hair all schtruwwlich, the rose-colored dress and white apron crumpled. Lettie couldn't help thinking of the little girl she'd given up and wondering if her adoptive mother had held her so very close in this way.

In two weeks or so, she'd hear something back from the Ohio Adoption Registry, or so Dr. Hackman had assured her. She hoped the time would go quickly till that important letter arrived in the mail. By then, she would have told Judah about the child and what she'd done in an attempt to gather information from the Ohio court system. Lettie yearned to lay bare her many secrets, bringing peace to herself and even offering forgiveness to Mamm. Truly, these long weeks away from home had worked to soften her heart. No longer did she ponder what her life might've been with Samuel; that curiosity had vanished for good. She'd begun to fully understand — and cherish — what God had given her. It was by no means perfect, but it was hers all the same.

Twilight hung like a blanket as they approached Bird-in-Hand. A slight haze was present, reminding her of Holmes County, Ohio, where she'd spent the bulk of her time away from home.

Lettie was wide-awake as the driver made a left-hand turn off Route 340 onto Beechdale Road. She sighed as the familiar sights came into view — Judah's new lambs wandering the pasture, the field mules and driving horses plodding along, heading toward the stable. *Where's Willow?* She looked but didn't see her favorite mare.

Staring longingly, Lettie wondered if she would ever live there again with her husband and family. She wished it was possible to spot Judah . . . near the barn maybe. Oh, to lay eyes on her man!

Hungry to take in every speck of the landscape, she gazed at the north side of the house, where her parents resided, and pressed a hankie to her quivering mouth. *Does Mamm miss me?*

A stream of tears came suddenly, arriving with a strange yet freeing understanding so powerful Lettie could hardly wait to throw her arms around her mother to tell her how sorry she was. "I can forgive her now," she whispered into her hands. "Thank you, heavenly Father!"

In a few short minutes, Preacher Smucker's place would be in full view. She'd get out, the driver would retrieve her suitcase from the back of the van, and then she would be at the mercy of Josiah and Sally, who might not want to receive her whatsoever. At least once the preacher knew of her sins. And then what? Once Lettie disclosed why she'd left her husband and children, there was no telling what the Smuckers or anyone else would say or do.

By the moon's radiant light, the stream looked exceptionally swollen. *From recent rains,* Grace thought as she walked along Mill Creek.

Two full hours had passed since her brother and sister departed for the Singing, and she'd waited till after sundown — coming later each day — to go walking. For while Grace had said she wasn't up to going, she couldn't bear to sit in the house. She felt terribly restless as she recalled her siblings' reaction on Friday to the news of Mamma's leaving Ohio. Adam had looked downright forlorn, while Joe, on the other hand, had frowned and shook his head in disgust. Most surprising was Mandy, who'd seemed to take it more in stride. Still, the knowledge Mamma hadn't come home with Grace was difficult to accept all around, even for her grandparents, who had been very quiet when she'd talked gently with them.

Now, wishing to rid herself of her heaviness, Grace reached inside her dress pocket and touched the marble-sized Cape May diamond Yonnie had found at the seashore and given her. Never before had she seen anything like it. Would it be rude to offer to return it? *It wasn't a special gift to an intended, like Henry's chime clock.* She wondered what her former beau had done with the lovely clock.

She held the quartz crystal up to the gleaming white moon, fascinated by the way the silvery beams shimmered through it. *Such a pretty token.* The only other time a fellow had given her something so eye-catching was back when she attended the nearby one-room schoolhouse. Her brother Adam had found some "fool's gold" during recess one morning. It had looked so pretty, so convincing, that Grace had known it was an extra-special gift, whether real gold or not.

Presently she strolled past the old run-down woodshed, covered over in thick kudzu vines, her mind still on her childhood. She could smell summer lurking, even though the days were still cooler than she liked, especially for going barefoot. Anymore she much preferred socks and shoes to the feel of the cold grass against her bare feet, at least on this side of the season. *Must be I'm no longer a child,* she thought, remembering how eager she used to be to abandon her shoes nearly as soon as the trees started to bud.

Glancing across the way at Becky Riehl's house, Grace saw faint golden light radiating from each of the upstairs bedrooms on this side of the big farmhouse. *Which is Heather's room?* she wondered. Perhaps Heather was packing her things at this very minute, preparing to move to the Wellness Lodge tomorrow. It was worrisome to consider what might be ahead for her new friend. And she *did* consider Heather a friend. After all, they'd spent a good many hours together traveling to and from Ohio, and Heather had shared something of her heart regarding her deceased mother. Grace would not quickly forget the tender remarks coming from the typically tight-lipped young woman . . . so reticent about personal things.

So far, though, Heather had not hidden inside a turtle shell like Becky had warned she might soon after Grace had met the girl. If anything, Heather had carried a good half of the conversation on the drive home. Grace found it amazing that an Englischer was so empathetic, even caring, about Mamma's whereabouts.

She continued walking, surprised there were no courting buggies in sight. Almost certainly Adam was out riding with Prissy. While the girl could be outspoken, even sassy, she *was* exceptionally smart and had always gotten good grades in school. And, too, you never had to wonder where you stood with someone like Priscilla Stahl.

Not like Mammi Adah, who tries to hide things.

Grace couldn't get over the fact her grandmother had worn full funeral attire to Preaching this morning. Even Mammi's grave look had matched her somber dress and apron. Had she given up hope?

Now, as Grace walked in the stillness of twilight, she doubted she'd ever sleep soundly again — not till Mamma returned. Until that time, there would be no end to the turmoil. Mamma's indifference toward all of them was reflected in the faces of everyone who'd ever loved her, especially in poor Dat's. And even though Susan Kempf had maintained Mamma was surely coming home, there was still no sign of her.

Chapter Thirteen

Sally Smucker was known throughout the community as a gracious and submissive woman. The wife of the younger of the district's two preachers and mother to six children, she'd followed the Lord in holy baptism at the youthful age of sixteen, when other girls were more interested in attending Singings and pairing up with potential beaus. Sally was not only a dutiful woman; she was a good friend to everyone who'd ever known her. Lettie included.

Sally had nearly died of cancer, which may have contributed to the gentleness of her mannerisms, although Lettie had always known her to be a tender soul, offering a kind touch and a soft voice to her little ones.

Now, as Lettie carried her suitcase up the lane to Sally's back door, she wondered just how cordial her longtime friend might be tonight. Would the preacher's sympathetic wife open the door wide and invite her in?

Lettie's heart was fragile yet hopeful as she stood silently at the back stoop. She rapped on the door, her heart beating ever so fast. Then, so as not to frighten her dear friend, Lettie called quietly through the screen door, "Sally . . . it's Lettie Byler. Did ya get my message?"

In an instant Sally was at the door, smiling. "Oh, goodness . . . you're here at last!" Even with a toddler in her arms, she gave Lettie a generous hug. "Come in, won't ya?" Then, stepping back, she said, "I was getting worried 'bout you — expected you sooner."

Lettie explained that the van had broken down, and how they'd had to wait for someone to come replace a part under the hood. She told about the Amish family from Indiana traveling with her; the young mother had fretted they'd have to spend the night on the side of the road.

"I was prayin'," Sally said, looking quite relieved. She motioned her inside the kitchen, past the pretty shelves of soaps out on the porch. "I've got your room all ready. Well, actually, you can have your pick of two rooms — one down and one up."

Lettie followed her to the bedroom on the main level, which was the obvious choice, since the children all slept upstairs and she would be more out of the way there. "Did you tell Preacher Josiah I was comin'?" she asked hesitantly.

Sally's eyes turned serious and she glanced at the little blond girl in her arms. "He'll be wantin' to talk to you first thing tomorrow. You assumed that, jah?"

Lettie said she had. After all, there were important rules that must be followed, generations of tradition to uphold. She would do her part and submit fully.

"Josiah's mighty cautious, truth be told." Sally moved to the doorway of the small guest room. "He wondered why you didn't go directly home to Judah."

"Naturally, he would."

"Wouldn't your husband want to know you're safe?" Sally's eyes probed her own. "Judah's struggled so . . . since you left. I thought you ought to know."

Oh, she was heartsick hearing it. Hurting him that way had been all her doing.

"Would Josiah be willin' to pave the way for me?" Lettie asked, going to sit on the edge of the bed.

"I'll talk to him." Sally stood with her wee one on her hip, rocking back and forth. "You've come this far, Lettie. Don't lose heart."

Lettie looked around, feeling a bit displaced in yet another woman's house. "It feels *gut* to be here." Her gaze stopped on the oak bureau Judah had helped Josiah make some time ago.

"Well, I'll let you be. You're tired from traveling," Sally said with a concerned frown. "There's plenty to eat — just make yourself at home. You're welcome to anything." Sally pulled the door closed and left, and Lettie looked about for her suitcase. But she stayed put on the bed, too weary to search for it.

Leaning against the pillows, she hoped she'd done the right thing, coming here. Sighing, she had the distinct impression Preacher Josiah had said more to his wife than what Sally had shared. In fact, Lettie had a feeling there'd been a long discussion about how to handle her return with the brethren and the membership. And her husband. *To think Judah is aching over my absence.*

Turning, she looked out through the window at the darkening sky. *Oh, Father in heaven, please soothe my husband's broken heart. Mend our marriage. In Jesus' name, I pray. Amen.*

After some time had passed, she remembered where she'd left her cumbersome suitcase . . . right where Sally had first welcomed her. Making her way back to the little soap shop on the porch, she suddenly realized how very quiet the house had become. Where had Sally gone? Upstairs to tuck in the children, perhaps?

As she approached the porch, she overheard Sally talking softly to her husband outdoors, the toddler making little bird sounds nearby. They must've been standing out behind the wide sycamore tree somewhere.

"Ach, she looks ever so weary," Sally was saying.

"I 'spect she is." Josiah's words sounded detached.

"Please, won't ya spare her, 'least for now?"

A long pause. And then, "Lettie's breached the *Ordnung.*" It was the reply Lettie had expected.

"Not to argue, dear, but what can be accomplished tonight?" Sally asked gently.

Reaching for her suitcase, Lettie hoped the minister might heed his wife's request. She felt nearly limp and on the verge of tears as she carried her suitcase into the kitchen, past the table, where a basket of fresh fruit graced the center. Too exhausted to stop and reach for even a few ripe strawberries, she headed for her room.

Closing the door, she felt certain the preacher would not offer his counsel tonight — urging her to own up to her sins in his hearing. No, Preacher Josiah Smucker had a real compassionate side to him. Surely Sally's earnest pleading would allow Lettie one peaceful night before tomorrow's dreary talk.

Grace was glad she'd worn shoes as she continued her amble near the creek bed. Tree roots had pushed out of the ground, causing her to stumble on the uneven ground, though she had not yet fallen. Being more careful now, she was grateful for the abundant light of the moon. Such a pretty night — ideal for courting.

She imagined Mandy with her beau, wondering if she was indeed seeing Becky's cousin. Then she thought of Adam. Sometimes it was hard to picture him riding contentedly with Prissy in his open buggy. Of course, there was really no need to borrow trouble over their coming union this fall. Even so, there were times she wondered why Henry Stahl's sister hadn't called things off with Adam. Why hadn't Prissy used Mamma's mysterious absence as an excuse when she'd been so outspoken against Grace's going in search of Mamma?

Was she just determined to marry Adam in spite of Mamma's bewildering behavior?

Unable to shake off the wretched musings, Grace let herself cry. *Better out here, where no one will feel sorry for me.* Tears rolled down her cheeks and dripped off her chin onto the cape part of her apron. She wished Prissy kept her thoughts to herself more often. Adam deserved as much.

"Hullo," someone was calling to her just ahead.

Startled, she stayed mum.

"Who's there?"

The voice sounded familiar.

Grace continued walking, less sure of herself now and looking around her carefully. She made no response.

"Grace Byler, is that you?"

Oh no . . . Yonnie! She picked up her pace, hoping she wouldn't end up walking directly into him.

But as it turned out, she most definitely did. He laughed and seemed pleased, if not overjoyed to see her. "Well, isn't *this* interesting?" He fell into step with her immediately, going now in the opposite direction he had been coming. "I didn't expect to see you here," he said boldly.

She glanced over her shoulder, aware now that Uncle Ethan's house was only a half mile away. "Goodness, I didn't realize I'd come so far."

"I'm glad you did, Gracie."

Gracie . . . She liked the sound of her nickname on his lips. She brushed back her tears, hoping the trees concealed her sadness. The last thing she wanted was for Yonnie to see her this way, especially when he had cast several quizzical glances in her direction during the common meal today.

"I looked for you at Singing," he said. "But Mandy said you weren't up to goin' after your trip."

She felt sheepish at Mandy's excuse. *He talked to my sister about me?*

"A pleasant stroll by the light of the moon is a *gut* way to relax," he said, letting her off the hook.

Turning, she looked at him — this handsome fellow who effortlessly said the nicest things. "Just so you know, Mamma wasn't in Baltic, after all."

"I heard that."

" 'Least not by the time I got there." She explained that Mamma *had* been there. "My family was so disappointed when I returned without Mamma."

"But it's not your fault you didn't find her."

"I s'pose not."

"No, no . . . I mean it," he said. "I'm concerned for you, Grace. You need to get past this."

"How would *you* feel?" she asked quietly.

"Prob'ly exactly like you do." His voice was gentle.

She didn't want to discuss this further. Not now, with the night so painfully sweet and the moon nearly too bright. She felt too susceptible to his kindheartedness.

The Cape May diamond shifted in her pocket as she walked. *Dare I bring up his question about us courting?*

He continued talking, saying that a few of the young men were getting together tomorrow after supper to chop down the kudzu vines across the road from Andy Riehl's. She mentioned that Adam and Joe might want to help and glanced up at him, breathing easier suddenly.

"We'll be glad for any help we can get."

She told him what Adam had said about not wanting to get the Lancaster authorities involved by reporting the vine. Dat had read that some communities were being coerced to spray the toxic weed. "They've had to bring in outsiders to do it."

"I can see why the bishop wants to handle things. Daed says there's something like over a hundred sites in Pennsylvania where the vine is thriving. And from what he heard over at the buggy shop, the state doesn't have any funds for an eradication program."

"Sounds like it's just as well we're taking care of it ourselves, then," Grace commented. "Hopefully you'll have a nice day."

Their conversation turned to the exceptionally warm night, and then Yonnie mentioned an upcoming work frolic at the nearby schoolhouse. "The school board wants to get it all spruced up and painted for next fall," he said.

Grace listened, but his important question of the other day — and her obvious lack of a reply — nagged at the corners of her mind. Still, Yonnie's easygoing and down-to-earth manner was so pleasant, she felt less inclined to broach the subject. She wanted to be in the right frame of mind, and just now she was anything but.

Meanwhile, Grace and Yonnie talked and walked deep into the night, farther and farther away from her father's house. . . .

Chapter Fourteen

All day Adah had fretted and fussed over Jakob. He wasn't himself during Preaching, nor at the common meal, when he had sat and picked awkwardly at the food on his plate. But when he had passed up the *snitz* pie, Adah knew for sure something was wrong.

Now, as she sat in bed, she watched him thrash about, muttering futile words in his fitful sleep. His breathing, too, was shallow — sometimes he didn't breathe at all for fifteen or more seconds at a time. *What the world's wrong? Is Lettie weighing on his mind again?*

Her husband had always been strong as a mule, the healthiest son of all Mother Esh's boys. Strong mentally, too. If only he'd wake up so Adah could talk to him and ease his worries. She wanted to take his hand and offer a prayer for peace. During his waking hours today, she'd tried to soothe him by diverting his attention to mundane things, especially during their ride back from Ethan's — their former homestead.

Jakob wasn't the only one who'd seemed agitated today. She'd noticed Judah shifting his weight from one foot to the other as he waited to go inside the house with the other men, and she'd seen the terrible disappointment on his face.

"Oh, Lettie . . . if only you had an idea of what sufferin' you've caused here," she whispered into the stillness. *I'm a big part of it, too,* she thought, tears burning her eyes.

Her husband stirred in his sleep, muttering sadly as he turned over yet again.

Jakob needs Lettie home, O Lord, she prayed, getting up and walking from the room to the very end of the hallway. *So does Judah.*

She peered through the dormer window into the nearly iridescent moonlight and wondered if Grace had returned. The girl had slipped out of the house some hours ago. Adah had strained her neck to watch her head north, past the Riehls' place, walking fast, like she had someplace to be.

Like Lettie used to rush off to meet her first beau. The jolting remembrance rushed over her. Like most mothers, she'd merely watched from the house, hoping the best for young Lettie and gritting her teeth all the while. Never once had Adah attempted to follow her, although she'd known of one mother who'd silently chased after one of her rebellious brood during his Rumschpringe, just to see what he was up to.

Maybe if I'd done that, things would've turned out differently . . . and Lettie'd be at home even now.

She wandered back to the bedroom, where Jakob had begun snoring loudly. Going to the oak blanket chest he'd made before their wedding day, she dug clear down and found what she'd been thinking about nearly all day: an envelope with the name of a doctor printed on a letter inside, along with other information written in midwife Minnie Keim's own hand.

Moving to the bedroom window, Adah opened the letter and read the kindly man's name: *Dr. Joshua Hackman.*

"Lettie . . . have you finally found what you're longing for?" she whispered. "I wish now I'd helped you find your child." *My own granddaughter . . .*

Grace and Yonnie walked north together, bathed in moonglow, the white light shining on their shoulders like shimmering butterflies. Pleasantly they discussed the many ways to keep the Lord's Day. Grace listened as Yonnie told of his family's surprisingly strict approach to keeping the day holy.

"Some of my cousins, out west — Indiana, ya know — were allowed to go fishin' or even swimming when I was a boy, but Daed never let us," Yonnie told her. His voice was clear but quiet, and the rhythmic sound of it made Grace want to soak up every word.

"We know some folk down near Quarryville who let their young children swim or run through sprinklers on a Sunday," she said. " 'Specially the no-Preachin' ones."

Yonnie shook his head. "Daed wouldn't allow that. He believes that each and every Lord's Day is to be reverently observed, no matter if we gather for worship or not."

Grace could remember sitting on the wood floor in young Becky's bedroom, playing with their faceless dolls on Sunday afternoons. Sometimes, when they were older, they even discussed sewing projects on those quiet days, and she wondered what Yonnie might make of that. Not that she wanted his approval; she just wondered how dogmatic he might be . . . if he knew.

"What about volleyball?" Yonnie suddenly asked. "Have you ever played on a Sunday?"

"A few times, but Dat always cautioned us to keep our voices subdued."

Yonnie chuckled. "Well, how's that possible?"

"Jah, it's hard to play without makin' a sound," she agreed, deciding she wouldn't bring up playing jacks out on Becky's sidewalk, either. No, their occasional squeals of delight whenever they'd get all the jacks in a swift sweep of the hand would undoubtedly not have been to Ephram Bontrager's liking.

Now, considering it, she saw that she and Becky — and sometimes Mandy — had spent plenty of Sunday afternoons in fun. She and Becky would ride their scooters lickety-split down the road, then throw their scooters into the shade behind the old telephone shanty and sit back there under the trees and whisper secrets. Sometimes they'd even listen in on folks' phone calls — which they knew was wrong — watching dust particles hang in the air like the thin curtains some Englischers had in their fancy bedrooms.

Grace shrugged away the frivolous memories and wondered how long Yonnie was going to follow the creek before turning back. Would he walk her to her house yet tonight? The thought of going alone all that way suddenly seemed very unappealing, and she sighed.

"What is it?" Yonnie looked down at her.

"Nothin', really."

"Thought you were 'bout to say more."

She shook her head, changing her mind. They were quiet for a time, the only sound the snapping of twigs beneath their feet.

Then, a few minutes later, Yonnie spoke. "Have you thought about what I asked ya, before you left for Ohio?" His voice was soft again.

She felt sad that he'd brought it up. "Jah, quite a lot."

He slowed his pace, waiting.

"Oh, Yonnie, I'm in no position to accept your offer of courtship. Not yours or anyone's." She faltered. "My mother wasn't out in Ohio visiting a friend when the Fisher girls saw her last week. She'd only just met Susan Kempf when Mamma accepted her offer to stay at her house for a while."

"I see." Yonnie's words hung there, as if they'd gotten caught on a tree branch overhead.

"Susan told me that Mamma was on some sort of search."

"She left home on a search?" Yonnie asked.

"Susan seems to know more than what she told me." Grace felt much too comfortable talking to him like this — she'd explained too much already.

Stricken, she reached into her pocket and pulled out the beautiful Cape May diamond. Raising it, she held it out before her and stopped walking. "I don't know how to say this, but I think I ought to return this to you."

He placed his hands over hers, curling them around the stone and giving a gentle squeeze. "No, Gracie, it's yours."

"Denki," she whispered, afraid he might hear the tremble in her voice. "Ever so kind of you."

"A gift from a friend is meant to be kept." His words might've sounded like a reprimand had anyone else spoken them. But his considerate tone made it possibly the sweetest thing she'd heard a fellow say.

"Friends, then?" she said shyly.

"Sure, Gracie. If that's what you need."

She knew what he meant, and she was thankful she hadn't offended him.

A full hour before dawn Monday morning, Grace was up and already starting the washing in the cold cellar. There, in the dingy area across from hundreds of canned goods on rows of makeshift shelves, she sorted through yet another pile of dirty clothes. She couldn't stop thinking how nice it was of Yonnie to walk her all the way back home last night. If not for the situation with Mamma, she could certainly see herself regularly enjoying the company of this young man.

Hearing someone on the stairs, Grace looked to see Mammi Adah moving toward her empty-handed, her hair tidy and neat. Her eyes had gray shadows beneath them, and her thin mouth was drawn as she shuffled across the cement floor.

"Mornin', Mammi." She felt as tired as her grandmother looked.

"Heard you up, dear."

"Wanted to get an early start."

Mammi smiled wryly. "Earlier than usual."

"Jah." *Need to keep myself busy.*

Just then, Grace remembered seeing Mammi Adah, as a much younger woman, herding a whole group of towheaded grandchildren outside to pick blueberries very early in the day. Mammi had touched the top of each little head, smoothing hair as soft as corn silk before Grace and her small cousins had all marched across the yard, carrying their buckets to the berry rows. Oh, but Grace wished she could recapture the happy, safe feeling she'd had then.

"I wish I'd found Mamma and brought her home," Grace said. "I wish it every day."

Mammi Adah fluttered her wrinkled hand.

"You're not to blame."

"But still."

Mammi's eyes were suddenly moist, and she moved toward the pile of the boys' clothes and leaned down to help sort the whites, colors, and darks. "We'll work hard and keep caught up with chores," she said more softly. " 'Tis best thataway."

Jah, 'tis.

Once the whites were loaded into the wringer washer, Mammi asked, "How was it . . . traveling with the Englischer to Ohio?"

"Just wonderful-*gut,* really. Heather's very nice, and we did a lot of visitin'." Grace measured out the laundry soap and sprinkled it over the clothes. "It's funny, but her birthday's in April, too."

Mammi nodded absently.

"You know," Grace said, "I think you'd like Heather if you got to know her better."

"Keep in mind she's English, so she may not be the best choice of a friend."

She bristled at her grandmother's pointed remark. There were other worldly outsiders who'd become fast friends with some of the People, and as far as she'd heard, no one seemed to quibble over that. Martin Puckett, their driver, came to mind. Why, she'd observed her own father talking quite spiritedly with Martin on several occasions.

But seeing her grandmother glower presently, Grace knew better than to press things further about Heather Nelson.

CHAPTER FIFTEEN

Heather finished up her last-minute packing long before she heard the clink of silverware and dishes downstairs in Marian's kitchen. She also managed to respond to well-wishing text messages from her online friend Jim, as well as from her father, who said he was definitely coming tomorrow.

On Heather's second trip to the car, Marian stopped her in the kitchen and offered to store her extra clothing and books. "Just till you're ready." Heather smiled and thanked her. "I mean it. I'd love to help out," Marian said. "You might even wish for a nice, hot, home-cooked meal by that time."

It was obvious that very few folk understood what transpired at the lodge, something Heather was about to experience firsthand. "I really haven't decided what I'll do after my juice fast," she told Marian, "but I appreciate the offer."

"Oh, but surely you'll want to stay round here while your father's house is built?" A smile flickered across her face. "Won't ya?"

Even though it was a mere ten days until the lodge stay was finished, Heather couldn't allow herself to think that far ahead. "I have no idea where I'll be, but it's very nice of you to offer, Marian. Thanks so much."

Marian called for one of her teenage sons to *"Kumm mit!"*

"Oh, that's all right," Heather said. "There's really not much luggage left."

But Marian insisted, and by the time the trunk was loaded and Heather was waving good-bye to nearly the whole family, lined up like birds on a power line, she almost felt sad. Backing up to the road, she recalled her mood the first time she'd pulled into this lovely long lane, nearly a month ago. She gave one last wave to young Rachel and Sarah, who'd run barefooted all the way down to the road after her, flapping their little hands in the air.

Should I have told Marian about my Ohio Amish roots? she wondered during the short drive. *What about Grace — should I tell her?*

When she pulled into the parking lot of the lodge, Heather was feeling rather blue. She breathed deeply and straightened, putting on a smile as she trudged up the sidewalk. *Buck up, girl. This could be the first day of the rest of your life. . . .*

Inside, Heather was impressed by the airy, bright entryway and plant-filled common area, as well as the exceptional congeniality of the staff. A petite, blond young woman named Arielle showed her to a small but cozy room upstairs. The space was modestly furnished and had a west-facing window, which Heather preferred, being a night person. When Arielle left the room, Heather stretched out and tested the mattress on the oversized twin bed. It was not on par with the pillow-top mattress she was accustomed to at home, nor was it as comfortable and firm as the bed at Marian's, but it would be fine for the duration of her stay. Already, though, she missed her cheery room at the Riehls', as well as her larger suite of rooms back home, so ideally removed from the main part of the house. *Like a miniature Dawdi Haus,* she mused, missing her childhood home so much she felt pulled back to it like a magnet. *The house where Mom fought her final battle so bravely.*

But today was about Heather's battle, and she knew she'd better get on with it. Downstairs, Dr. LaVyrle Marshall, dressed to the nines in a peach-colored suit and tan heels, was smiling and talking with different people in the gathering room, welcoming the new patients — eight in all, including Heather. The naturopath's eyes were kind and her expression disarming as she began to discuss the "daily program here at the lodge." *A regimen,* Heather decided as she once again heard the numerous aspects described, including how to begin and break a fast. The level of detail made it evident LaVyrle believed in treating the whole body. "Your time here is about helping your body to find the problem area, and letting your *body* get to work on it."

There were other elements that brought healing, as well, LaVyrle said. "For instance: drinking pure water, breathing deeply, loving fully, having faith, embracing hope . . . and nurturing friendships. I consider all of these vital to optimal health." She then launched into the differences between acidic and alkaline foods, emphasizing the importance of achieving the right balance in one's diet. She handed out a list of alkaline fruits to each patient before moving on to discuss the benefits of neutral fruits — all kinds of melons, peaches, and strawberries — then talked about the slightly acidic fruits. "Grapes, bananas, avocados, and dried fruits."

Karl, a middle-aged man from Texas with an appealing drawl, asked, "How would someone know if his body's off-kilter . . . er, balance?" Karl went on to tell the group he'd undergone cancer surgery and numerous rounds of chemo and radiation and was still terminally ill. "With only a month or so left to live." He paused. "I've got four grandchildren who put all kinds of zing in my life. . . . I'm doing this for them — and for me." His voice cracked so that he could hardly get the words out.

LaVyrle's eyes glistened as she moved to his side. Touching his shoulder gently, she replied, "Thanks for sharing this with us, Karl."

Heather noticed other heads bobbing in agreement, and she found herself aching for the man.

LaVyrle continued, still standing near Karl. "To help you understand what I mean, a body that is out of balance is an acidic system," she said. "That can cause a number of problems, such as a quick temper, stress headaches, and addictions to everything from alcohol to coffee. At its worst, an overly acidic system creates conditions ripe for deterioration . . . and the growth of cancers." She looked again at Karl, then the rest of them.

"Keep in mind, it's essential for good health that we find the proper balance between alkaline and acidic foods," LaVyrle said, explaining how primitive people groups all over the world seemed to have an innate understanding of this. "For all of you here, that will mean learning to consume more alkaline-promoting foods. The diet of our Western civilization is obviously overly acidic . . . which is why our country leads the world in degenerative diseases."

Heather was riveted, hungry to learn everything she could. She texted Jim later that afternoon, feeling as upbeat as the blogger had said he'd felt at the outset of his time at a similar lodge. He'd never mentioned where he had gone for his detox, and she'd decided not to inquire. Not that Heather wasn't curious. She scanned through his blog archives to see if he'd stated any particular lodge but found no mention.

To think Jim was becoming a good friend, someone she could turn to with her many questions . . . even rely on. Heather was undeniably relieved that she didn't have to go it alone on this somewhat foreign path she'd chosen to regain her health.

From her cheery kitchen, Adah watched two

yellow warblers in the birdbath, flicking water over their backs with their little wings. Another bird joined the others, and the splashing began all over again. She thought of Lettie each time she watched the many birds that visited their yard. And she prayed for her, especially today.

She heard rustling about in the hallway and found Grace out there redding things up. She and Mandy must have made quick work of hanging out the washing. Adah poked her head around the corner. "Gracie," she said. "I've been thinkin' that I'd like to return to cooking in my own kitchen . . . for Jakob and me."

"Well, Mammi, we like havin' you with us for meals," Grace was quick to say.

"Oh, we enjoy the company, too . . . but it's not necessary for us to eat every meal together."

"Ain't a burden at all, Mammi."

"No . . . I never thought that," Adah said. "You and Mandy *do* have an awful lot on you, though."

Grace looked glum. "But let's not go back to the way things were before, ya know."

Before Lettie left . . . "How 'bout if we still join you for the noon meal, then?"

Grace brightened. "Jah, *gut* . . . 'cause it sure seems Yonnie likes talkin' to Dawdi Jakob at dinner."

"I've noticed that, too." Adah tried her best not to grin at the mention of the handsome young fellow, not wanting to embarrass Grace.

"All right, then . . . we'll see you at noon."

Adah felt better already. She'd wanted to bring this up earlier this morning, but Grace had other things on her mind, downstairs with all that washing. Smiling over her shoulder, Adah hurried back to her own kitchen, eyeing it with renewed interest. Oh, she was so eager to cook and bake again.

Jakob wandered in from the back porch just then, huffing and puffing as if he'd walked too far. "Goodness, but that Marian's a magpie." He put his straw hat on the wooden peg near the back door. "She was over talkin' to Yonnie, who's out exercising Willow."

Adah paid little mind as she looked in her pantry for some flour and salt, ready to bake something. *Anything.*

"The young Englischer moved out of Marian's place this morning," Jakob remarked, dropping into his favorite chair with a sigh.

"Marian said something a few days ago." Adah glanced at him, sitting there like a bag of potatoes. "Thought she'd already told you, too."

He looked unconcerned. "Marian's not sure, though, if the girl's stayin' round here much afterward."

She looked out toward Riehls' farm. "Wonder what our Gracie thinks of that . . . if she knows."

"But what's really bothering Marian," he said, "is Lettie staying away. She hardly knows what to think of her disappearing from Ohio."

Adah held a can of baking powder, staring at it. "Well, now, all of us are troubled by that. Ain't so, love?" The rattle of a horse and buggy rolling into the driveway caught her attention. She peeked out the back window to investigate and saw Preacher Josiah Smucker leaping down from his carriage.

Adah was gripped by sudden fear. "Ach . . . has he come to put the Bann on Lettie?"

CHAPTER SIXTEEN

"Well, what's this?" Judah muttered from where he stood just inside the stable. He could see Preacher Josiah coming toward the barn, his long stride marked by the thud of his work boots on the pavement.

Judah stepped forward to meet Josiah, who stretched out his hand right quick. "*Wie geht's,* Judah?"

"Oh, fine . . . just fine."

Josiah looked like he'd slipped out of bed without a thought to his appearance, his straw hat pushed back a ways on his disheveled hair. He glanced about the stable. "Judah . . . are we alone?"

" 'Cept for the animals."

The young preacher placed a hand on Judah's back and led him into the stillness of the stable. "Might be best if ya sat down somewhere," he said, his voice low.

"No . . . I'm all right." He looked at Josiah. "What's on your mind?"

Frowning, the preacher eyed him cautiously. "Lettie's back . . . came in last night. Stayin' over at our place."

Judah's heart fluttered against his rib cage. "Lettie, you say?" He could hardly get the words out.

"She asked me to come see you."

Not waiting to hear more, Judah swept past him, rushing toward the barn door. He never once stopped to consider that acting so impulsively — not even taking leave of the man of God — might be wrong. Only one thing drove his actions now, and he heaved open the barn door and set off running down the driveway, toward the road. Tears stung his eyes as he went.

Lettie's back!

Adah noticed the preacher follow Judah out of the barn, shaking his head as Judah scuttled down the driveway. For the life of her, she couldn't figure where her son-in-law had taken off to, all red in the face.

She tried to return her attention to mixing the dough to make noodles. A nice hot supper of chicken and homemade buttered noodles might just put a smile on her husband's face.

"Mammi!" Grace called to her from Judah's side of the house. "*Kumme* quick!"

Well, now. She'd have to clean the wet dough off her hands before dashing over there — and from the urgent sound in Grace's voice, she'd best do it fast.

She nearly bumped into Grace in the center hallway; the dear girl's eyes were all lit up. "Mamma's back! Preacher Josiah just told me so on his way to his carriage. Oh, can ya believe it, Mammi Adah?"

Her breath caught in her throat and she looked around her. "Where?"

Grace said that, according to Preacher Josiah, Lettie had shown up on the Smuckers' doorstep and spent the night there. "Dat's on his way to see her . . . on foot, of all things." She was smiling to beat the band.

"I saw him dart out to the road," Adah told her. "Oh, Gracie . . . such wonderful-*gut* news!"

Without saying more, they hurried to the front room windows and peered out. In the near distance, Adah spotted Judah still trying to run, huffing and puffing as he stumbled along. Preacher's buggy was bumping down the road after him.

"Well, I'll be," she whispered.

Judah's chest burned with every breath, yet his legs had a mind of their own. Lettie — his Lettie — was but a mile or so away!

She'd come home on her own, just as he'd wished. The thought impelled him onward, despite the cramping pain in his hip.

Then, suddenly, Preacher Josiah pulled up next to him, motioning from the right side of the carriage. "I'll take ya, Judah . . . you'll get there faster."

Stopping, Judah tried to catch his breath but could only pant. "Jah, prob'ly . . . a *gut* idea," he murmured, going around to the left side and climbing up. "Denki, Josiah . . . ever so much."

Grace watched the preacher's horse slow and her father limp around to get into the gray buggy. She glanced at Mammi Adah, who also was still staring out the window. Grace's heart beat so hard. She was thrilled beyond words, wishing she might've thought to dart after Dat and catch up with him. *Oh, to see dear Mamma again!*

"Maybe we should hitch up the horse and head over there, too," she said suddenly.

Mammi Adah shook her head. "Better to give your parents time to work things out."

"Puh, maybe so."

Looking more solemn, her grandmother blinked her big gray eyes. "Trust me, Gracie . . . 'tis best we stay put."

Disappointed, Grace felt helpless to step

away from the window. With all of her heart, she yearned to go to be with her mother. She could just imagine Mamma surrounded by Sally's youngest children, maybe balancing one of the littlest on her hip and walking round the kitchen, cooing in her ear. "Why'd she stay at Smuckers', do ya think?"

Mammi brushed a hair away from her face. "Your Mamma's not one to push her way back, I daresay."

"But this is her *home.*"

"Well," said Mammi, "she may need some time, is all."

Is she sticking up for Mamma?

"Your mother would've come home straightaway if all was well," said Mammi Adah. "That's what I'm sayin'."

This response frustrated Grace no end. She looked hard at her grandmother, knowing for certain she *did* know more than she'd ever let on. *And all along, no doubt!*

A raucous chorus of tree frogs had kept Judah awake last night as they called back and forth over yonder by Mill Creek. The reverberation of the frogs had progressed in his mind to the sound of *Lettie . . . Lettie* as he lay in his bed, trying unsuccessfully to fall asleep. And to think she'd been only several farms away!

Judah sat pitched forward on the buggy seat to the left of Josiah, who held the reins. "How's Lettie look?" he asked, impatient to know more now that he could speak again.

Josiah took a few seconds to respond. "Very tired."

She's traveled a long way. . . .

"Seemed well, though?" Judah asked, struggling for more information.

"You'll soon see for yourself."

Jah, slow down, Judah told himself, aware that his heart was still beating much too fast. He also wanted to inquire about whether the Bann remained an issue now that Lettie was back from her wanderings. But Judah could not bear to ask, and the more he mulled things over in his mind, the more he hoped the ministers would go easy on his wife. After all, she'd returned before the stipulated time they'd set.

One step at a time, he told himself as the short distance to Preacher Smucker's seemed to stretch onward unendingly.

The kitchen was thick with the chocolate-like aroma of naturally sweet carob chips. Lettie was eager to help Sally all she could, baking "healthy treats," as Sally called them. All the while, Lettie tried to picture Judah's reaction to her returning unannounced. *Is he at all happy about the news?*

She spooned out the cookie dough, placing each lump carefully on the greased cookie sheet. As she worked, she wondered what Judah might say to Preacher Josiah . . . to their children, too. Would he allow her to return, or had her selfish decision to set off in search of her eldest child, telling no one, strained the fabric between them beyond what it could bear? Lettie had been so blind to the possibility of a permanent tear that she had been willing to jeopardize her life here in Bird-in-Hand for a child she'd never known. *Chasing dreams . . .*

Yet wasn't it too late to ponder any of this now?

Such thoughts distressed her, especially knowing Preacher Josiah had gone to speak with Judah this morning, after a brief word with Lettie. She heard the clatter of Josiah's buggy returning now all too soon, and a thin strand of dread wrapped around her as she worked alongside Sally. *What's it mean?* she wondered, her heart sinking. *Has Judah rejected me?*

Lettie forced her trembling hands to keep busy with cookie making . . . and looked over at Sally to see if she might be wondering the same.

■ ■ ■ ■

When, at last, Preacher Josiah made the turn into his dirt lane, Judah looked for Lettie outdoors. But apparently she was inside cooking or cleaning with Sally . . . or helping with the youngest girls. Lettie was so good with little children. *The dearest mother my children could've had!*

He noticed the old tire swing out back swaying slightly. The older boys must be off at a fishing hole somewhere, he guessed, seeing no signs of them. As he followed the preacher up the back stoop and through Sally's little soap shop, he felt a pang of sadness, and by the time he looked past Josiah and into the kitchen, hoping for a glimpse of Lettie, the feeling had swelled to grief.

Will she want to see me?

Following the preacher into the kitchen, Judah heard his wife's gentle voice before he ever laid eyes on her. She was talking quietly to Sally . . . something related to baking, he thought. Then he smelled the fresh cookies, and in that moment all the years of their marriage raced back. Lettie was a mighty fine cook indeed.

"Judah's come to see Lettie," he heard Josiah tell Sally, probably hinting for them to skedaddle as Judah stepped into the bright kitchen.

Lettie looked his way and their eyes caught. He saw her lips move silently as she mouthed his name. Her eyes were pretty and blue, as always, but this minute, as she smiled at him, they were filled with expectation. He wondered when the preacher and Sally would scram.

"Lettie, you're here," he whispered, moving toward where she stood at the woodblock worktable, an oven mitt on one hand, holding a cookie sheet. He stopped within a yard or so of her, still caught up in her loveliness. It seemed they were the only two people on God's green earth.

Her lips parted. "Hullo, Judah." She smiled tentatively.

He nodded, wanting to say, *It's wonderful-gut to see you.* But in the background he heard Sally mutter something to one of the children who'd wandered into the kitchen. Just that quick, Judah's awareness of others in the room jolted him back into his usual self-consciousness.

Undoubtedly sheepish, Lettie turned back to her work and removed the warm cookies onto the wax paper on the worktable. Her face was flushed, and if he wasn't mistaken, a tear rested in the crease under her eye.

"Would you like a cookie?" he heard her say.

With a trembling hand, he accepted the warm treat. His fingers brushed against her cool hand, and he felt like a schoolboy at forty-two.

Then, by some small miracle, Josiah was herding the child and Sally out of the kitchen, heading for the front room. Judah waited till they were out of earshot before he spoke again. "Lettie . . . so nice to see ya." He touched her dimpled cheek with the back of his hand.

She put down the cookie sheet and removed the oven mitt, turning to him with a full smile. "It's *gut* to see you, too, Judah."

He moved toward her and kissed her soft cheek, and the sweet smell of her provoked thoughts he'd nearly forgotten. "Come home with me. Will ya, Lettie?"

Her eyes searched his; then she surprised him by reaching for him. "Oh, Judah," she whispered against his chest, starting to cry. He held her close, cherishing the moment he'd yearned for all this time.

The days and weeks of waiting seemed to dissipate with the warmth of her, and he wanted to hold her for hours on end. "I hoped you'd return." He kissed her other cheek. "Truly, I did."

She looked up at him and a great sadness swept her face. "Preacher Josiah wants to speak more with me. Then . . . with the two of us."

He let her step back slightly, away from him. "Jah . . . in due time."

"Today," she said. "Before I can return home with you."

He nodded, immersing his eyes in hers . . . admiring the way her pretty lips moved.

"There is much to tell you." She blinked back tears. "Ever so much, Judah."

Something about the way she said it caused a heaviness to crowd out his breath.

"Where can we go?" He pulled her near again.

"Let's walk," she said.

He reached for her hand and led her toward the soap shop, filled with the sweet-smelling things Sally made for sale. But his surroundings were of no consequence to him now. His wife's small, lovely hand clung to his big, callused one, and she was following him toward the back screen door, then down the back steps, not so much as uttering a word.

Gladly, he would listen to Lettie *this time,* hear her out. And they'd return home together and be done with whatever had caused such an uproar in his wife's poor heart that she'd run away. Soon — very soon — they'd get on with their lives . . . somehow find their way again.

As they walked toward the springhouse, Judah fought hard the urge to simply wrap Lettie in his arms right there and then. He set his jaw, fearful of what might be in store. *Do I really want to know why she left me?*

Chapter Seventeen

Lettie began to tell her secret slowly at first, with Judah still holding her hand. She skipped parts that were unnecessary — such as the times Samuel had urged her to ride in a car to destinations their parents would've frowned upon. Or how Samuel had talked privately with her about *not* joining church.

"I should've told you the truth 'bout Samuel and me . . . right away when you and I first started seein' each other." She paused, gathering strength. She recalled writing her thoughts while visiting Cousin Hallie — her tender thoughts about the hummingbird . . . how it could fly backward. And likening that to her yearning to revisit the past.

The breeze that had cooled her face earlier as they walked down here to the springhouse abruptly stopped. The stillness seemed remarkable to her, and Lettie glanced at the sky in wonderment. "But all that's behind me now."

"I'm not surprised you were fond of him," her husband offered kindly. "I'd guessed as much."

"Well, you were never told why I went with Mamm to Ohio, though. I'm awful sorry 'bout that, Judah." She hesitated a moment. "Maybe you figured that out, too."

Her husband's gaze held her own. "To help a family member, your father said."

"But it was only part of the truth." She must continue and not lose heart. She'd come home to tell Judah everything. Oh, but her words would hurt him terribly, she realized yet again — the reason she'd never wanted to come clean with Judah. Such shame she felt, just looking into his sincere and trusting eyes.

"What I'm tryin' to say, Judah, is ever so hard," she said, her heart breaking. "You see, I had Samuel's baby in Ohio. Mamm and I went to Kidron for the birth . . . and to give the baby away."

His mouth dropped open, and he let go of her hand.

"My parents thought it best . . . that no one should know." Her lip trembled. "In so many ways, I was deceitful, goin' along with it."

His ruddy face had turned white, devoid

of color. "You had a child together?" He looked like someone had struck him square in the face.

"It's nagged at me all this time. Oh, Judah, I'm ever so sorry for keeping it from you!"

He shook his head. "I suspected things . . . that you'd made a mistake."

She nodded, understanding what he implied.

"But I never suspected you'd had Samuel's baby." He turned slightly, facing toward the road. "I never dreamed *this,* Lettie."

"Daed and Mamm advised me against telling you for this very reason."

His ashen face filled with misery.

"I was young, Judah. Ever so young and foolish."

"But you knew better. You know what the Good Book says."

I've wounded him.

He tugged at his suspenders and stared at her, his feet firmly planted in the soil before her. His eyes were like coals of fire. "Who else knows?"

"The doctor who placed the baby . . . and the midwife." She told how she'd found midwife Minnie Keim in Baltic, that she'd only then discovered she had birthed a daughter. "I selfishly went in search of Minnie. I felt I had to do it, but I was wrong to leave you as I did."

"Did ya search for Samuel, too?" His eyes were moist, but not, she thought, with sadness. His resentment formed his tears.

Lettie admitted how sorry she'd felt for Samuel after encountering his twin sister at the spring barn raising in Bart. "It was the first I knew that Samuel's wife had left him a widower . . . and childless. I thought it might ease his pain to know of our child." Weeping now, she covered her eyes.

"He left Bird-in-Hand — he and his family — before knowing?"

She looked into the pain-ridden face of her husband, stunned at how his words seemed to pour out. Stunned, too, that he still stood before her. "Samuel never knew about the baby. Not till I told him a little more than three weeks ago in Ohio."

Judah folded his arms across his burly chest.

"I asked Samuel's forgiveness for what I'd done — for not bein' forthright." She struggled to go on. "I wanted to make things right with him, just as I want to make amends now with you."

"Samuel's held first place in your heart for too long." He said it so quietly, she wasn't sure if she'd heard clearly. Yet, seeing him this distraught, she didn't have the heart to ask her husband to repeat himself.

"I was wrong, Judah." She wanted to add, *If I could do it all again, I'd do things differently.* But her tongue remained locked in place.

"I wish I didn't know this, Lettie." He shook his head repeatedly.

"I'm askin' for your forgiveness, Judah." She almost sobbed the words. "If you can find it in your heart somehow . . ."

His eyes held hers for a long, awkward moment. "I don't know what to say." Then he turned his back to her and waved his right hand absently before walking forward in a daze toward the road.

She wouldn't call after him. No, she deserved exactly this . . . just as she'd known deep within herself on their wedding day.

With a sigh, Lettie walked back toward the Smuckers' house, knowing full well that the bishop and all the ministers had the power to dole out the harshest discipline possible. It was the kneeling confession she feared most. If required, she'd be expected to disclose her many sins before the entire membership of the People.

But Judah's response, and the pain she had carried for too many years, were entirely different matters. Judah was clearly displeased with her. Bewildered too. She had no guarantee he'd ever extend the forgiveness she longed for . . . just as her parents had predicted so long ago.

What right do I have to expect it?

Lettie reached for the screen door and heard the happy sounds of Sally and Josiah with their children — a toddler's soft whimper and the giggle of a youngster, maybe bouncing on someone's knee. The door made a creak, announcing her entry. And the house fell suddenly still.

While Grace waited for the next batch of clothes to dry — and while her hotdish was baking — she wandered out to the stable to see Willow. Yonnie had been walking the recovering mare little by little, back and forth in the barnyard. Yonnie grinned when he saw her, waving her over. "Come help me," he said.

As cheerful as Yonnie always was, she was glad to comply. "Looks like she's not favoring her hurt leg anymore." She touched Willow's shoulder, and Yonnie covered her hand with his own.

"Willow's goin' to be all right," he said. "Like I told ya all along."

She laughed softly and slipped her hand out from beneath his. "Did you hear my mother's back — over at Preacher Smucker's house?"

"Jah. Preacher told Adam and Joe before he left for home."

"Ach, I'm so happy, Yonnie." She smiled up at him. "I wish I could go over there this minute."

He pushed his straw hat firmly down on his head. "If you're happy, then I am, too," he said more seriously.

"I see you're wearin' a broader hat brim than before."

"Wondered when you'd notice." He winked at her.

"When did ya change it?"

"My father and I decided it was time."

"The ministers didn't prompt you, then?" Her smile was wide; she couldn't help it.

"*Nee* — no. We just finally got around to it."

She couldn't stop smiling. Yonnie was the kind of fellow who brought life into any room — or any barnyard. He had an uncanny way of making her feel like he was paying close attention when she talked, too. Like right now. There was no getting around it: Yonnie made her want to be around him.

Even so, what she'd told him last night remained true — with so much about Mamma still up in the air, now was not a good time to begin courting.

Judah walked, stunned, for a half mile before his brother-in-law Ike Peachey happened along in his hay wagon. He accepted the ride without saying why he was heading home on foot from the direction of Preacher Josiah's farm.

"You gettin' your lambs all fattened up?" Ike asked.

"Some."

"Des gut." Ike eyed him askance. "You look like you just lost your best horse."

Judah shrugged. Ike was a friendly sort, but he had no idea of the pit Judah was in.

"Wonder if Adam and Joe could come over and give me a hand with haying this week, maybe."

"Don't see why not."

Ike went on. "Heard that a bunch of fellas are getting together tonight, over at Andy's."

Judah knew all about it. "Bring your sharpest ax."

"Think they can clear out that kudzu vine?"

"We'll sure try."

Ike clicked his tongue, urging the horse to go faster. "Heard any more from your wife?"

"Jah." No need to check his words. "She's stayin' over at Josiah's for the time bein'."

Ike's eyebrows rose. "Well, now . . . so she's back." He smiled. "Grace must be mighty glad, 'specially after her recent trip."

"Grace hasn't seen her yet."

"Well, for pity's sake."

"She'll go and see her mother soon," Judah muttered.

"So, then, Lettie's not goin' home just yet?"

"It's up to the ministers."

Ike looked serious. "Any idea why she left?"

Judah leaned forward. "Wanted to make peace with her past."

"Well, jah, that's a mighty smart thing to do," Ike said. "But only if it don't cause more trouble in the doin'."

Ain't that the truth. . . .

Lettie had looked awful vulnerable standing there before him at Josiah's springhouse. He wished he'd never let her talk so much — just pulled her near and held her for dear life. Because the way he felt now, his love for her seemed mighty desperate . . . even out of place. Lettie had opened her mouth and destroyed his heart with her talk of Samuel and their baby.

Another man's baby? How could she have kept such a terrible secret for so long?

Samuel Graber. The mere thought of his

name made Judah's legs feel stiff as boards. Lettie'd gone all that way to ask *him* to forgive her? Judah was still so jealous, he couldn't shake off the animosity that plagued him. *She chose to comfort Samuel with the news of their child . . . never caring enough to tell me anything at all!*

This was not the time to think again of those maddening frogs that had tormented him last night! They would surely besiege him again tonight, only it would be far worse, knowing what he knew now. And Lettie would sleep in the Smuckers' house, waiting for the next Preaching service to confess her rebellious ways.

Hopefully, the People will forgive her. . . .

Chapter Eighteen

"The ministers want to meet with you in a day or so," Preacher Josiah told Lettie after she had admitted her grave misdeeds to him later that morning. "At that time, we'll decide on the type of confession you must offer the church."

There were four kinds of disciplinary actions, including the kneeling confession, as well as the Bann, which could last as long as six weeks. Members who were in rebellion and not attempting to adhere to the Ordnung could be shunned for life if they refused to repent and come under the authority of the church.

"Will I be allowed to return home in the meantime . . . see my children?" Lettie asked tearfully as she leaned against the side of the corncrib, where they talked privately. She knew that, because of the gravity of her sin and the years of covering it up, there would be dire consequences.

Josiah frowned thoughtfully and removed his straw hat. He ran his long fingers through his matted hair. "For now, that's up to your husband."

She nodded slowly. Everything was being decided by others — her husband, the ministers, and the membership as a whole.

"Sally'll help you move to our smallest Dawdi Haus, since it's vacant," Josiah said. "Just till the bishop makes a ruling."

Deciding my fate. She wondered how long it might be before Judah received her back — if he would at all. She couldn't help but think they might be apart for a long time, given his response to her confession. *Maybe for the rest of my life.*

As for the church vote, if a wayward person sincerely repented and turned from his or her wickedness, the bishop would offer the hand of fellowship within two to three weeks. But Josiah hadn't mentioned any of that.

"Denki, preacher, but I don't have to stay here if it's too awkward," she offered, not knowing where else she'd go.

"We don't mind." Josiah put his hat back on and excused himself to the barn.

Lettie stood there, facing the wooden slats of the corncrib, and leaned her head on its sun-drenched side. Oh, she needed the comfort of Judah's arms . . . and time spent reading the Good Book, especially the more soothing psalms.

But she must not think too far ahead; she must simply manage to live *this* day without fretting or borrowing trouble. As Proverbs 27:1 said, *thou knowest not what a day may bring forth.* Preacher Josiah had said she was welcome here, with him and kindhearted Sally. Perhaps, in due time, Judah's heart would soften. If not, Lettie must keep her chin up — with God's help.

Still shaken, Judah bent low to pull a weed near the edge of his property where the road and the driveway made a T, and the sheep fence edged the grazing land. He stood back up with a groan and looked toward the house, rubbing his soiled hands together. Adah was up there leaning on the porch railing, staring across the road, evidently lost in thought. He dusted his hands against his trousers.

I must speak to Jakob. He wondered if he shouldn't sit Adah down, too. Sure seemed like the two of them needed to hear what was on his mind. Did he dare to let out all the pent-up frustration he'd experienced since seeing Lettie? Her shocking admission still pounded in his head. His sense of reasoning was askew. Truth was, he had little regard for his wife's efforts to soften the blow of her confession. *If she'd just confided all this business about having Samuel's baby before I ever asked her to marry me . . . Well . . . no.* Now that he considered that, he wasn't sure if he would've gone ahead with it, even though he'd loved Lettie then. He loved her even now.

Knowing she'd carried and birthed another man's child — and that she'd conspired with her parents to hide that fact — gnawed at his core. He could not shake it, particularly when he thought back to Lettie's shining joy at the births of their four children.

Looking again at Adah, he stiffened. To think Lettie — and Jakob and Adah, too — had succeeded in keeping their wretched secret from him. He muttered in Deitsch as he walked to the backyard, then made his way to the Dawdi Haus. There, he saw Jakob puffing on his old pipe while sitting on a wicker chair in the screened-in porch. *"Guder Mariye,"* Judah said, wishing he'd had more time to contemplate what he might say to Lettie's father. But he was here now and so was Jakob. He'd have to make the best of it.

"Mornin'," Jakob said, his pipe wobbly

between his white teeth. His hair was combed and he wore his tattered work hat, the straw sticking out in places.

"Got your cane nearby, Jakob?" He thought they might mosey out to the woodshed, maybe — someplace out of hearing, away from the house.

"Right here." Jakob reached to tap on the crook of his cane.

"Time we talk man-to-man." *Again . . .*

Jakob's eyes locked with his. "If it's about Lettie, then Adah ought to be privy, too." No sooner had Jakob uttered this than here came Adah, pushing open the screen door. By the look of concern on her face, Judah knew his father-in-law was right.

"So be it." Judah pulled over another porch chair for Adah and pushed it next to Jakob's. He perched on the porch rail and waited for her to sit, all the while sorting out his thoughts.

"There," Adah said, reaching behind her to situate the yellow-checkered pillow on her chair.

"Lettie will be stayin' on at Josiah's," he began, "till the ministers put their heads together." *And I decide what to do about her living arrangements. . . .*

Adah nodded ever so slowly, her gray eyes serious. But, surprisingly, the more he told them what he knew about Lettie's time as a teenager in Kidron, Ohio, the more relaxed her face became. "I never thought I'd say it, but I'm relieved someone else knows Lettie's secret now . . . 'specially *you,* Judah."

"Oh jah," Jakob piped up. "Adah and I never should've asked Lettie to keep this quiet . . . never should've interfered 'tween you and her. For that, I'm most sorry."

Adah's mouth twitched. She looked at her husband and tears spilled down her face. "It's been just awful livin' with this . . . for so long. And for Lettie, too."

"What'll happen, do ya think?" Jakob asked Judah.

"For now, we'll just have to wait 'n' see," Judah said finally, knowing he was also a big part of the decision-making process, at least when it came to Lettie's relationship with him. Because if he'd wanted her to come, Lettie would already be home.

"Can we visit her?" Adah asked. "And Adam and Grace — won't all the children want to see her?"

"They can go." Nothing like this had ever happened in this church district — not that he knew of, anyhow.

The fresh, pungent smell of late spring drifted lazily through the morning air. A cluster of birds flew out of a stand of bushes over yonder, near the property line of Andy's pastureland. The grazing land literally shone in the shifting light.

"So, then, did Lettie find what she went lookin' for in Ohio?" Jakob had extinguished his pipe and was gripping his cane with his bony hands.

"Never even thought to ask that."

Adah's brow knotted into a deep frown. "Well, either she found her child or she didn't." She turned to Jakob and looked at him for the longest time before she continued. "I have information — had it all these years — if you . . . or Lettie want it. About the private adoption." She sighed heavily, as if an enormous weight was slowly lifting from her.

Jakob's eyes lit up; he was obviously as surprised as Judah was. So there were more secrets hidden away from view than even *Lettie* knew!

Judah glanced again in the direction of Andy's cow pasture, marked with dozens of dairy cattle. In certain patches the meadow grasses were already knee-high. *Ach, too much has happened too quickly for a single morning.* He was a man who preferred order and predictability. All this personal information seeping out first from Lettie . . . and now Adah, was more than he cared to hear.

"Will she balk at makin' a public confession if it's required?" asked Jakob.

"That may be why she came home." Judah felt as if someone else were saying the words.

Adah let out a little wheeze and reached under her sleeve for a handkerchief, which she pushed hard against her mouth. Her face wrinkled up beneath it, quivering, but she said no more.

From the barn, there rose a piercing wail — the sound of one of the last ewes delivering her young. Judah slid off the railing and mumbled that he must see to the keening ewe. With that, he hurried to the barn, relieved to put the tense moment behind him.

O dear Lord, this just cannot be! Grace prayed silently. Her stomach felt cold, and panic bubbled up as she carried the heavy basket of clothes inside from the line. She hadn't meant to, but she'd overheard some of Dat's conversation with her grandparents.

Mamma had a baby before she married Dat!

She didn't want to believe it. And oh, goodness, Mamma might have to confess it in front of the entire congregation!

She stumbled into the house, where Mandy was trying to keep ahead of the folding at the long table. Quickly, Grace concealed her tears by looking away, shaking as she did so. She didn't want her sister to learn such heartbreaking news from her.

She set the wicker basket down right away. "There's more clothing yet," she said over her shoulder, heading back outdoors. Dawdi Jakob and Mammi Adah were still sitting on their porch, and for the life of her, Grace couldn't understand how they could appear so calm.

Making her way through the grass, she eyed the clothesline. There were plenty more damp dresses, aprons, and trousers, but few that were anywhere near dry enough to take in. She had to keep her wits about her, even though she'd love to stop everything and take the pony cart up to see Mamma this very minute. No, Grace would have to wait till later, after making the noon meal and washing dishes, to go visit Mamma at Smuckers'. Maybe she could simply walk, stopping on her way home to see how Heather Nelson was settling in at the lodge. A visit to Heather would certainly provide a welcome distraction.

Still shaken, Grace thought about Mamma's being intimate with her first beau like that . . . back when. Recalling the remarks she'd overheard from her mother's sisters clear last month — when they'd come to help prepare Dat's house for worship — she wondered if the baby's father was the young man who'd given Mamma the poetry books, some of which were now missing from her bedroom bookshelf.

Just then, she saw Yonnie and Joe coming out of the barn, slapping high-fives and talking loudly. "We've got us another healthy new lamb!" Yonnie called to her.

He talks like he's one of the family. She smiled fleetingly at Yonnie, her heart aching at the prospect of his hearing this news.

Downright blue, Grace considered Mamma's plight. Fact was, all the People, Yonnie and his family included, would soon know why Mamma had gone to Ohio.

Sometime after the noon meal, Dat returned to the house and asked Grace and Mandy to go with him into the front room. His eyes were so dark and solemn, Grace's heart skipped a beat.

Slowly, he informed them that Mamma would be staying with the Smuckers for the time being. He added that he'd just told Adam and Joe the same thing, out in the barn.

Mandy appeared bewildered. "Why doesn't Mamma come back home, Dat?"

He bowed his head for a moment, his

hands limp in his lap. Then he raised his head. "The ministerial brethren are deciding how to handle Mamma's disappearance and her return."

"But I want to see her!" Mandy said, dismayed.

Grace reached for her sister's hand as she sat next to her on the little settee. "We all do, Mandy."

"It's all right to go to her at Smuckers'," Dat said, "when there's time."

Chores came first, he meant. After all, a visit over there with Mamma could stretch on for hours.

"I've urged Adam and Joe to go, too," Dat added, to Grace's relief.

But it was clear that Mandy was baffled by the apparent need to keep their mother at bay. "Try and look on the bright side, Mandy," Grace told her sister after Dat left the room. "At least Mamma's within walking distance."

"Well, it makes not a whit of sense!" Mandy rose with a sigh and ambled through the sitting room to the kitchen. She kept going as if she might follow their father clear out to the barn, but then stopped at the side door and peered out. "Ever so peculiar, ain't?"

Maybe not so peculiar, Grace thought,

recalling what she'd so recently overheard. She went to stand behind her sister, placing a hand on her arm. Then, seeing Yonnie push open the barn door for Dat over yonder, she flinched. She hoped their father hadn't included Yonnie in his talk with her brothers, like a third son. Dat was fond of him; she knew that much.

I have a sister I've never met, one who doesn't even know she has four half-siblings. The concept was so foreign, Grace scarcely believed it. She could see why Mamma might be curious to find her grown daughter at this stage of her life, but why had she left her family to do it?

Glancing up at the clock, Grace knew that if she hurried and helped Mandy finish cleaning the kitchen — and bring in the rest of the clothes — she might be able to rush off to see Mamma. Grace wanted to do whatever she could to get her mother home.

Surely Mamma will return soon with Dat's blessing . . . surely.

Mandy agreed, though a bit reluctantly, that Grace should visit Mamma first. Grace was relieved as she hurried past the Riehls' house on foot, waving now to Becky, who was carrying in the washing from her family's clothesline. She made a mental note to catch up with her friend in the next couple days. *It'd be interesting to hear if she* is *seeing Henry Stahl — if she'll even own up to it.*

Temporarily shrugging off Mamma's own secret — stunning as it was — Grace sped up her pace, eager to get over to Smuckers' place. *Oh, Mamma . . . I miss you so!*

Through the screen door, Grace saw her mother folding a heap of children's clothes in the small kitchen of the three-room Dawdi Haus, where Sally Smucker's maternal grandparents had lived before they passed away. Sally had directed Grace to go there, all smiles when she met her coming up the lane. *"Your Mamma surely needs a hug,"* Sally had whispered on the back walkway.

When Grace rapped on the rickety door, she had to steel herself so she wouldn't cry. "Mamma . . . it's me, Grace," she said, touching the screen.

Her mother dropped the little dress she was holding and came swiftly to the door.

Grace opened it and flung her arms around Mamma. They held each other, her mother's breath warm on Grace's neck.

"I missed you ever so much . . . *all* of you," said Mamma, looking into her eyes when they parted slightly.

Grace's own gaze remained glued to her mother's face as they gripped each other's arms. "I'm so glad you're back — oh, you just don't know . . ." She was surprised to note Mamma looked nearly the same — bright blue eyes, plump face — but the sweet new light on her countenance was a welcome change from her former melancholy.

In that moment, Grace fully remembered what hope felt like. How her heart had wrenched with ongoing concern through all the days of waiting till Mamma might come to her senses. And now she was here!

Tears rolled down Mamma's cheeks, and she cupped Grace's face. "It's awful *gut* to see you, Gracie. How's your sister . . . and Adam and Joe?"

"Just fine . . . all of us workin' hard, as always." She told how anxious Mandy was to see her. "I 'spect she'll be over here real soon."

The light dimmed in Mamma's eyes, and she touched her chest, mouth drawn suddenly. " 'Tis a hard time for your father . . . and for me." She said it ever so quietly.

The questions spilled from Grace's lips almost before she realized it. "Ach, Mamma . . . is it true we have an older sister — a half sister?" She could hardly breathe.

"Did you look for her in Ohio? Is that why you went there?"

"Jah." Mamma gave a slow nod. "I see your Dat told ya, which is his right — I should've told you myself." She sighed. "I'm waiting for some word back from the Ohio Adoption Registry, but all that's up to the Lord now."

"You mean you're still hoping to hear something from her?" Grace's voice quivered and she felt helpless to stop it.

Mamma reached for her, pulling Grace into her ample arms. Her mother's tears spilled onto her own face. "Let's not talk 'bout that now. I'm sorry for hurting all of you," Mamma said softly. "I have much to make up to your father for . . . and to you and your sister and brothers."

The sunlight fell on the table, laden with the Smucker children's tiny nightgowns and socks and little aprons. It splashed onto the gleaming wood floor and came to a stop on the far wall, across from the table. In the midst of her own sorrow, Grace was surprised to feel a new kind of love for her mother, who'd suffered these many years under the weight of this burden.

"We love you, Mamma. We never stopped." She said what surely Dat had this morning when he rushed off to see Mamma

— at least Grace hoped this with all of her heart. "And Dat didn't say a word to me about the baby. . . . I overheard him talkin' with Mammi and Dawdi."

At Mamma's pained look, Grace quickly changed the subject. "You know, I came lookin' for ya in Baltic, Ohio." She hadn't planned to tell her, but there she was saying it all the same.

"Oh, Gracie? When?"

"Just this past week . . . I went with Heather Nelson, an English girl who's been stayin' at Riehls'." She told her about Heather's kind offer and how they'd gone together and spent the night with Susan Kempf, after word had come via the Fisher girls that Mamma had been seen at a local hen party. "But since you weren't there, we drove right back last Friday. I was hopin' . . . you'd want to come home with us, Mamma." It was all she could do to keep her emotions in check.

Her mother's jaw sagged, and she let out a loud sigh. "Aw, you poor girl."

"Susan told me you would return to us . . . once you finished searching," Grace said. "At the time, I didn't know what she meant."

Then she began to cry, sobbing into her hands, all the emotions of the past weeks spilling out. Mamma stroked her back and said in soft tones that the elusive daughter somewhere out in the world would never take Grace's place in her heart. "You will always be my sweet Gracie. Always."

Such dear things her Mamma was saying. It took a few minutes to pull herself together. When she had blown her nose and straightened herself a bit, she said, "Sorry, Mamma . . . I shouldn't have. It's just —"

"A terrible shock."

"Is it a shock for Dat, too?" Grace blurted. "Did he know 'bout the baby . . . before now, I mean?"

Mamma's head moved painfully slow. "I never told him." She looked away. "Another one of my sins," she said in a near whisper. "One I regret to this moment."

Suddenly, Grace understood the source of the unmistakable pain in her mother's eyes.

Chapter Nineteen

After her tearful visit with Mamma, Grace was all wrung out, yet she still wanted to see how Heather was faring on her first day at the lodge. Grace found her friend sitting on the lawn beneath a shade tree, her fingers flying across her laptop keyboard. "Hullo," she called, hurrying over to Heather.

Her friend's blue eyes danced when she saw Grace. She put down her laptop and rose to pull a spare lawn chair over for Grace. "I'm glad you came, but I'll only be out here a short time — we're having a little break from classes." Heather explained that each day began with a question-and-answer session, plus "re-education classes," as Dr. Marshall referred to the instruction. "It's fascinating to get a better understanding of how the body works."

Grace glanced back at the big house, where several patients sat on the long front porch. "Are they treating you well,

Heather?"

"Oh yes. But . . . I'm already getting tired of *drinking* my meals and it's only the first day. Boy, am I in trouble!" Heather laughed a little. "But I knew coming here would be a challenge." She shared some of the concepts she was learning. "Chewing is instinctive, so missing it is something that has to be overcome when fasting with liquids."

Grace wondered what it would be like to live solely on juices made from powdered kelp and wheatgrass and other greens. *I'd do it to keep from dying,* she decided.

Heather mentioned two new acquaintances — a teenage girl named Tessa, with leukemia, who had been given only a few months to live; and Jeannie, a young woman whose cancer had spread to her bones. Jeannie had already been on a juice diet for several weeks before coming to the lodge. "Such sad stories." Heather glanced over her shoulder. "I wish I could introduce you to both of them . . . but I don't want to make a spectacle of them." She smiled. "Or of you, either."

Grace looked about her. "They might ask who that Plain girl is you keep company with, jah?"

"Hey, when you're seriously ill, you don't care about other people's business. It just doesn't matter."

Grace leaned into the comfortable lawn chair, glad for the warmth of the late-day sun and the fragrant breeze. Her concern for her mother had subdued a bit now that she was thinking of cancer patients, and she felt ready to share her news with Heather. "My mother's back from Ohio," she announced.

Heather's mouth gaped open. "Are you serious?"

"Jah, it's wonderful-*gut* news."

"You must be thrilled, Grace."

She nodded. "I'm ever so happy."

The cool breeze blew Heather's light brown hair away from her pale face. She seemed more ashen than the last time Grace had seen her, on their trip home.

"Are you getting plenty of rest?" Grace asked.

Heather laughed again, the sound ringing in the air like a melody. "That's practically all we'll be doing when we're not taking walks, drinking juices, or doing other cleansing therapies. Uh . . . don't ask." She gave a half smile.

"Well, I don't want to tire you out." Grace rose from her chair. "Just had to see how you're doing."

Reaching for her laptop again, Heather

said, "I'm documenting these ten days for posterity." She looked up at Grace and their eyes held. Then Heather glanced over her shoulder again, lowering her voice. "I'm not sure some of us are going to make it, Grace." She sighed, her expression sad. "Some are getting this kind of help too late."

"Ach, so very sorry . . ." She couldn't bear to look up at the porch, thinking Heather must've meant someone, or more than one person, sitting there.

Heather closed her laptop and placed it on Grace's chair, then got up from her own chair. They strolled out toward the road. "Thanks for coming, Grace. It was really great seeing you."

"I'll come again tomorrow on my way home from work at Eli's." Grace squeezed Heather's arm as she mentioned the natural foods store where they had met. "Take *gut* care, all right?" Grace waved good-bye, hoping her friend hadn't noticed she was somewhat preoccupied with her mother. Tomorrow was plenty soon enough to reveal that Mamma and Dat were living apart.

The air was muggy and close — *too warm for a late May evening,* thought Judah.

An occasional breeze carried the sounds of insects and the crackle of leaves. Several men had gathered, including Judah, who'd put his ax down only once to catch his breath and in hope of a breeze. The massive kudzu vine had not only taken over the woodshed; its roots were entrenched in the soil. *Like Lettie's secret.*

If Lettie had repented when she was a teen, none of this business with the ministers would be happening now, he felt sure.

He watched Adam, Yonnie, and Joe slash away at the tenacious vine. They'd positioned themselves at various spots around the woodshed. Two of Yonnie's cousins were also helping to eradicate the vine. Judah had noticed the way Yonnie appointed himself the one in charge. *Unlike Adam, who's taken a backseat in things lately.* Judah hoped his eldest wasn't feeling henpecked already, when he wasn't even hitched yet.

If Adam's betrothed was indeed Priscilla Stahl, as Judah supposed, he wouldn't be surprised. Her mother, Susannah, had been anything but agreeable back when she was courting age. After he and Susannah had become friends, Judah had taken her out several times before courting Lettie. At the time, she'd confided in him about her desire to someday run a quilt shop someplace other than her house. He'd found this startling and had told her so, but she had not been deterred.

Of course, he shouldn't have taken her out more than once. Because later, when he didn't continue asking Susannah to ride home with him, she'd been very hurt. Word had it she'd liked him . . . a lot. In hindsight, he was both sorry Susannah had been so fond of him and was hurt by him. But he had never been able to think of her in that way. No, even during those months while Lettie was away with her mother in Ohio, Lettie Esh had always been the girl for him.

Behind the vine-covered woodshed, a mourning dove sang in the stand of oaks. Lettie once had told him the mourning dove's call had sometimes made her sad. *Like she must be right now.* Before he came here to lend a hand with the removal of the vine, Grace had told him that Lettie had moved into the Smuckers' little Dawdi Haus, *"till things get sorted out."* Grace had looked downright miserable as she insisted that Lettie needed him. *"I'm concerned 'bout Mamma,"* Grace had said, wide-eyed and so serious he wasn't surprised when she confessed she now knew the reason for her mother's search.

Judah's mind returned to the task at hand as, all the while, he resented Lettie's deception. The years of their marriage seemed like a lie . . . the sin's menacing tentacles stretching out to destroy and cover over everything in sight.

Will Lettie's past swallow up our family, too?

Heather stayed up longer than the suggested lights-out that night — *like summer camp,* she thought while sitting in bed. She at least wanted to answer Jim's most recent text message before going to sleep. *I breezed through my first full day here,* she wrote back. *A piece of cake . . . um, you know.*

Well, the toxins are still roaring around inside you. Just be ready to feel worse before you feel better, he replied.

I expected to be hungrier than I am! she told him. *You'd think the stomach would go completely crazy with all that juice.*

LOL — just you wait, he wrote. *You'll be hungry eventually . . . really hungry.*

She wondered how he sounded when he laughed. Staring at the ceiling, Heather couldn't believe how comfortable she felt "talking" to him. *Would I still find him interesting, if we ever met?*

Quickly she pushed the preposterous thought away. Getting involved with another guy wasn't wise, especially now. Plus, she absolutely refused to get hurt again. She had a transitory thought of her former fiancé, but she dismissed it. Even fleetingly, she didn't want to think of Devon.

But she *was* concerned for Jim's own health struggles, which were ongoing, he'd said earlier today. So, despite his radical diet and previous lodge stay, he wasn't out of the woods. She shivered at the thought. *All that effort and he's still sick. . . .*

Does the doctor there suggest dry brushing the skin? This can be very beneficial, he wrote.

Absolutely, she typed back. Later, she added: *My Amish friend came to visit this afternoon. She says she's going to visit every day to cheer me up. And guess what? Her mom is back — the woman we went looking for a few days ago in Ohio.* Heather wouldn't go into detail or say how elated Grace was now that Lettie had come home on the heels of their futile trip. None of that concerned Jim. He, too, restricted his comments to the ordinary stuff of his life, or to things pertaining to health — buying groceries at a co-op after getting off work, going for a run. Things like that. But he didn't say where he worked, and she hadn't asked.

Too nosy.

Fighting sleep now, Heather signed off after his last text and slid down into bed.

She placed her iPhone on the small table nearby. Then, pulling up the sheet, she relaxed her arms on either side of her, pulling the sheet taut across her chest.

Will I hit the proverbial wall soon . . . the one Jim warned about? Her eyes slowly adapted to the darkness as she lay there wondering how things would play out. How would she feel on the fourth . . . sixth . . . tenth day? What about weeks from now, after her time at the lodge?

She breathed deeply, as she'd learned to do — four counts as she inhaled, then eight long counts to exhale. She tried to imagine her mom praying for her as a baby, before her parents had even heard about her or knew she was available for adoption. Evidently, waiting for a baby through the local agency in Virginia had taken far longer than her parents had ever envisioned. Mom had seen it as divine intervention when she and Dad had learned through Ohio friends of Heather's availability.

Dad said they fell in love with me at first sight. She felt peaceful with the thought, as she had back home in her own beautiful room. If only her father would reconsider selling the house she and Mom had loved so well.

Should I bring it up again? She wondered if

he'd gone home to put the house on the market. *Is it too late?*

Tomorrow, if he visited, she would stick her neck out and ask.

Long after the Smucker children were tucked in for the night, Lettie opened the back door of the little Dawdi Haus and waved Sally inside, glad for the company. "Are the children asleep?"

"For now, but Isaac tends to walk in his sleep," Sally told her, going to the table and pulling out a chair. "It started after he saw his uncle accidently cut off his thumb while splitting logs."

Lettie cringed. "No wonder."

"Happened more than a year ago."

"Children react differently to troubling things." Lettie got up to put some water on for tea. She hoped her own children would not be severely scarred by what she must tell them. Although her visit with Grace today seemed to indicate otherwise. *Knowing the truth didn't change her heart toward me.* It seemed to Lettie a kind of miracle.

"Not sure how any of us gets through life without some scars," Sally remarked.

The psalm Lettie had read this afternoon came to mind as she set the kettle on the stove. *For thou art my rock and my fortress;*

therefore for thy name's sake lead me, and guide me.

Sally turned in her chair to look at Lettie with concerned eyes. "Are you comfortable over here?"

"Jah . . . fine. And I'm grateful to you and Josiah." She wouldn't say she missed Judah, especially after his warm and welcoming greeting in Sally's kitchen earlier. She'd thought of little more than his tender touch all day — the way he'd stroked her cheek, his eyes glistening. His fondness touched her even now, and she wished he might've forgiven her then and there.

"I hope things improve for you." Sally's words were soft yet strained.

Lettie understood and appreciated her concern. It was important for the People to have the opportunity to extend mercy to those who wished to repent — their age-old tradition. The significance of the degrees of confession set down by their forefathers was revered by the bishop and the church membership, despite the fact that many in their church district embraced Scripture as the ultimate authority. *All for the good.*

"What things are bound and loosed on earth will be so in heaven," Sally whispered.

"*Das alt Gebrauch* — the Old Ways are best," whispered Lettie.

"Anything else would be considered worldly."

But as serious as Lettie's situation was with the ministers and, ultimately, the People, her heart was equally heavy for Judah. If she could, she yearned to help him through the hurt of betrayal and maybe, someday, receive his forgiveness.

"Will you offer to be shunned for a time?" Sally asked, her eyes sad. "Josiah looked dreadfully concerned after the two of you talked today."

Lettie thought of Judah again. In spite of his reserved nature, he had always been loyal to her, even compassionate. With Sally talking like this, she wondered if Judah would also eventually ask her some of the same questions. "I've carried the pain of my sins too long," she said. "I'm ready to make things right before God and the church."

Sally opened the small cupboard and reached for two teacups and saucers, as well as raw honey for sweetening. "I'll keep you in my prayers, like I did all the weeks you were gone from us."

Lettie's eyes filled with tears. "I need prayer now more than you know," she said, remembering again Judah's earlier sweetness toward her. How quickly his tenderness had turned to disbelief . . . and rejection.

She wiped her eyes on the hem of her black apron. *How could I expect otherwise?*

Chapter Twenty

The night was a canker on Judah's heart, knowing Lettie was back in the area but not with him tonight. He'd remained silent at her plea for forgiveness and didn't know what to do about it.

He turned his attention now to his newest lamb. Already he'd spent hours making sure it was nursing from its mother. Sitting on an old barn stool, he replayed Grace's words from this afternoon again in his mind. They haunted him — to think his wife had moved from Preacher Josiah's main house to their little Dawdi Haus, as if she might be there a while.

Staying all alone . . .

He considered what Lettie must be feeling. Surely she had demonstrated a submissive spirit toward Preacher Josiah. And surely she was willing to be shunned for a period of weeks, as was their way. Not in hopes of being quickly forgiven — or having her sin concealed. He'd seen in her eyes that she was truly sorry. Yet he had utterly abandoned her.

There was a rumble of thunder, and he went to stand in the doorway of the barn, watching the lightning rupture the sky. The musky smell of coming rain pervaded the air, and he pulled it deep into his lungs. Too restless to think of going back to bed, he looked across at the dark silhouette of the house, quite satisfied the young lamb was going to thrive. She'd finally latched on to the ewe and was bonding with her mother even now.

He stepped out of the barn and pushed the door shut behind him. The grass beneath his feet was damp with dew. He felt it flatten beneath his work boots as he walked to the front of the house. Stepping lightly onto the porch, he fixed his gaze on Lettie's beloved swing. *Impossible not to.* He went to sit there and leaned his head back, stretching his sore neck.

Missing Lettie had been agonizing when she was out of reach, but now? He exhaled. The Lord commanded forgiveness, no matter the offense. The Sermon on the Mount said it was expected. *But I'm just a man . . . not God,* thought Judah ruefully. *I need a divine measure of grace. O Lord, help me!*

He sat there for a good twenty minutes, waiting out the rain that came like silvery arrows out of the black sky. *Forgive and your heavenly Father will also forgive you.* He winced at the thought.

When the storm had blown itself out and was moving rapidly east, Judah rose and walked down the steps and through the front lawn, bypassing the walkway. With his wife's despairing look embedded in his memory, he headed around the side yard and into the kitchen.

The front porch creaked, awakening Adah out of a deep sleep. Who'd just come and sat on the porch at this late hour? In her weariness, she raised herself on one elbow, then after a moment leaned back into the soft mattress once more. Jakob needed her there next to him. This had been his most agitated night yet, despite Lettie's return. Adah had hoped he might settle down a bit now that Judah had told them Lettie was back. But, truthfully, it wasn't enough for them to know their wayward daughter had returned. Things were still undone, and Adah and Jakob both suffered with similar guilt.

For Lettie's sake, she'd begun to pray about what to do. Receiving forgiveness from the People was a good and holy thing. Something she had yearned for, as well. And Lettie's coming back to confess to Judah was a fine start. *For all of us.* The festering burden Adah had also carried was beginning to lift; she could feel it slowly easing. Now if she could just be free of it completely.

Looking over at Jakob, who'd finally given in to sleep, she assumed he, too, needed to be released from bondage. If only she could talk with Lettie to find out what she'd told Preacher Josiah about her past. *If anything.* And, too, she was anxious to know what Lettie was willing to do to again become a member in good standing, once the ministers agreed upon the discipline.

But Adah knew her own guilt would not be dealt with by her daughter's repentance. She must do what the Lord required of *her,* with or without Jakob's blessing — and without Lettie's say-so. Adah's harbored sins were her own. *From the first time Samuel laid eyes on Lettie till now, I resented him. And worse.*

She clasped her hands over her bosom and squeezed her eyes. *O Lord, forgive me for despising him.* Sorrowful tears trickled down her face and onto her nightgown. *First chance I have, I'll ask Lettie to forgive me, too. The very first chance,* she prayed.

Then, as if Jakob was somehow aware of her prayer, he rolled over and sighed. Adah scooted over next to him, leaning her head on his big shoulder. Her long hair fell around her as she nestled closer than she'd done in years.

Grace awoke to the dawn the next day, a warm and golden Tuesday. The high-pitched staccato song of a house finch perched near her window sent Grace's thoughts flying to Mamma. She whispered a prayer, asking God for a quick resolution to her parents' separation.

She dressed quickly and went down to the kitchen, where she and Mandy cooked a hearty breakfast of scrambled eggs, French toast, and fried potatoes for their father and brothers. Dawdi Jakob and Mammi Adah were clearly missed at the table, but Grace honored their wish to have two meals a day in their own kitchen.

"I'll need to work most of the afternoon today," she told Mandy and suggested that Mammi Adah might help with making supper.

Mandy insisted she could handle it.

Grace gathered up the ironing. She tried to count her blessings as she set to work, thinking what a relief it was that Mamma was at least back in the area. As a little girl, she had been totally taken with her mother. And now . . . well, it was a horrid feeling to go from such admiration, to wondering what folks might think of Mamma. For her part, Grace was surprised Mamma had been so open about her youthful error, telling even Mandy and Joe and Adam when they visited. How would they feel toward the eye-rollers once word got out about Mamma's first child . . . if it did? Not knowing what upheaval was ahead of their family was most disturbing.

Adah's heart was hammering as she rode with Jakob in Judah's family buggy after an exceptionally early breakfast. She could hardly wait to lay eyes on Lettie and was grateful for Jakob's willingness to accompany her to Smuckers'.

When they pulled into the lane, she said right quick, "If ya don't mind, I'll go in and talk to Lettie first."

Her husband scratched his beard, saying he'd assumed as much. His hands remained on the reins, even though the horse had come to a halt.

"She'll want to see you, too," she added.

"Just give a wave . . . I'll come on in."

Adah nodded and climbed out of the buggy to make her way to the Dawdi Haus where Grace had said Lettie was staying.

She was met at the door by Lettie, whose eyes brightened at the sight of her. "Oh, Mamm . . . it's ever so *gut* of you to come!"

Her heart warmed at the unexpectedly kind reception, and Adah's eyes filled with sudden tears. She moved to embrace her daughter.

It was Lettie who pulled away first and motioned toward the little sitting area. "I wondered if you knew I was back."

Adah nodded. "I came first chance I could. It's wonderful-*gut* to have you back." She glanced out the window, then back at Lettie. "I've thought of little else since you left."

Lettie seemed relieved to see her and began to share what she'd encountered in Ohio, telling of her journey. "I located Minnie Keim, who told me that, to the best of her recollection, I gave birth to a baby girl." Lettie regarded her. "Mamm, I never knew I had a daughter!"

"I should've told you." Adah worked her mouth, trying not to cry. "I kept other things from you, too, Lettie." She bowed her head. "Failed you miserably."

"None of that matters now, Mamm, really."

"But I —"

"Mamm . . . *please.*"

"You couldn't possibly know how difficult that all was for your father and me."

"I *do* understand. And I forgive you . . . for the things I know, and for the things I still don't." Lettie brushed back her tears. "Most of all, I don't want to carry any more bitterness toward you."

"You suffered terribly because of me." Adah struggled to speak. "I knew you cared for Samuel and for your unborn baby. I knew it then, and yet I did everything in my strength to keep the two of you apart. Didn't want him to influence you, keep you from joining church, too. Ach, his family was just so different. . . ."

"No need to rehash this, Mamm."

Adah asked hesitantly, "Did ya find . . . the child?"

"No." Lettie's eyes squinted, tears welling up. "But I've filed the necessary paper work with the state of Ohio."

"I'm so sorry to have put ya through this."

"If God wills it, I'll find her yet."

They were quiet for a time, absorbing each other's presence.

At last, Adah spoke. "I wish I hadn't hated

Samuel so . . . and I'm sorry for that." She reached for Lettie's hand. "We loved you, dear one. Your father and I surely did. We thought it best we conceal your pregnancy."

"Any parent would want to protect their daughter," Lettie said. "You wanted me to have a chance to wed a man like Judah . . . wanted to spare me the disgrace and to protect our family's name."

"Jah . . . all of that."

"I've longed to talk to you, Mamm — to ask you to forgive me for holding this grudge against you and Daed." Lettie wiped her eyes. "It took finding Minnie for me to understand that I'd buried my pain over the loss . . . what it was doin' to me."

"Of course I forgive you," Adah said. "Can you ever forgive *me,* Lettie? For makin' you give up your first wee babe?" She paused, gathering herself. "Such an awful long time you've waited for those words, I'm afraid."

"Ach, Mamm . . ."

"No, no — let me finish. I never should've forced you against your will. You loved your little one so."

"I've already forgiven you, Mamm." Lettie smiled sweetly.

In her deepest heart, Adah knew Lettie had harbored resentment these many years. But now, seeing her daughter's lovely face radiate such mercy, Adah sensed she spoke the truth. "Ach, Lettie, you've made me feel whole again. Truly, you have."

Lettie's arms flung wide. "Let's try and put the past far behind us, jah? Can we?"

"Oh, we must," Adah managed to whisper as she stepped into her daughter's waiting arms. "We surely must. . . ."

When it was time for Grace to leave for work, Joe volunteered to take her. During the ride to Eli's Natural Foods, Joe brought up his visit to see Mamma yesterday with Adam and Mandy. "Brief as it was."

"I'm sure she was glad ya went."

He nodded. "She had plenty-a hugs and kisses for all of us."

"Adam must've enjoyed that," Grace joked.

"Well . . ." Joe rolled his eyes. "It *was* nice to see her. Just surprising when she told us why she might not be coming home for a time." He glanced down at the reins in his hands. "Never imagined Mamma was hiding something like . . . well, you know."

"No, and poor Dat in the dark 'bout it," Grace said. She was quiet a moment before adding, "It's probably for the best that Mamma's keepin' busy helping Sally out."

"Just hope she doesn't get too comfortable over there," Joe commented.

Grace sighed. "Hopefully she and Dat will work something out . . . in time." Now that he and her other siblings knew about Mamma's past, she hoped they would keep it quiet. It was enough of a transgression for Mamma to have deceived their father all this time — not to mention leaving the family for all those weeks, too.

When they pulled into the parking lot for Eli's, Joe said, "Mandy's somehow run out of vanilla for whatever she's makin' for supper. Do ya think you could grab some right quick?" He looked sheepish as he asked, but of course he wouldn't know where to begin to look for such a thing.

Grace smiled. "Wait here, and I'll go right in." She hurried down from the carriage and headed inside.

The store was busy with customers, typical for this time of day. She shouldn't have been surprised to see Prissy Stahl shopping there. Grace waved to her in her rush to the baking aisle.

Prissy was still pushing her empty grocery cart around when Grace came back down the aisle, heading for the front entrance with the vanilla for Joe. "Hullo, Grace," she said.

"How're you, Priscilla?" She moved past her and toward the cashier. "Excuse me . . .

Joe's waitin' to take this home to Mandy." She hoped Prissy wouldn't think she was impolite.

When she returned from the parking lot and Joe, who'd left with a grand wave of his straw hat, Grace searched reluctantly for Prissy without success. Not wanting to delay the start of her shift, she went back and punched the time clock, then donned her work apron.

Grace was eager to dive into her first task of the day: setting up an attractive display of chemical-free sun blocks. Later she'd need to help customers in the bulk food section, weighing and bagging grains, nuts, and dried fruit.

Only a few minutes had passed when Prissy snuck up on her, smack-dab in the middle of the store, where Grace was counting out the sunscreen products. "Is your mother home yet?" she asked, her eyes blinking steadily.

Grace regarded her, wondering how much Adam had told her. "If you'd remember us in your prayers, we'd really appreciate that, Prissy." She surprised herself with her calm response to the sometimes feisty girl.

Prissy reached for a bottle of sun block and seemed terribly interested in the ingredients. She must've stood there reading them at least a half dozen times.

At last, Prissy said, "I guess you know from Becky Riehl that Henry's been seein' her lately."

"I'm glad for Henry," said Grace, turning back to the display.

"But not so happy for *Becky* . . . do ya mean?"

Oh, for pity's sake!

"You'll have to excuse me, Prissy. I really shouldn't talk while I'm workin'."

Prissy nodded her head. "Jah, you've been pretty busy lately. But you still find time to talk a-plenty to that fancy friend of yours . . . what's her name?" She snapped her fingers. "Heather something."

"Heather Nelson . . . and she, too, could use your prayers."

"Oh?"

Grace thought of saying she planned to visit Heather later today, but there was no need to fuel this flame. It wasn't Prissy's business that Heather was staying at the Wellness Lodge — or why — and Grace didn't want to risk Prissy's passing on word to everyone within hearing distance. No, she knew Adam's fiancée too well to mistake her interest now as anything other than fishing for gossip.

"Have a nice afternoon," Grace said, ready

to bring an end to their conversation.

This time, Prissy took the hint and replaced the bottle of sun block. And when she pushed her grocery cart away, she walked with quicker steps than before, her head tilted high.

Relieved that Prissy wouldn't be bothering her anymore — at least for today — Grace resumed her work.

Chapter Twenty-One

Later that afternoon, when Joe dropped Grace off at the Wellness Lodge, she offered to walk home.

"Ya sure? I could come back for you," her brother offered kindly.

"Well, I can't be certain how long I'll visit with Heather. But thanks."

He held the reins and gave a nod. "Say, before I forget, Martin Puckett stopped by while you were working and asked Dat if you'd want to help his wife plan an herb garden. In exchange for some free transportation."

The thought of designing an herb garden scarcely seemed like work to Grace. "What'd Dat think of it?" she asked eagerly.

Joe grinned. "Well, any time he can get a free ride . . . ya know?"

"So he's in agreement?"

"He asked me to mention it to you. Just give Janet Puckett a call tonight if you want to help."

"All right, then." Grace would go to the phone shanty right after supper. She watched Joe leave, then made her way down the lane toward the Wellness Lodge.

She found Heather sitting in the backyard again, facing the creek, her laptop nowhere in sight. Heather smiled to see her. "I'm famished, Grace! Never been so hungry in my life."

Grace couldn't begin to imagine what she was going through, having only experienced the twice-yearly fast before communion Sunday.

"Naturally they're giving us plenty of liquids." Heather went on to mention that her father was expected to arrive this evening. "He had some business to wrap up at home," Heather told her. "Sure hope I'm good company for him."

"Well, he's comin' to see *you,* however you are," Grace reassured her friend.

Heather slumped in the lawn chair beneath the tree. "I can't explain how I'm feeling today. It's a drastic change from yesterday," she said quietly.

"I'm thinking 'bout you, Heather . . . and prayin'."

"Thanks. Jim is, too." Heather told her more about the fellow she'd met online.

"He's terribly ill — even worse off than I am, I think." Heather struggled to talk. "It really weighs on me."

"Sorry to hear that."

"He sent a text today, something from the Bible about the importance of focusing on things that are true and good — whatever is right, pure, lovely . . . whatever is admirable. Things like that."

"For healing in soul and body?"

"Right. I think he's a little God crazy."

"Evidently he knows his Bible, too." Grace found it sweet how interested Heather was in talking about Jim.

"It might sound kind of strange to you, but I'm fascinated by his comments." She paused. "He's been sending me text messages every few hours lately."

"Ah, well, he must like you, then."

Heather smiled. "Just trying to encourage me . . . that's all."

"Right, and you sound just like I did when you said you'd overheard Yonnie talkin' to me last Wednesday. Remember?"

Heather grinned. "So . . . how *is* Yonnie?"

That brought a good laugh from Grace. "We've decided to be friends."

"*Just* friends? Everyone agrees to that when they wish they could be more." Heather shifted in the lawn chair. "I don't know if Jim likes me that way or not, but, like I said, he's crazy for God."

"What a wonderful-*gut* thing, ain't so?"

Heather shrugged and stared at the row of willow trees, their branches sweeping forward and down to touch the lush green lawn.

Grace breathed deeply. "I visited my mother yesterday before comin' here to see you." She pointed in a northerly direction. "Up yonder."

Frowning, Heather asked, "She's not at home?"

Grace explained gently that things were up in the air right now. "I pray she'll be back soon, though."

Heather turned to face her. "Oh, Grace . . . I feel terrible about this." She blinked her eyes and tears welled up. She struggled to regain her composure. "I'm really sorry . . . what's wrong with me?" she mumbled, shaking her head. "This must be what Sally Smucker described — I'm on emotional overload."

Grace remembered Sally telling them about it. "Jah, she said there were days she just sat and cried."

"And I've heard it can get even worse." Heather wiped her tears, sighing.

"Is that what Jim told you?"

Heather pulled her hair back. "He's worried about me, I think. Maybe I should be, too."

Grace didn't want to be pushy when talking about her faith, but she felt compelled to say something. "Ever think that God sees you here?"

Heather was silent for a moment, a faraway look in her eyes. "Sometimes," she whispered.

"He cares about what's happening to you."

"Funny you should mention that. I've been thinking all day about something my dad told me."

"What's that?"

"Evidently my mom prayed for me . . . back when they were getting tired of waiting to adopt a baby. She was really discouraged."

"Maybe like you are today?" Grace touched her hand.

"Knowing that gives me a wonderful comfort, especially at times like this. It's as if God's had His eye on me."

"That He has." Then Grace had an idea. "Would you like to see Sally Smucker again?"

Immediately Heather brightened. "Only if she's not too busy. . . ."

"I doubt she's ever *that* busy. Where Sally's concerned, the best thing 'bout life is people and makin' time for them. People and time, that's her motto."

"Whenever Sally can squeeze in a few minutes to visit, that would be great. Thanks."

Grace hated to leave Heather there looking so frail in the canvas lawn chair, but Mandy would be setting the supper table soon. "I'll see you again tomorrow, all right?"

Heather clasped her hand. "Grace, it's really kind of you to visit."

"I like to. And know that tonight, before I sleep, I'll be whispering your name to Jesus," Grace said.

Heather's face showed a flicker of hope. "I'll count on that."

Grace waved, then walked down the lawn toward the road. When she turned to look back at Heather, she saw that her chair was already empty.

After a delicious supper of roast beef and onions, cooked carrots, and buttered potatoes, Grace hurried to the phone shanty and left a message for Martin Puckett's wife, agreeing to help with the herb garden. Then she dialed the number for Sally Smucker's soap boutique. "My friend Heather's discouraged, and I thought you'd like to know," Grace told Sally once she'd reminded her that Heather's lodge stay had started. "Would ya want to visit her sometime soon, maybe?"

"Poor girl . . . I'll stop in to see her tomorrow morning."

"Denki, Sally. I know it'll mean so much."

"Glad to help."

They said good-bye and hung up. But walking back home, Grace wished she'd asked about Mamma — how *she* was doing. In fact, considering all the many directions Grace felt pulled in, she nearly understood why Englischers — like their neighbors the Spanglers — enjoyed the convenience of a car.

She glanced over at their big brick house. Seeing not a single vehicle parked in the driveway, she assumed Jessica was at work, trying to make enough money to fund her December wedding. Carole Spangler wasn't at home, either. In fact, the windows were all closed up and dark, which was rare this time of year, and the Spanglers' golden Labrador was nowhere to be seen. Recalling the worrisome things Jessica had recently shared about her parents' pending separation, Grace breathed a prayer for them as she walked briskly home. *There's so much sadness in this old world, Lord. Please surround the Spangler family with your presence . . . and love.*

Then, thinking again of Mamma, she asked God for something beautiful to come of the jagged edges in folk's lives all around her — a mending of shattered hearts and dreams.

Heather spent the first few moments of her dad's visit that evening crying in his arms. Overwhelmed, she felt helpless to stop the flow of tears. As many times as LaVyrle and others had warned her that such reactions were common during a cleanse, Heather never dreamed she'd feel this depressed by the end of only the second day. *All the toxins in my body . . .*

Later, Dad tried to distract her when she dried her eyes. He led her outdoors to sit with him on the wide porch. He was beaming with his news that the excavation had begun today, and soon the foundation would be poured. "After the foundation has cured, I'm told things will move along quickly." He paused and looked at her tentatively. "I also contacted a real estate agent to look over our home and see what might need to be done to get it ready to sell."

She groaned. "Oh, Dad . . ."

"Honey, what?"

"I can't bear the thought of losing that terrific house — Mom's and yours. My entire life is wrapped up in it."

"Maybe you're being overly dramatic."

"Is it really necessary to sell it?"

He looked toward the road. The new house was only a long stone's throw from where they sat. "This is where I want to live . . . and retire someday."

She refused to back down. "Can we please just keep our present house, too?"

"Well, I won't rush into anything . . . not now." He seemed to imply that he would hang on to their home until he was sure Heather felt stronger.

"Selling our home makes me feel . . . disloyal somehow."

He smiled knowingly. "I understand, honey."

The screen door opened and LaVyrle came out to sit with them. "Hello, Mr. Nelson. So nice to have you visit." She glanced sweetly at Heather. "I know your daughter's very happy to see you."

He brightened. "Oh, please just call me Roan." He leaned toward LaVyrle as he shook her hand, holding it slightly longer than necessary. "How's Heather doing?

You're taking good care of her, I hope."

I'm right here, Dad!

LaVyrle explained to him once again the stages of the body's cleansing process. "Some patients have emotional reactions, experience weepiness —" She stopped and offered a sympathetic smile to Heather. "Everyone responds differently to juicing and fasting. Tears can be part of an emotional cleansing."

This fact hardly made Heather feel better. She wanted something to chew on. *God made teeth for a reason, right?* She almost smiled at her private little joke.

Dad and LaVyrle talked about the lovely location of the lodge, something LaVyrle seemed to take great pride in. And they talked of the pleasant springtime weather — all positive things. LaVyrle was the ultimate upbeat PR person.

Heather's stomach lurched, and she felt seriously nauseated. "Uh, please excuse me," she said quickly, heading inside. Arielle helped her upstairs to her room, where she rested on the bed.

Various staff members checked on Heather over the next few minutes, but neither LaVyrle nor her father came up immediately. She assumed her dad was bending the naturopath's ear. But she dismissed the notion that her father might be attracted to the woman. She had to. There was no way she wanted to let her brain latch on to that!

Judah's exhausting day was long finished when he took off walking Beechdale Road, determined to see Lettie tonight. He was too aware of the empty ache within his chest, and he wanted to make up for turning away from her so abruptly yesterday. The memory of that continued to plague him as he made his way up the dark two-lane road.

The moon was well concealed behind a mass of clouds, and the musty smell of rain hung in the air as he reached down for a sturdy walking stick from the roadside. *Exactly what I need on such a murky night.* He'd already walked a mile north of his house, so he knew Josiah's place was just around the next bend.

Until he reached the Smuckers' Dawdi Haus, he foolishly didn't consider that his wife might be sound asleep. And she was just that when he found her in the small bedroom, just off the kitchen. He'd let himself in the back door, and now he stood mutely in the doorway of her room, watching her sleep, her hand limp on the white sheet. Oh, but he wished to awaken her, take her in his arms, and say how much he loved her and always had. Tell her, too, that he was wrestling against the jealousy he'd long held against the man she'd loved first.

Judah leaned against the doorjamb. "I shouldn't have rejected you yesterday," he whispered, not wanting to startle her. "And not ever."

He thought of their years together. *Was I aloof because of the barrier between us?* He guessed that was so, although his tendency toward being standoffish was also a culprit. But it was not an excuse.

No, they were beyond that now.

Leaning forward, he listened to her gentle breathing. He should've kissed Lettie instead of rushing away from her — should've promised to help her through the days ahead, before her coming confession.

Wanting to touch her hair, her forehead, Judah reluctantly remained in the shadows . . . and instead whispered, "*Gut Nacht,* love."

Chapter Twenty-Two

Judah stepped back into the kitchen and went to sit on the rocking chair, aware of a distant hoot owl. With a sad sigh for the additional pain he'd brought his forlorn wife, he leaned his head against the wood and fell swiftly asleep.

Hours later, he awakened with a start and glanced about the room, not knowing at first where he was. The night hour pressed in — he heard the faltering sounds of crickets in the background — and he knew he'd fallen asleep.

Best be getting home, he thought groggily, getting up and heading out the back door. He closed it behind him quietly, his heart racing.

On the walk home, he met not a soul the first half mile on the narrow road, moving slowly due to his limp. The vision of Lettie resting on the bed in sweet repose, her long blond hair mixed with only a few streaks of gray, sustained him somehow.

Mindful of his surroundings, Judah glanced ahead and saw a parked car sitting along the shoulder. Someone sat inside the vehicle, and he heard the sound of a woman weeping. As he approached the vehicle, he realized it belonged to the Spanglers — their English neighbors to the south. The windows were down and Carole Spangler was leaning her head against her arm on the steering wheel and crying as if someone dear to her had just passed away.

"Mrs. Spangler," he said softly, so as not to frighten her. "It's your neighbor Judah Byler."

She jerked up. "Oh, I didn't see you there."

He assumed she wondered what he was doing out at two in the morning . . . just as he wondered about her. "Are you all right?"

Pushing her hair away from her face, she laughed darkly. "Nothing's right anymore. My husband and I . . ." Her voice trailed off.

There had been occasional rumors about the woman's family situation, but Judah rarely paid much attention to the doings of fancy folk. "Sorry to hear it," he replied.

As if encouraged by his words, Carole told of her separation. "I should probably hire an attorney to protect everything I've brought into this marriage," she ended bitterly.

Judah's toes curled inside his work boots. Was this what happened when two people grew apart — the world's way of describing a broken heart? Hearing the woman pour out her sorrows, he could only think of his poor Lettie, slumbering under another man's roof, alone and comfortless. All that way she'd come, and look what he'd done — made her nearly an outcast!

Standing with his hands on the walking stick, and heartsick at the reminder of where things stood between him and Lettie even now, Judah worried about what to say to his distraught neighbor.

"I'm sorry, Mr. Byler. You . . . you must be walking off your own problems," she said suddenly, looking up at him. Her right hand grasped the steering wheel. "This has been absolutely selfish of me."

"Not to worry," he mumbled.

"You go ahead," she told him. "Your family will wonder what's become of you." She glanced up the road. "Or would you like a ride home?"

"Not necessary," he replied, even though if Martin Puckett or another male driver had offered, he would have taken him up on it for certain; he was that drained. "Mighty kind of you to offer, Mrs. Spangler. Mighty kind." Adjusting his hat, he thought he must seem distracted. Did he? *Like during Lettie's attempts to make conversation with me . . .*

Slowly he made his way toward home, with only so much strength left to kick himself. *When Lettie needed me most, I walked away. I walked right down the stairs and out to the barn the night she left!*

The years of emotional distance weighed on him like the heavy ax he'd used to sever the kudzu vines.

When he arrived at the turnoff to his driveway, Judah paused to draw a breath. He saw a dim light coming from the sewing room on Jakob's side of the house. *Adah must be up, too.*

Needing more rest than the forty winks he'd already gotten, he plodded around toward the back of the house. And he would've stumbled right over his own son had he not been looking down. "Ach, Adam, is that you?"

The lad had been muttering into his arms, his head bowed. Startled, he looked up, the whites of his eyes nearly all that could be seen of his face. "Dat?"

"You all right, son?"

Adam straightened from his waist up. "It's my girl," he said guardedly. "She heard that Mamma's home but . . . well, she ain't *really,* ya know. Guess one of Preacher Josiah's older boys told it around."

Judah cringed, certain Lettie's past sin would see the light of day all too soon. "Did you keep what ya know of your Mamma's situation private?" he asked quickly.

"Wouldn't think of spreadin' *that.*" Adam stared at the barn and sighed loudly. "Sure would hate to see Mamma livin' over at the preacher's place permanently."

"She won't be there for long," Judah blurted, knowing he'd do whatever he could to bring her back straightaway. As soon as it was daylight, even.

"Prissy'll be relieved at that," Adam said, then caught himself. "Puh, I mean . . ."

"No, no . . . 'tis all right." Judah would keep that in confidence.

"Denki" was all Adam said, but with a great sigh of relief, as though he knew his courting secret was safe with his father.

Well, well . . . Susannah Stahl's daughter, thought Judah, reaching for the door to let himself in.

While Grace was down scrubbing the kitchen floor Wednesday morning, she heard

Dat take the horse and buggy lickety-split out to the road. She dropped her sponge in the bucket of hot, sudsy water and went outside. "Where's Dat goin' in such a big hurry?" she asked Adam, who was coming back from the springhouse.

"To fetch Mamma." Adam wiped his forehead with the back of his sleeve.

"Des *gut!*" Grace could hardly stand still.

"Dat urged us to show mercy when she arrives," Adam said, his eyes serious.

"We'll welcome her home, all right!" She turned and ran to the house to tell Mandy. "Mamma's comin' home!" she told her sister when she found her upstairs redding up. "Oh, Mandy, this is ever so wonderful-*gut!*"

Mandy's eyes popped open. "Are ya sure?"

"Adam just said so."

Mandy sat on her bed, then fell back onto the pillows. "It'll be so nice to have her home again."

Just then Grace thought of their parents' bedroom. "Ach, I best look and see how Dat left things." She darted down the hall to check on the bed and see if he'd picked up his dirty socks, which he wasn't known to do. She made a sweep with her eyes from the doorway. The space was spotless — bed made, clothes picked up. *Jah, Mamma is definitely returning today!*

Grace headed downstairs, where she heard Sally Smucker visiting with Mammi Adah across the hall. She hurried to see if she might be on her way to see Heather, as well, and found that she was indeed. "Heather will be so glad," she said, having interrupted Sally and Mammi Adah's tea. "But where are your little ones?"

"Your mother's with them, back at the house." Sally set her teaspoon down.

Sally must've just missed Dat. She doesn't know Mamma's coming home. . . .

Oh, but Grace could scarcely stand there and be still, not with Mamma soon on her way. Glancing again at Mammi Adah, Grace doubted her grandmother had any idea of her father's plan, either.

Sally sipped her warm tea while the pair discussed the jam making they wanted to do. Grace looked over at Dawdi Jakob, who sat in the corner of the kitchen, observing the songbirds he loved. *Like Mamma . . .*

Did her grandfather sense a change in the wind? *Like the shifting of a tide . . .* She'd once read in a library book that some folk who'd lived by the sea for many years were uncannily sensitive to the changing of the tides, able to feel the split second when the cadenced washing of the waves reversed direction. Inland dwellers said it was impossible to feel the rhythm of the tides change, but lovers of the sea knew. Perhaps, like them, Dawdi Jakob could tell something was coming . . . even now.

Grace went back to the kitchen and set to work on the floor again, all the while waiting for Dat to bring Mamma home for good.

Judah hardly noticed the stray chickens on the road as he turned into Preacher Josiah's lane. Two other gray buggies were parked in the side yard, minus the horses, so he pulled in behind them and tied his own horse to the fence. He figured he wouldn't be long enough that his horse would need water or feed.

Taking off his straw hat, he mopped his face with his old kerchief, then put his hat back on and pushed his handkerchief into his pocket. *The bishop and the other preacher sure are here early.* He recognized both buggies and guessed Deacon Amos had gotten a ride with one of them.

At the back door, he raised his hand to knock, but as he peered through the screen, he realized the main house was empty. The sound of voices came from the small back porch around the side, and he followed the walkway to the former residence of Sally's grandparents, now gone to Glory.

Children's voices wafted from within the cottage-like Dawdi Haus, although Lettie was sitting outside on the porch with the brethren. *Must be Sally's children,* he assumed, noticing now that Josiah's family buggy was missing.

Deacon Amos fluttered his hand at Judah, signaling for him to wait right there. Respectfully, he backed away, but not before he saw Lettie's red and puffy eyes.

In the field to the north, two of Josiah's uncles and several nephews were making hay — a mighty good day for it. He considered going to lend a hand to occupy himself but then decided against it, wondering if Lettie might not want to talk over the ministers' decision later.

Several grackles flew toward the backyard feeder, where they pecked at the grains of corn, then flitted back into the sky, toward a grove of distant trees. It crossed his mind that he hoped Lettie's bird feeders were all filled at home. Surely, Grace would see to it — she and Yonnie. He smiled whenever he thought of the well-mannered lad. The fellow was just so likeable. And it looked as if Grace might be warming to Yonnie, too. After all, it was mighty clear he'd taken a real shine to her.

Walking to the barnyard, Judah thought of all the many chores he ought to be doing. But, no, he wouldn't permit himself to think that way today. No longer was his work more important than Lettie. He would remind himself daily, if that's what it took. He wasn't ever going to lose her again!

At last, he heard the ministers coming near, talking amongst themselves as they fetched their horses from the stable. Instead of offering to help hitch up the horses for the bishop, deacon, and older preacher, Judah made a beeline back to his wife.

She'd already gone inside when he walked up the few porch steps. He could hear her talking softly to the preacher's children, and through the door, he watched her lightly touch their little blond heads, running her hand over their necks and shoulders. "Your Mamma will be here soon," he heard her say, her voice raspy from crying.

Then, when he could stand it no longer, he lightly tapped on the screen door and announced himself. "Lettie . . . it's Judah."

Her eyebrows rose and her face broke into a sweet smile. "Oh . . . I'm so glad you're here."

She had one of the little girls in her arms, carrying her about as the child whimpered for her mother. Lettie hurried to the cupboard and gave her a graham cracker to nibble on. "There, there, honey-girl. This'll make ya feel better."

Food always does. He smiled and glanced out the back window, where the bishop and the deacon were getting into the same buggy, talking a blue streak.

"Would ya care for something to drink?" Lettie asked, getting the little one settled in the playpen again with her sister.

"Just cold water," he said, unable to take his eyes off her.

Lettie went to the sink and ran the water, her fingers under the tap. "Can we talk 'bout the ruling the ministers made?" She carried the glass of cold water to him.

" 'Tis *gut* they came," he replied. "I was here last night, Lettie . . . hope I didn't wake ya," he told her. "Wanted to see you . . . apologize."

Her lower lip quivered. "Aw, Judah."

"I wish I'd stayed after we talked Monday. I shouldn't have run off like that." He took a drink, then set the glass down. "Seems I've made a bad habit of that in recent years, and I'm sorry."

They sat on the worn sofa, facing each other. Lettie told him what the ministers had decided, calling her situation a special case. "They said if I choose to reveal my sins to the church, I won't be shunned. If not, then I'll be shunned for six weeks. After that time the bishop would welcome me back as a voting member once again."

He studied her eyes, the way her delicate brows framed the blue of them. Such pain she'd always carried there, and now he knew why. "What will you do, Lettie?" he asked.

"When I first spoke with Preacher Josiah, I told him I was willing to be shunned, not knowin' I could avoid it by revealin' my sins." Her words lodged in her throat. "But now, knowin' this . . . I'll most likely tell everything before the membership. Not to avoid the Bann, mind you, but so that I might feel free of my transgressions once and for all. And, too, I feel almost like I've already been shunned . . . by my own doin', too. Bein' gone so long and all."

Judah sensed she was willing to do whatever it took. He thought of pointing out the possible drawbacks to her but decided against it. After all, Lettie was the one who yearned to be free of her guilt. Who was he to say she couldn't reveal to the membership the sins of her youth, just so they might spare the family's name?

"Are ya praying 'bout this?" he asked.

"Ever so much."

"Then so be it."

For the first time ever, he helped her get a toddler down for a morning nap, then set up the other little Smucker girl with some blocks. Then, together, he and Lettie went to sit at the kitchen table, where he reached for her hand. "I'll help see ya through what's ahead."

Tears ran down her face. "Oh, Judah."

"I mean it . . . from here on out."

She wiped her eyes, her face so white. "There's something else I've wanted to apologize for." She sighed. "I never should've withdrawn all that money from the bank. I should've asked you first."

"Shh, love." He stroked her face.

"Should've told you what I had in mind."

"What's done is done."

"But, still, I —"

"We'll start fresh from this day forth." With that, Judah rose and pulled her to her feet, taking her in his arms. "I've always loved you, Lettie. Always."

She nodded slowly and looked up, gently touching his beard. "I'm going to need you, Judah . . . for what's comin'."

He slipped an arm around her waist, knowing she meant the kneeling confession. "We'll trust the Lord for the outcome."

"Whatever it may be," Lettie whispered, leaning her head on his chest.

Chapter Twenty-Three

Heather felt encouraged later that morning, and a visit from Sally Smucker — a true cancer survivor — was a big reason for it. She and Sally walked together along the creek bank and discussed Heather's daily routine, as well as the various methods of cleansing. Everything from herbal methods to deep tissue massage and hydrotherapy — alternating hot and cold showers to jump-start the immune system. They both had a little laugh over people like the Polar Bear Club enthusiasts, who swam in icy waters in January, claiming it made them stronger.

"But, hey, I'm open to anything natural that's worked for others," she said to Sally. "Within reason."

"An open mind and a cheerful spirit can be mighty helpful," said Sally. "I needed a plucky attitude to help me get through detox . . . and beyond. The work of healing needs to continue when you leave this place, too," Sally added. "The staff here gave me suggestions about further ways to continue healthful eating," she said. "I was so grateful."

"I worry about that sometimes," Heather admitted.

Sally stopped walking and turned to face her. "What would you think of coming to live with me for a while after the lodge stay? I'd be happy to help oversee your diet, if you'd like." She smiled with understanding. "It'd be too bad if you couldn't continue, 'specially when you're already making this kind of commitment." Here, Sally glanced back toward the lodge.

"You must be my guardian angel," Heather said, greatly relieved.

"Goodness, I've never been called that before."

"Well, I'm surprised."

"So, you'll come?" Sally asked as they walked on toward the road.

"It's very nice of you, Sally. Maybe for a few days." Heather wondered what her dad would say to this, since he'd mentioned last evening he was set on their seeing her oncologist as soon as possible to get a *"medical opinion"* of the results of her treatment here. Heather, though, thought she'd possibly seek a second opinion from another doctor.

Dad might dig in his heels again. . . .

But . . . wait. What if LaVyrle was the one to suggest Heather stay on at Sally's? She might simply put a bug in Dr. Marshall's ear and let *her* persuade Dad. *Perfect!*

Sally and Heather continued walking, the midmorning sun warm on their faces. The light filtered over them like a happy memory. Soon they came to a flat ledge overlooking the briskly flowing creek. "I came here to pray sometimes," Sally said in a near whisper. Even to Heather, it seemed the ideal location for someone who felt they had to talk to God.

"On my fifth day here, I actually felt like I might die." Sally paused to look around. "I experienced a strange sensation over and over, like I was sinking. I can't describe it really, but it frightened me . . . and I called out to the Lord that day from this very spot."

When they began walking again, Heather was glad to get her mind off the dreaded "fifth day."

"My strawberries are near ripe," Sally said. "I'm goin' to make jam next week with Marian Riehl and Adah Esh at Adah's place."

"Oh, I'd love to observe your jam making, and I'd really like to see Marian Riehl again.

What would you think of that?"

"Comin' to put up jam . . . or visiting with Marian?"

Heather laughed at Sally's delightful teasing.

"You *should* join us, Heather."

"I certainly will."

"All right, then. A week from Friday's the day — come in the morning. We'll have us a right *gut* time together."

Lettie sat in their family buggy with Judah by her side, observing the beauty around them. It was the same stretch of road she'd ridden last Sunday night on the way to Preacher Smucker's place. But now . . . *now* she was going home.

Lettie suddenly realized she was literally holding her breath. She took in the verdant landscape surrounding Beechdale Road, seeing it with new eyes. *What will life be like for us . . . now that my family knows the ugly truth about me?*

She glanced at Judah, who seemed relaxed, the reins hanging loose in his tan, callused hands.

"Nervous?" He reached for her hand.

"A little hard not to be." She was thankful for his touch. "And, to be honest, sometimes I worry what might happen if the girl I gave up appears on our front porch one day. How would you feel?"

She couldn't blame him for not answering right away. It was obvious from his face that Judah was working through the idea now, finding his way through the emotional upheaval she'd caused. A life-altering circumstance, for sure and for certain. *I was awful selfish.*

She recalled Minnie's words: *"What if your daughter doesn't want to be found?"* She shuddered. She could only imagine what her poor children must be thinking; they'd said so little on the subject when she'd told them. Undoubtedly all the family preferred not to know.

"If your long-lost daughter comes callin', we'll be well-mannered," Judah said quietly.

She turned, surprised. "I'm walkin' on pins and needles . . . second-guessing near everything I've ever said . . . and done."

"Wouldn't be natural otherwise." He glanced at her, then back to the road. "Your mother says your child with Samuel wasn't placed with an Amish couple."

"What?" She shook her head, aghast.

"Adah has a letter with the doctor's name and whatnot all."

"She does?"

He merely nodded.

Why didn't Mamm tell me this yesterday? Unsure what to think, Lettie reminded herself to trust in the Lord. Oh, she must.

She watched as the edge of Andy Riehl's front lawn came into view, even before their grand old house appeared. Her eyes swept the sheep fence to the south and the grazing land closer to her own house. To the left, it looked like someone had come and scalped the little woodshed. She stared at it, taken with the structure, laid bare now for all to see. *Without those miserable vines.*

Then, looking the other way, Lettie spotted the familiar front porch and the wooden swing hanging there. The appeal of their home nearly took her breath away. "Oh, Judah . . ."

"You all right?" He looked at her tenderly.

In a minute or two she would see, once again, her handsome sons and sweet daughters. Yet her neck tightened at the thought of living again under the same roof with her parents.

Will things truly be different between us?

A refrain of birdsong met Grace's ears as she finished shaking the throw rugs outdoors before the noon meal. She glanced at the bird feeders, filled just so for Mamma's return.

The sky was nearly cloudless and as blue as she imagined the ocean might be on such a pretty day. A quiver of a breeze rustled her Kapp enough to send the long strings floating up momentarily, then down.

When she heard Dat's buggy pull into the driveway, she hurried inside and dropped the rugs in a heap on the kitchen floor. "Quick, Mandy . . . Mamma's here!" she called up the stairs.

Mandy came running down, past Grace and straight through the kitchen, bursting out the screen door. Going to stand by the door, Grace covered her mouth as Mandy rushed right into the buggy and hugged Mamma. Grace could hear her sister's endearing welcome mixed with joyful tears.

Show mercy, indeed . . .

Soon Adam and Joe came running from the barn to the buggy. Adam went to stand directly at the side of the carriage, waiting to assist their mother down. But when Mamma needed no such help, Adam grinned all the same, seeming to enjoy his attempt at chivalry.

Just as quick as Mamma had climbed down from the buggy, she opened her arms to Mandy and Adam and Joe, all of them jabbering in Deitsch.

Dat stood on the perimeter of the huddle

and tried to be discreet about mopping his brow. He glanced back at the house — at Grace — and their eyes met.

"Mamma's finally home," she whispered, looking at her father, his lined brow ever so soft now. *What he's been through . . . bless his dear heart.*

Grace pushed open the kitchen door and walked across the yard to join them, letting Mandy keep her place nestled against Mamma. "Willkumm home, Mamma," she said as Adam stepped back, then slipped his long arm around their mother's rounded shoulders. "Mandy and I'll cook whatever you'd like for dinner, won't we?" Grace said, smiling at her sister.

"What'll it be?" Mandy asked Mamma.

Their mother reached into her sleeve and pulled out a hankie. When she'd regained her composure, she said, "What if the three of us cook together?"

"Wonderful-*gut!*" Mandy exclaimed.

"Jah, I'd like that." Mamma exchanged loving glances with Dat.

Then, here came Dawdi and Mammi, smiling as they strolled outside together. Mamma burst into a smile at the sight of them. "We're glad you're home, Lettie," Dawdi Jakob said, his deep voice ringing out strong as he leaned on his cane.

Mammi Adah's chin quivered, and the three of them opened their arms to each other. Witnessing this loving embrace, Grace felt her heart might break anew. It was all she could do not to weep right along with them.

What joy it was, having Mamma working in the kitchen again! Grace kept looking over at their mother's gentle face as they set to creating a memorable feast.

Mammi Adah had already brought over freshly made bread and apple butter, and the ingredients for two side dishes — crushed corn fritters and sour cream cabbage — she'd planned for her and Dawdi. Grace was delighted her grandparents were still taking the noon meal with them. She certainly did not want to go back to the estrangement between daughter and parents that had existed prior to Mamma's leaving.

When it was time to call the men, instead of ringing the dinner bell, Grace hurried to the sheep barn. She could hardly wait for all of them to sit down as a family. *Together at last!*

Once she'd announced dinner was on the table, Adam and Joe ran ahead of her toward the house. It was Yonnie who fell into step with her while Dat made himself scarce, saying he needed to check on one more lamb. It seemed obvious to Grace that he wanted Yonnie to have a chance to talk with her alone.

"I won't be stayin' for the noon meal today," Yonnie said unexpectedly. "It's a special time for your family . . . a reunion, really."

"That's up to you." Her voice was a thin thread. She wanted him to know he was still welcome.

"Also, Daed wants me to start workin' with him — as his business partner at the buggy shop. I'm starting first thing tomorrow. I just told your father."

Her hands fell limp at her side. This felt so sudden. "I'm sure Dat will miss your help," she eked out.

He gave her a brief smile, then looked more serious again. "It must be mighty *gut* havin' your mother home."

She nodded, unable to speak.

"Well, I'd better get goin'."

Her heart pounded as Yonnie headed toward the road, on foot as was his usual way. Hoping he might turn and give her at least an enthusiastic wave, as he sometimes did, she watched . . . and waited.

Yonnie kept going, never once looking back. And Grace was startled at how quickly her happiness had waned.

Lettie could hardly keep her smile in check, moving about the kitchen as she served her family on this, her first day home. More than ever before she delighted in sitting near Judah, having sorely missed her place at this table. And while Grace and Mandy were clearly accustomed now to getting the meals and redding up the kitchen, she was sure they would gladly surrender the primary responsibility, given time. *It's my duty, after all.*

During the silent blessing, she thanked the Lord for traveling mercies . . . and for such a compassionate and forgiving family. When she raised her eyes at the amen, she caught her mother's warm gaze.

Suddenly, Judah covered her hand with his, just as Hallie's husband had done at their table. Lettie caught her breath — such open affection between them was entirely new.

"I want to say something before the food is passed." Judah looked her way, then around the table at each one present. "My wife has returned." His voice did not waver. "God has forgiven her and we, as a family, offer her our forgiveness, too."

Tears threatened her vision as Judah

squeezed her hand.

"Let's rejoice together," he said before reaching for the meat platter.

Lettie dared not look across at her parents, lest she weep openly. She was certain they, too, were moved by Judah's words. Oh, such love welled up for her husband. Never had she heard him express himself so freely. Never!

Once the leftover food was put away and the dishes and pots and pans were washed and dried, Lettie hurried across the house to find her mother. She fairly bumped into Mamm in the hallway. "Ach, sorry . . . are you all right?" She steadied her.

Mamm broke into a small smile. "I was just comin' to find *you,* Lettie."

Lettie bit her cheek, worried what she might have on her mind: She knew that look on her mother's face all too well. Somewhat reluctant now, she followed Mamm into the front room.

When they were seated, Mamm fiddled with her apron. Lettie looked into her deeply lined yet sincere face. "I'm awful concerned 'bout something."

"What is it, Mamm?"

"When you make your confession before the membership . . . must you reveal everything? I mean *all* the personal details?"

"I want to do the ministers' bidding . . . to come clean."

" 'Tis a thorny issue, the confession."

Lettie replied softly, "It's up to the bishop what questions are asked of me."

Mamm's lips drew into a stiff line, and her cheeks flushed. She sighed and reached into her pocket. "I've had this letter since Minnie Keim passed it on to me years ago — information about the doctor and the lawyer who placed your baby." She stared at it for a moment. "The letter was meant for both of us, but I was worried you might change your mind after the baby's birth, so I hid it away." She gave Lettie the envelope. "I did you wrong, Lettie. The information there might've kept you from leavin' your family as you did."

Lettie held the letter, unsure of herself. "Well, my search was only part of the reason I left." She drew a breath. "I wanted Samuel to know about our child, too, hopin' to soothe his sadness over his wife's death."

Mamm's eyes widened, and Lettie continued. "So Samuel would know he wasn't childless at all."

Frowning now, her mother looked befuddled.

"I realize I should've told him long ago,

since the baby was also his." Lettie shook her head. "And I never should've traveled alone to see him without Judah's permission. It was wrong of me."

"But what'll you do if your daughter wants to find *you?*" Mamma asked. "What then?"

"I think that's unlikely now." She paused. "And since visiting Cousin Hallie, I've been prayin' differently 'bout this."

Mamm let out a little gasp. "You mean Hallie Troyer knows?"

"I told you, Mamm. I'm weary of this secret." Lettie's throat tightened. "I've spoken with the ministers in confidence already." By the look of trepidation on her mother's face, she wasn't sure she should say more.

"Oh, Lettie . . . Lettie, dear."

She explained what she'd decided to do. "The brethren ruled that I won't be shunned if I fully reveal my sins to the congregation."

Mamm grimaced, shaking her head. And the silence that fell between them was thick as custard. Yet Lettie would not allow herself to be persuaded otherwise, because in her heart she knew this was the right thing to do.

"And Judah . . . what does he say?" asked Mamm.

"We must trust the Lord." *With all of our hearts . . .*

Mamm reached out and placed a hand on Lettie's arm. "I wish you'd give it more thought, dear. Consider the consequences that such a disclosure might cause."

"For me?" Lettie whispered. "Or for you?"

Mamm's eyes were grave. "Not just for your father and me. Think how it could affect Adam's pending marriage . . . and Grace's and Mandy's potential mates. Young Joe, too."

Lettie had witnessed firsthand the humiliation and embarrassment previous church confessions involved, so she understood something of her mother's reluctance. Yet, no matter how painful her declaration of guilt might be, she felt certain God was calling her to do this. No anguish could be worse than her — and her family's — bearing the ramifications of her sins in utter silence.

"I want to follow the Lord in this," Lettie said, hoping her determined stand would not create another wedge between them.

CHAPTER TWENTY-FOUR

When Martin Puckett pulled into the driveway that same afternoon, Grace went out to meet him. "My wife received your voicemail. She's thrilled you want to help," he said. "When would you like to come?"

Glancing back toward the house, she said, "I'd best talk with my mother right quick. She's just returned home!"

Martin's eyes lit up. "Well, what good news! I'm happy to hear it."

"There's a lot of happiness to go round." She turned toward the house. "Do ya mind waiting? I'll run in and check."

But her mother was not to be found on their side of the house, so she slipped across the center hall. There, in the sitting room, she found Mamma and Mammi Adah talking in low voices. Both looked glum, as if they'd just had the most dreadful news.

Her mother turned. "What is it, dear?"

"Don't mean to interrupt." Grace swiftly

explained Janet Puckett's interest in creating an herb garden. "Martin's here now. . . . If it's all right with you, I'll tell him I can help his wife this Saturday."

Mamma tilted her head slightly. "Gracie, you managed the entire household without my say-so," she said with a demure smile.

Grace had to laugh a little. "You're right. Thanks, Mamma." With that she returned to tell Martin, who said he'd pick her up after breakfast Saturday. Grace watched him drive away, pleased at the prospect of spending a morning working in such a pleasant way. Life seemed so good now that Mamma was home. She couldn't begin to understand why her mother and grandmother had looked so depressed just moments ago.

On the way to the Wellness Lodge later that afternoon, Grace stopped by the Riehls', eager to see Becky, whom she hadn't had a chance to visit with privately since returning from Ohio.

Her friend rushed out of the house, her long purple skirt swaying. "Gracie . . . it's been much too long!"

"I've missed you, too."

They fell into step and strolled toward the pond behind the barn. "I hear your Mamma's back," Becky said.

"Dat brought her home from Preacher Josiah's just this morning."

Becky was quiet all of a sudden, and Grace realized she must not have known Mamma had been staying at Smuckers'. Since she was hesitant to delve into that, Grace changed the subject quickly. "I thought you might want to know Heather's having quite a time of it."

"Awful sorry to hear that," Becky said. "I'll try and visit her." She smiled as they neared the pond out back. "I'm glad she's found a friend in you, Gracie."

" 'Tween you and me, Heather seems sad . . . even depressed."

"Well, I'd be sad, too." Becky stopped near the edge of the wide pond, near a tall willow tree. "Sally Smucker mentioned to Mamm that Heather has some form of cancer. Did ya know?"

Grace said she did. "I hope Dr. Marshall can help her . . . like she did Sally."

"Jah, I wish the best for Heather." Becky lifted her skirt slightly and dipped her toe into the pond. She motioned for Grace to do the same. "C'mon, it'll cool you off."

"Ain't *that* hot." She hung back, watching her friend. She looked over at Dat's sheep pasture. Soon it would be June and lambing season would be over. *Mamma came home at exactly the right time.*

"I'll tell you a secret if you promise not to repeat it." Becky grinned at her.

"Frankly, I'm full up with secrets."

"Aw . . . Gracie?"

Grace waved her hand vaguely. "If you must."

"Well, after the Singing last Sunday night, Henry and I snuck around the back of the barn and went wading."

"Here?"

"In this very pond."

"Becky, you didn't!"

"Clear up to our knees."

"Whatever for?"

Becky waded in a little farther. "It wasn't my idea, but Henry's."

"So . . . he *talks* to you, then?" Grace bit her tongue too late.

Becky's laugh was infectious. "Not much, no."

"Goodness, he must've suggested it somehow. Maybe sign language?"

"No, he just rolled up his pant legs and walked right on into the water."

"So . . . sounds like you might be a couple."

Becky's wide smile gave her away. "Ain't s'posed to ask such things, Gracie."

"Well, you don't have to say." Grace

hesitated, then added, "Henry might be just right for you."

Becky made no response; by now her friend was up to midcalf in the pond.

"If you're goin' in much farther, maybe you should wait till dark," Grace suggested.

"Are ya saying to make this visit quick, Gracie?" Becky turned, her Kapp strings dangling down her front.

"Thought you might want to be alone to remember last Sunday, out here with Henry and all." Grace covered her mouth, stifling her laughter.

"Aw . . . you're a tease." Becky started to head back to the grassy slope. "What 'bout you and Yonnie . . . doin' all right?"

Since she asked it like that, Grace guessed Becky was completely over him. "We've become friends," Grace said.

"*Just* friends?" There was a playful look in Becky's eyes again.

"Right."

Becky kept the hem of her skirt up a bit to let the sun dry her bare legs and feet. "Say, I hear Mamm's putting up jam with Sally Smucker and your Mammi Adah a week from this Friday."

"Must be strawberry."

"That, and some strawberry rhubarb, Mamm's favorite," Becky said, walking with

Grace toward the house.

"If I'm not scheduled to work at Eli's, I could help. Mamma prob'ly will, too — we could put up enough for several families, and a bunch to sell at the roadside stand, too. A jam-making frolic, jah?"

" 'Fraid you'll have to have fun without me. I promised Mamma I'll be home with my sisters," Becky said.

They hugged quickly and said good-bye, then Grace headed to the lodge, smiling to herself at the image of her friend standing there with the hem of her dress all sopping wet.

After supper, Lettie found it heartening that Judah had a longer time of family worship than usual. And when he finished, he told Adam and Joe they were to be in charge of checking on the lambs tonight. "Take turns wakin' each other up," he stressed, glancing at Lettie.

Mandy and the boys had been especially attentive to the worship this evening. Grace, on the other hand, had looked distracted, and Lettie feared she'd taken on too much of the burden for the family in her absence.

Was that the reason Grace seemed so interested in helping Martin Puckett's wife? Did she feel compelled somehow?

When Lettie climbed the stairs with Judah and they were finally alone, she mentioned Grace's eagerness to work for Janet Puckett. "If only for a day or two," she said.

"Janet must know of our Gracie's love for gardening," he said. "Certainly seems like a good fit."

It was remarkable how quickly Judah now offered his opinion. But Lettie didn't point it out, not wanting to embarrass him . . . simply enjoyed his willingness to share like this.

Looking around the bedroom, she stared at the headboard, which sat to the north, just as all the beds in their house were positioned. Her gaze fell over the pretty, handmade hope chest — Judah's handiwork — at the foot of the bed, filled with her blankets and quilts. She'd tucked the midwife's letter away there, as well as the poetry books from Samuel Graber, on the off chance their child might be reunited with her someday. Other than that, she did not care to read either the letter or the books ever again.

The eyes of her heart had led her home. *To Judah . . .*

Her husband removed his suspenders, humming all the while. The contents of her hope chest were the last thing she cared to think about this night. Once she was settled into bed, Judah carried the Good Book from the dresser.

When he sat on his side of the bed, he took her letter from the Bible and opened it. "These gave me hope while you were gone." He tapped the Bible, then her folded letter, looking at her with tender eyes. "I'm grateful to God you're home, Lettie."

She felt her own heart fill anew with gratefulness at his words. And when Judah reached for her hand and raised it to his lips, she immediately warmed to his touch.

Grace stood at her bedroom window, contemplating the day and Mamma's homecoming. If someone had once told her she'd be pondering an older half sister she'd never known, she would've said they were *ferhoodled.*

Is she still living in Ohio . . . this sister Mamma kept such a secret?

She raised the window, needing the breeze on her face. Curious about the child Mamma had given away, she breathed in the rain-fresh fragrance and wondered if the young woman was as strong-willed as Mamma had always been. *And Mammi Adah, too.*

It made her tremble to think her mother

might have to own up publicly about her long-ago baby. *Becky and her parents and older brothers will be there . . . and Yonnie and his parents, too.*

She went to sit on her bed, tapping her fingers over the quilt pattern. "Is Mamma up to confessing?" To think Mamma hadn't even told Dat about the baby till her return! Had she feared he'd refuse to let her search for her long-lost child? If so, was that reason enough to keep mum all those years, then leave so unexpectedly?

By keeping quiet, Mamma misled Dat terribly . . . lied to him every day of their married life, she thought. *Which makes Dat's forgiving her now all the more precious.*

Leaning back on the bed, Grace crossed her arms behind her head and watched the shadowy flickers on the wall, thinking again of Yonnie. She squeezed her eyes shut and remembered their walk along Mill Creek. *Is it possible I like him more than I even know?*

She asked God for an understanding heart — to know what part she should take as a voting church member when Mamma declared her guilt. *I don't want to be a stumbling block, O Lord.*

Beginning to rest more easily, Grace thought presently of her recent visit with

Becky. Hearing her friend describe the fun she'd had with Henry at the pond had been an eye-opener! That, and seeing the joy-light in her friend's eyes as she talked of her new beau — for surely Henry was that. Even so, it was hard to imagine him courting Becky. *To think Henry actually* talks *to her!*

It was not as hard, however, to picture what it might be like to be courted by Yonnie. Or maybe she shouldn't let herself imagine that. Grace rolled over and let out a little groan, wishing she knew her own heart.

The glimpses she'd caught of Dat's and Mamma's affection today surprised her. Were they falling in love again? Could it be? Had her mother married out of convenience, as she'd accidently overheard Dawdi Jakob and Mammi Adah indicate more than a week ago in the privacy of their kitchen?

Just then a crack of thunder shook the house. *Another late-night thunderstorm.* Grace sat up quickly and peered out the window from her perch on the bed. "Maybe I need a lightning rod to protect my heart," she whispered as she intently watched the sky.

After a time, she went to her dresser, where the gas lamp burned brightly. She found the beautiful, clear marble-sized stone from Yonnie. Turning it over in her hand, she felt its coolness, its lovely smoothness, and dreamed of the sea. What would it be like to watch the tide move in against the sand? Or to smell sea salt in the air . . . to feel the spray of waves on her skin?

Will I ever know?

Once the storm subsided, Grace tiptoed across the hall to join Mandy in saying their bedtime prayers. Together, they'd beseeched the Lord nearly every night for Mamma's safety and her return, missing only the evenings when Mandy was out with her new beau.

Grace knelt silently beside the bed, next to her sister, and each took turns thanking God for answering their prayers. All the while Grace remembered how desperate she'd felt, though never wanting it to show — for her family's sake. *Trying to be brave . . . always hopeful.*

Afterward Mandy hugged her and whispered, "Things are best when Mamma's home, ain't so?"

Grace tearfully agreed.

Long after their mutual prayers, Grace took her time talking to God in the stillness of her own room, asking for divine wisdom for Mamma as she offered repentance before the People.

Grace had to reject the temptation to fret. Instead, she would box up her fears and hand them over to her all-wise and all-knowing heavenly Father, whose love encompassed them all. After all, hadn't the Lord prompted Mamma to be willing to repent openly? Wasn't that His divine will?

God had also softened her parents' hearts toward each other, by bringing Mamma home and in opening Dat's loving arms. The Lord was at work in her family . . . and she must rely on His will and way, no matter how problematic their present situation might seem.

Chapter Twenty-Five

With nine siblings, Lettie should've guessed her sisters would be the first to drop by Thursday morning, staggering their visits over the space of a few hours. Their calls were punctuated by those of more than a half dozen nieces, several cousins, and three sisters-in-law.

"The grapevine's workin' overtime, I dare-say," her sister Mary Beth said, grinning as she carried in a hamper filled with food.

Older sister Lavina nodded cheerfully. "There's a salmon loaf in there, made with rice. We cooked up lots of roast, too. Gravy for the roast is separate and all ready to heat up." Lavina also set several containers of chocolate chip cookies on the kitchen table. "We can't stay long — we're makin' hay today."

Mary Beth said they were doing the same. "But we'll come again soon."

"I understand . . . and thanks ever so

much for your thoughtfulness," Lettie said between hugs, both glad and embarrassed to see so many of her extended family coming and going. Aside from the occasional furtive look, it was akin to a reunion. *They're scrutinizing me . . . but can I blame them?*

Later, when the house was not so bustling, she sat at the kitchen table and dashed off a note to Cousin Hallie, letting her know she was home. *Hard as it was, I've now told Judah — and our children — about the daughter I gave up. Please keep praying for peace to fill our hearts . . . especially on the day of the next Preaching service, one week from this Lord's Day.*

Lettie went on to note that the family was well, and a few other bits of local news she knew her cousin would appreciate hearing.

I'm so thankful for the time I could spend with you and Ben. Remember you're always welcome to visit anytime. Write when you can.

With love from your cousin, Lettie.

When she finished, she thought of writing to Susan Kempf, but there was work to be done in the garden. Grace was working at Eli's part of the day, so it was just Mandy and herself.

Lettie quickly addressed the envelope to Hallie and realized, as she glanced around the kitchen, she was still finding her place in a house that had managed to run quite well without her. A bit unsettling, but Mamm would say it was a compliment to her mothering skills.

She left the letter on the corner cupboard, planning to take it to the mailbox later. Then she headed outdoors to help Mandy hoe and weed the vegetable garden.

About an hour later, when she was washing her hands at the kitchen sink, she heard Mamm calling to her from the hallway. "Come on over," Lettie called.

Her mother appeared, hanging back a bit. "Guess I'm still getting used to havin' ya home."

"Well," she said, "I s'pose I am, too."

Mamm went to sit at the foot of the table and leaned forward on her elbows. "Marian's itchin' to put up jam a week from tomorrow. Told her I'd be happy to make it in my kitchen."

"Sounds just fine. Anyone else want to join us?"

"Sally Smucker does."

"Then it'll be the six of us, counting Grace and Mandy. If Grace doesn't have other plans," Lettie added.

Mamm looked up at her. "Ah, our Gracie." She sighed. "I've never said a peep before, but are you fine with her workin' for Englischers like Janet Puckett?"

"Frankly, the world's squeezing in around us, Mamm, and movin' closer all the time." Their eyes met. "Janet's a good woman, and Gracie comes in contact with English customers at Eli's all the time." Lettie sighed. "We can't shield her, ya know."

"Well, at least she's already joined church."

Lettie straightened her apron and went to sit with Mamm. "She joined so young . . . even before I did as a youth, remember?"

Mamm's eyes widened. It was clear she remembered, all right.

"Still, makin' the church vow is only part of what makes someone right with God and the People."

Mamm agreed. "And Grace, well, she surely lives up to her name."

"I'm thankful for that," Lettie said softly.

"Well, if you're up for coming, I'll organize things for the jam-making next week." Mamm said. "Maybe Mandy can help me wash the canning jars and whatnot beforehand."

"Sure, and we'll all be out in the strawberry patch first thing Friday morning."

"We can eat the firmest ones for supper," Mamm suggested.

"And use the bigger ones for jam."

Mamm nodded but her eyes reflected her weariness. *No doubt from all the wondering and waiting,* Lettie presumed, still aware of the lingering ache in her own heart. *Ach, such a bittersweet time of reunion!*

From her window Heather saw several patients having a short break after their classes that morning. Three were strolling along the creek below the formal lawn, and two others were milling around the rose gardens. One woman linked arms with another, which put a lump in Heather's throat.

We're all in the thick of it now.

She wondered if any of the others felt as weak as she did. After the hot and cold showers, the nausea had hit her hard. It might be a textbook response to a cleanse, but it still felt perfectly miserable. To think Heather had hoped she might not experience much of a reaction.

Boy, was I wrong! She shivered as she headed back to bed, unable to get warm as she curled into a tight ball beneath the sheet and lightweight blanket. She was aware of her pounding pulse, and in her heightened anxiety and discomfort, she wondered if she might be dying.

How can anyone feel like this and survive? The intense nausea made her weaker than any bout of stomach flu she'd ever experienced. Every time she raised her head, the room began to spin rapidly, competing with the violent churning of her stomach.

She lay there, gripping the pillow and moaning. Squeezing her eyes tight, she clenched her teeth and tried with everything in her to regain control. But thoughts of her deceased mother swam in her dizzy head, causing hot tears to trickle toward her ears. *Oh, Mom . . . I wish you were here to help me.*

She contemplated her master's thesis, sadly unfinished. Of course, she hadn't really expected to wrap it up this summer, but its incomplete state evoked further anxiety. If she died today, she'd never complete her graduate degree . . . never see her academic dreams fulfilled.

Unable to relax, a list of must-do's formed in Heather's head — other things she wanted to accomplish: land a great-paying job, buy her own place, tuck money away for the future. *A future that might not exist . . .*

Suddenly she was startled by a vision of her young Amish mother, a mere teenager dressed in the style of clothing she'd seen in Ohio. This unfamiliar likeness collided with her earlier recollection of her modern, adoptive mother.

Heather tried to make sense of the contradictory collage in her mind as the two images merged into one vague apparition. And, just as quickly, the two began to separate and her adoptive mom's face reappeared — she looked healthy and whole — leaving the other filmy and featureless. What played most strongly in Heather's mind was the fact that if she died now, she would never meet the Amishwoman who'd given her life.

I'll be dead and gone before we have a chance to find each other. She was seized by an urgency unlike any she'd ever known. *Has she even looked for me, God?*

Gasping for air, she rolled to her left side, just as LaVyrle had said to do when nauseous. But even the change in position made no difference. If anything, the pain was increasing, along with her irrational thoughts.

If she hadn't felt so deathly ill, Heather wouldn't have been thinking in such morose tones. Was it the release of toxins that was producing these crying jags . . . even her depression? *Can that also make me suddenly want to locate my biological parents?*

She tried to shrug it off, but try as she

might, she could not dismiss this new, unforeseen desire. Her mind was in turmoil over her Plain origins and the very real likelihood of never connecting with her natural mother. Such a strange and perplexing fear! For the first time in her life, Heather literally yearned to find her original family, and above all, the woman who'd given birth to her. Before today, such thoughts had felt somehow awkward. Even as a little girl, whenever she had thought in passing of her biological parents out of mere curiosity, she had quickly pushed the interest aside for love of her adoptive parents.

Was this longing due to the cleanse . . . or to the seriousness of her illness? Whatever its source, she was determined to act on it — if only she could find the strength. Another wave of nausea overtook her, and Heather clutched her stomach and willed the pain away. *How much more can I tolerate?*

She made an attempt to double up the covers for additional warmth but was fearful to raise her head in case she lost consciousness. Instead she leaned up slightly to scan the room, hoping to spot another blanket. *It can't be so chilly this close to June . . . my body's thermostat must be completely out of whack.*

When Arielle came to check on her, Heather felt too hazy to explain what was happening, except to point to her stomach, indicating pain. She wanted to vomit.

"Continue resting, Heather, and I'll give you some peppermint essential oil — three small drops in a cup of warm water will settle things," Arielle suggested, coming to stand near her bed. "You'll need to sip it slowly and keep it away from your eyes. It's quite potent and can sting a bit."

"Why do I feel like this?" LaVyrle's instruction had flown right out of her head.

"Most likely the pain is due to the dying yeast and other unfriendly intestinal bacteria. Remember, your body's cleaning house." Arielle explained that yeast was "an opportunistic parasite. It's a friendly environment for cancer cells."

Trying to be polite in the midst of her pain, Heather struggled to keep her eyes open, willing herself to understand what was happening.

"Your body's in fight mode, just as it should be — cancer is a very real battle," Arielle told her. Her expression was gentle, caring. "The goal is for your body to become inhospitable to cancer cells."

Heather made an attempt to nod her head in response to what she was hearing, but right now she wasn't sure who was going to win.

"We have to work *with* our bodies to fight the disease." Arielle smiled down at her. "I'll run and get that peppermint oil for you, okay?"

"Thanks." *Please hurry,* thought Heather, thinking again of her mom. *If she prayed for me . . . why couldn't I pray for myself now?*

Lying there, she reached gingerly for her iPhone on the table near the bed. She wasn't the best pray-er on the planet, but her friend Jim was. Maybe he would agree to talk to God for her. But when she tried to key in a text message, she couldn't see the letters due to wooziness. The phone fell, clattering, to the floor, and she was too weak to reach for it.

The thought of losing her ability to connect with Jim or anyone in her address book — despite the fact Arielle was coming right back — put Heather in a panic. *I don't want to die like this, God. Please don't let me die alone!*

CHAPTER TWENTY-SIX

Martin Puckett was pleased the day was warm and sunny. Two very talkative Amish carpenters were his passengers today, telling humorous stories about filling silo and shoe-ing horses. He'd also heard much about the "Englisher building the Amish house" — enough that his curiosity was piqued. Today he hoped to finally meet Roan Nelson himself at the house site, where Martin was presently heading.

When he pulled up, he noticed several men already on the site. Two were Amish; the other two were not.

The forms had already been set into place for the foundation. Once it was poured and cured, the house could literally be framed within days. He'd observed barn raisings and Amish farmers supplementing their income by building gazebos and toolsheds. But this would be the first time he had seen them build a house up close.

Early on, when Roan Nelson first purchased the property, he'd had a driveway put in on the north side, carefully avoiding the mature trees. *Somebody's on the ball.* Martin respected home builders who didn't tamper with nature.

"Here we are," he said, pulling onto the shoulder. An attractive-looking tan Camry was parked nearby. He assumed it was Roan's as he got out and went around to open the van door to let out his passengers, accepting the cash payments as they exited.

When he asked Josiah Smucker, the preacher-carpenter, to point out Roan Nelson, Josiah replied, "That's him over yonder, standin' near the foundation."

"Thanks." Martin closed the door and walked toward the Virginia man. "Hello, I'm Martin Puckett. . . . I drive the Amish for a living. I'll be bringing a lot of the men here each day." He shook the well-dressed man's hand. "Josiah says you're in charge."

Roan smiled. "I wouldn't go that far." He glanced at Josiah. "I try to stay out of the master carpenter's way. From what I've heard, the man was born with a hammer in his hand."

Martin laughed, having heard the same. "He's the one to turn to if you want an Amish builder in these parts."

"I'm lucky to have caught him at the right time," Roan admitted.

"Anymore the Amish around here are having to find work other than farming — farming's just too costly."

Roan nodded. "And some have found pretty creative niches for themselves, like making baseball bats."

Martin was pleased at how well-informed Roan already seemed to be about the area. He wondered how the man had come to take an interest in the Amish.

But Roan obviously had other things on his mind, and he waved at Martin to follow him around the house in progress. "Would you like to hear about the floor plan?" Roan asked. "You have time?"

"Sure do." As Martin fell into step with him, they also talked of the ingenious ways the Amish workmen were able to get by without electricity, powering their building tools with compressed air pumped by diesel engines. "There's an Amishman not far from here who builds modular homes in his warehouse — makes ten or eleven a year. It takes only about five weeks to put each one together," Roan said, walking the area where he said the foundation was to be poured today. "I understand it's a lucrative family-run business."

Martin hadn't heard of that operation. "How big are the houses?"

"Average size is fifteen hundred square feet. The cabinet maker I'm working with told me about the operation."

Martin pushed his hands into his pants pockets, imitating Roan's relaxed manner. "If you don't mind my asking, why did you choose to build here, in a mostly Plain neighborhood?"

"Well, my wife and I liked to come here on family trips quite often for years before she passed away." Roan glanced over his shoulder, then back at Martin. "We'd planned to retire here . . . always enjoyed this area."

"It's about as nice a place as I can imagine living in," Martin said. "My wife and I grew up in Lancaster County, so we've always been near Amish."

Roan smiled amicably. "A unique people."

Martin nodded wholeheartedly. "They certainly are. I, for one, admire their work ethic — their honesty, generosity, cordiality . . . the whole nine yards."

Roan showed him the location of the well, already dug and installed. "We found it by water witching," he said, "with the help of a guy named Potato John. Sounds fictitious, doesn't it?"

Martin grinned. "You'll hear all kinds of nicknames round here."

They walked in silence for a while. Then Roan mentioned that his daughter was presently at the nearby natural treatment center for cancer. He pointed in the direction of the Wellness Lodge, which Martin had heard good things about.

"Certainly hope all goes well for her . . . and for you."

"Thanks." Roan offered a warm handshake. "Very nice talking with you."

"Same here." No matter how many people he ran into in his line of work, Martin was always amazed whenever he hit it off so well with someone he'd just met. "Feel free to look me up anytime." He dug into his wallet and pulled out his business card. "I'll be glad to show you around Lancaster County — have you and your daughter over for dinner sometime."

Roan's smile was wide and sincere. He glanced in the direction of the lodge. "We might take you up on that."

Martin headed back to his van, wondering if Roan had put any money down on the project or even signed a contract with Josiah Smucker. From what he'd heard about such dealings with Amish, the only thing required was a firm handshake.

The old-fashioned way.

While Heather waited for the peppermint oil to take effect, she tried to remain calm. Arielle had retrieved the iPhone from the floor and placed it on the bedside table with a smile when she'd returned with the warm drink. She sat near the bed for a time, not saying much — just offering her presence as comfort. Then, after a while, she got up. "If you feel worse, just call me at the number downstairs, Heather," she said.

"I hadn't thought of that." Heather reached for the phone and cradled it in her hands. Dare she contact Jim? Typically, he was the first to text her each day. *But, hey, this is the new millennium,* she told herself and sent him a greeting.

Within seconds he replied. *Hope your day's off to a great start. Let me know how it's going.*

Got slammed by my first cleansing crisis, she wrote. *Thought I might not make it.*

He wrote back: *How well I remember. Hang in there — I promise it gets better.*

Still feeling too ill to even get out of bed, Heather told Jim she'd actually contemplated trying to find her biological mother. *A completely radical thing for me.* She sent the text before realizing he didn't even know she was adopted. *Yikes,* she thought. But it was too late now.

Soon he wrote again. *I'm composing a prayer for you. OK if I send it by email?*

Now, this was some way to get a girl's attention!

I need all the help I can get, she typed quickly and sent it before she could change her mind. The truth was, Heather felt desperate. Staring at her phone, she waited to read Jim's prayer, written on her behalf . . . to God.

After ten minutes passed and no email appeared, she filled the time by looking up the Ohio Adoption Registry online, hoping to get information on how to locate her birth parents. From perusing the site, it appeared to be rather easy, although the court records were sealed for adoptions that had occurred between January 1, 1964, and September 18, 1996. She bookmarked the adoption registry site and decided she'd go to a twenty-four-hour copy shop to print the form, then submit it once she was released from the lodge.

If I survive this . . .

Chapter Twenty-Seven

With the last of the lambs birthed and thriving, Judah could finally turn his energies to fattening them up for market. And tomorrow, what with the sunniest weather in days, he hoped to begin raking hay. Most every neighbor in the community was already doing so, including Andy Riehl and his boys up the way. Only the Spanglers were not, because they didn't work the soil or raise animals for a living. It crossed his mind that Lettie should go over and visit Carole Spangler. The woman had been so upset on the road, in the pitch-darkness. He made a mental note to ask his wife to look in on her. But no, Lettie might not be the best choice just now. Grace was the one he would ask.

He had seen Lettie and Mandy at work in the vegetable garden earlier, and he'd stopped what he was doing to admire his wife, mighty glad she was home. Despite his initial negative response to her shocking secret, his mind had cleared swiftly — a real change of heart. *The Good Lord's doing.*

Judah had been praying about the types of questions the bishop might ask Lettie during her confession. That day was coming too soon for his liking. Yet his wife was unwavering in her decision to do so in public, despite grave concern from her mother. Nevertheless, Judah would not stand in Lettie's way, not when she felt so certain of the Lord's leading. She had never been one to put too much stock in the opinions of others. No, his wife was unlike any Amishwoman he'd ever known.

Even so, she's mine, Judah thought with a chuckle before he turned back to mucking out the barn.

Heather was relieved when LaVyrle came into her room that afternoon to reassure her that what she was experiencing was not uncommon.

"Before bed tonight, help yourself to an extra serving of the veggie broth," LaVyrle suggested kindly. "It will keep your electrolytes up." She explained that Heather was losing more bodily fluids than usual, and the broth provided an important sodium-potassium balance.

Heather recalled the powdered broth she had earlier mixed with hot water. It had a pleasant, satisfying taste, but she now wondered aloud if she had the energy to even navigate her way to the kitchen area where it was stored.

"No problem. I'll have Arielle bring you some. You just rest." LaVyrle pulled up a chair and sat down. "Something else, Heather . . . Sally Smucker mentioned her invitation to you — to stay with her next week, after you leave here. I took the liberty of suggesting this to your father. I hope that's all right."

Heather was surprised this had already been discussed. "What did Dad say?"

LaVyrle smiled readily. "He agreed rather quickly."

Interesting . . .

"Given his initial hesitation, it's very nice your dad's become so supportive," said the naturopath. "Quite remarkable, really."

Heather agreed, noticing how LaVyrle's eyes sparkled when she mentioned her dad. *What's going on here — a budding romance?* The thought was a bit awkward, but if Dad was bouncing back from his deep grief, she was happy for him.

"Thanks for discussing Sally's idea with Dad," she said. "Maybe I'll find some time to return to working on my thesis while I'm there. I feel like I've been derailed."

"I won't be surprised if you're feeling well enough to start working on it again soon." LaVyrle squeezed her hand. "I can see the fight in your eyes . . . you want to live."

"I'm trying hard; I really am."

"I know you are, Heather. And that goes a long way toward getting your health back."

"Thanks." As she watched LaVyrle leave, it was all she could do not to call after the woman and thank her again for this amazing opportunity.

Heather was just awakening from a surprisingly restful sleep when she heard the pronounced chime signaling a new email. Hoping it was from Jim, she opened it quickly, still groggy from her nap.

> Hey, Heather:
>
> Here's the prayer I wrote and am praying for you. Rest assured God is there with you.
>
> Concerned, yet trusting Him,
>
> — Jim

She began to read his poetic prayer. . . .

A Prayer for Heather

Lord, You know well my friend.
You see her tears,
You hear her cries,
You alone understand her fears . . .
because You made her,
crafted her in Your very image.
Grant her persistence for this difficult
journey,
help for the long night
and stamina for the fight.
Thanks for being with her . . . always.
Surround her with divine guidance and
light.
Be her healing presence
and her constant friend.
Bless her abundantly with You,
the best of gifts.
Amen.

Heather's tears flowed freely. The prayer was the kindest, dearest thing a guy had ever done for her. *This Jim . . . he's really something,* she thought.

She wanted to read it again but first wiped her eyes dry. The kind of trust apparent in his words was mindboggling to her. Jim patently believed this stuff.

How can I thank him? She scrolled down

to reread the final lines. The fact he'd written the prayer in free verse had also caught her attention. Since coming to the lodge, she'd occasionally taken a similar approach to her daily journal. *To think he took the time to do this . . .*

She caught herself. *Am I falling for this guy?*

Her feelings were a mix of emotions as she let his prayer saturate her heart, bringing a momentary peace. After a time, she emailed Jim a thank-you, hoping he might know how sincerely appreciative she was.

The lights were on at the Spanglers' house after supper as Grace walked down the road with a loaf of homemade bread and apple butter. Dat had asked this afternoon if she might look in on their neighbors, a solemn expression on his sunburnt face. *He's concerned for them.*

At the time, she'd wondered why he hadn't asked Mamma, but then, considering that Dat might not want her mother exposed to the neighbors' questions, Grace understood.

The sky was a slate gray and growing darker by the minute. Hopefully this evening would find Carole and her girls — Grace's friend Jessica, especially — at home. She asked God to help her encourage Jessica and her family. *You know just what they need, dear Lord.*

As it turned out, Carole was away from the house. "At a Bible study," Jessica said, then thanked her for the "treats," as she called the bread and apple butter. She placed both on the kitchen counter.

"Oh, it's nothin'," Grace said.

"Don't sell yourself short, Grace. You should see Brittany and me devour your fresh-baked bread."

"That's nice to hear. Denki."

They headed upstairs to Jessica's room, and when her friend closed the door, she leaned against it. "I'm really glad you came, Gracie."

"I've been thinking 'bout you."

"Well, you might be surprised — and happy to know — that my fiancé and I have started taking premarital classes since the last time we talked. We're receiving a lot of practical counsel."

"Oh?" Grace had never heard of such classes. Their Amish church district gave no counseling either before or after marriage that she knew of.

"I wanted to take the classes because of my fears over my parents' problems," Jessica added quickly.

Grace was reticent to ask about that.

"Actually, it's become a blessing — what Quentin and I are doing for our upcoming marriage. We're addressing potential problems ahead of time . . . so we'll know how to tackle things that could threaten our love." Jessica's eyes grew more serious. "Quentin and I are becoming best friends because of it."

Jessica led her to the computer desk across the room and got online to show her several places she and her fiancé were considering for their honeymoon — several featured ocean settings Grace found most appealing.

"Oh, I should have asked . . . but did you get to visit your mom while she was in Ohio?" Jessica said after she'd closed down the travel pictures.

Grace told her about the quick trip with another English friend, then shared with her the big surprise of Mamma's recent return.

"Oh, Gracie . . . what a relief!" Jessica frowned suddenly. "I felt badly that I couldn't take you . . . and Mom was so worried about . . . well, Dad."

Ach, we all had our worries.

They headed back down to the kitchen, where Jessica toasted two pieces of the homemade bread and spread the rich apple butter, giving a slice to Grace. "Amish-made bread is the best," Jessica said. "Brittany and I will make quick work of this."

After she'd enjoyed the toast along with Jessica, Grace said she had to return home for family worship. "I'd better be goin'."

"Come anytime," Jessica called after her.

On the walk home, Grace was relieved Jessica hadn't asked her about her own romantic prospects — not that Jessica was so nosy as to inquire. But Grace wouldn't have known what to say, since Yonnie had so quickly exited her life and was working for his father now.

She breathed in the minty scent of the lavender-blue catmint from a nearby garden. The night was filled with the familiar sound of crickets. Yet, staring into the darkness, Grace realized she no longer enjoyed walking alone. And she missed seeing Yonnie around the house and barn . . . especially during the noon meal.

Just then it dawned on her that Mamma didn't even know of her breakup with Henry Stahl! *After the reservations she expressed to me 'bout him, no doubt she'd be glad about it.* Then Grace laughed into the night. "But she'd like Yonnie, that's for sure!"

Too bad Mamma hadn't been around to see Yonnie help fill the bird feeders or to hear him talk a blue streak with Dawdi Jakob at dinner. Or to observe him carrying a stack of dishes to the sink. Truly, Yonnie was unlike any other fellow she'd known.

Right then, Grace wished she might see him again, especially before the Preaching service. *When Mamma confesses . . .*

CHAPTER TWENTY-EIGHT

The sky was past its twilight the next evening when Heather's father came to visit. "I'm sure you're tired, kiddo, so I'll only stay a short while." He kissed her forehead and they settled into a private corner of the comfortable commons area, green with a wealth of indoor plants to keep the air rich with oxygen.

"The peppermint oil is helping," she told him. "Magical stuff."

"I'm glad." He looked tired, but she could tell he was making an effort for her.

They talked about the perfect weather for pouring the foundation. Like everything else thus far, this aspect of the project had gone very smoothly.

"How soon before the framing will begin?" she asked.

"A week." He crossed his legs, and she noticed his hands were trembling slightly on his knee. "Heather, how are you doing . . . really?"

"Dad, please don't worry."

"Well, fathers tend to do that."

She forced a smile. "What I've experienced is fairly normal. Some patients just have worse reactions than others."

He frowned and still appeared to be worried.

"I've started to wonder if Mom's death sapped my health somehow." She didn't mention the shock and subsequent heartache over her breakup with Devon Powers.

"Lots of folk have unresolved issues, but those don't necessarily affect their physical health," said Dad.

"I think that's debatable. I've been learning a lot here about stress and how it affects the body." She explained some of what she'd gleaned in LaVyrle's daily classes — how she'd read that stress was the number-one killer in the country. "We have quite a lively daily question-and-answer time."

Dad chuckled. "I'll bet you do." He slipped his arm around her. "And I can see your point about stress. I've definitely been one to internalize it."

"Don't we all?"

"You're getting excellent care here."

She nodded and decided to test the waters. "Yes . . . and it's hard to believe the good doctor is single."

"Actually, she was married once . . . years ago. Her husband died of a rare form of leukemia, which is the main reason for her work here at the lodge. She wants to help as many people as possible."

"Sounds like you know more about my doctor than I do."

There was a convincing twinkle in his deep-set eyes. "I'm discovering she's one special lady." He glanced around the well-decorated room, with its rustic but comfortable furniture, greenery, and bold, deep colors. "I hope you don't mind if I get to know her better, Heather."

"If you like her, go for it. That's your business, Dad."

He smiled and pushed back a wisp of hair from her face. "Are you sure, kiddo?"

"You don't need my permission to ask LaVyrle out."

His eyes searched hers. "What else is on your mind tonight?"

"Oh, I don't know," she hedged.

"You're being elusive."

"No . . . just don't want to hurt you."

He took her hand. "Hey, I'm tough."

She second-guessed whether she should say anything about her recent decision to search for her birth parents. After all, it was doubtless hard enough for him to see her fighting this illness. They really didn't know if the cleansing fast would ultimately make a difference in her cancer . . . or if she'd have a wonderful suprise for her oncologist.

"You can trust your old man, Heather. C'mon, give it a shot."

He was right. "Well, I've been thinking about looking for my Amish mother . . . and possibly my birth father, too," she said.

A solemn wave swept his face. "I wondered if you might want to do this someday."

She said the idea had come when she'd felt so deathly ill. "I'd just like to meet them . . . nothing more," she explained. "I honestly thought I was going to breathe my last upstairs in my room yesterday."

"Oh, honey."

She leaned her head on his shoulder. "Please, don't be upset with my wild idea."

"You have every right." He kissed her forehead.

But the crimp in his voice was obvious, and later, when Heather went to her room for bed, she wished she hadn't brought it up at all.

Adah felt greatly relieved as she stood in her kitchen, making homemade popcorn for Jakob. Her heartfelt confession to Deacon

Amos this afternoon had been short and to the point, as she had just been telling Jakob. "Amos asked if you were in on the arrangements for Lettie and her baby," she added.

"Not nearly enough, I daresay." Her husband leaned forward in his chair, eyes fixed on the deep pan.

"I admitted it was mostly my doing. Guess the deacon wondered if you'd thought of goin' to speak with him, too. Confess, ya know."

"I guess if I don't feel convicted 'bout it, then I won't be goin'."

She eyed his ruddy face, wreathed in smile lines. "Do as you see fit . . . just so the deacon doesn't suspect a defiant spirit in you."

"Not the case," he said, watching her pour the hot popcorn into a large bowl.

She took the entire bowl and set it in his lap. "Don't eat it all, love."

He grinned and reached into the fluffy white mound. "Care for some?"

"Thought you'd never ask." She sat next to him to share the evening treat. "Tastes *gut,* jah?"

He nodded, reaching for another handful. "Supper was delicious, but I needed something salty."

She smiled at him. Her beloved Jakob . . . he knew what he liked; no getting around it. "So you don't feel the need to visit Deacon Amos, then?"

"I made things right with the Lord God long ago . . . and I've spoken to the bishop directly." His gaze remained on the popcorn. "Quite recently."

Adah was surprised at this but said no more about it . . . ever so glad Jakob had made things right with the man of God.

Later, after they'd nearly eaten all but a dozen or so unpopped kernels, she looked at the day clock. "It's getting late."

He licked his fingers. "You know, I only hope the brethren will go as easy on Lettie as they did on you, dear." He cleaned off his buttery hands with his blue paisley handkerchief, then handed her the popcorn bowl before gripping the arms of the chair to ease himself up.

"Who's to know?" she said.

"The Lord does."

She placed the bowl in the sink and turned as he limped across the room. "I am glad I spoke to the deacon," she said quietly. "The Lord's been workin' on me for some time now."

"Then you must feel as free as the songbirds I watched with Lettie this afternoon."

He gripped his cane as he walked toward her.

"And you? I can tell you're feelin' much better, too . . . just havin' her back," she said.

Jakob smacked his lips. " 'Tis funny how the head and the heart work together in such things."

Adah couldn't agree more. "Jah, 'tis."

Chapter Twenty-Nine

Saturday morning Lettie washed and dressed quickly, then went outside to check on the bird feeders, enjoying the way the meadowlarks, jays, and chickadees landed on them, pecked at the grains, and fluttered away. One lone blue jay eyed her from a nearby branch, as if gauging her proximity to the feeder. Soon he flew back for seconds, plucky enough to return, even though she stood near. *They feel safe here, sharing this peaceful spot. Just as I do . . .*

She liked to think of the morning feeding as a time of gathering, when the whole of the day stretched out before these beautiful, trusting birds. *A day with a clean slate.* " 'Thy kingdom come, Thy will be done,' " she whispered, giving up her will again to the Lord — relinquishing concern for the whereabouts of her daughter, too. Sometimes it was a twice-a-day occurrence, sometimes more. She'd carried the memory of her firstborn close to her heart for so long, it was difficult to fully surrender. Yet Lettie believed that by lifting her eldest child to the Father each and every morning, she was doing just that.

"I will never forget you, dear one," she whispered to the breeze. "And I long to meet you . . . to know you . . . in God's timing."

Grace was both surprised and pleased to see Yonnie already sitting in the van when Martin Puckett came by to pick her up at the house. She secretly wondered if this was an answer to her prayer last evening. *Well, more of a wish than a prayer,* she realized.

"Fancy meeting *you* here," Yonnie teased from his seat near the window in the middle row of seats.

"I was thinkin' the same thing," she said, unable to conceal her smile.

She slid in next to him, since there was another passenger up front — an Englischer — sitting with Martin. It seemed providential, because this way she and Yonnie could talk privately in Deitsch, and Martin and the talkative older man would be none the wiser.

"How're the youngest newborn lambs doin'?" asked Yonnie, his smile almost too wide for his handsome face.

Dat and her brothers hadn't mentioned any problems. "Oh, fine . . . far as I know."

"And your mother . . . is she settling in all right?"

She nodded, not sure how to answer.

"Wonderful-*gut.*" But there was some hesitancy in his voice.

"Mamma is spending plenty of time now reading the Bible with Dat . . . more than ever," she volunteered.

"My father always says the Good Book has healing power."

"Jah, I believe that, too."

Leaning closer, Yonnie said, "Ever hear a story about the man who decided to ride his horse backward so he wouldn't be sidetracked by where he was going?"

"Nee."

"That way he could pay closer attention to where he'd been instead."

"Where'd ya hear this?"

"Don't remember, really . . . but it made an impression on me."

"Denki for sharing that," she said quietly.

"For some folks, where they've been — the past — has important meaning for their present circumstance."

"And for the future, too," she replied, surprised at his perceptivity. She guessed he knew about her mother's search for her child. Goodness, but she was glad Martin Puckett and his other passenger were involved in animated conversation up front!

"Oh, definitely for the future," he said.

She fell silent, pondering the significant things he'd conveyed in such few words. *He's so interesting,* she thought, folding her hands in her lap.

The sunlight played off the windshield of the van. She turned to look out her window, thinking just then of the changing ocean tides — and the way Mamma's confession might drastically alter her friendship with Yonnie. "Have you ever heard of folks who live near the ocean . . . who can feel the actual moment when the tide changes?" she asked timidly.

He looked at her with a quizzical expression. "Honestly, Gracie, I have! And I've never known of anyone else who thinks about such things . . . at least out loud."

She smiled. "Well, I read this somewhere, and I really love the idea."

He slipped off his straw hat. "You just keep surprisin' me."

Grace laughed softly, letting her imagination fly. What if someday she and Yonnie could visit the ocean and walk along the water, watching the tide creep farther and farther ashore? Might they be able to sense the moment when the tide reversed?

"Will you be at the next Singing?" he asked, sounding more serious now.

A lot would depend on how things went with Mamma's confession, but she certainly didn't want to mention it now. He might not want to have a thing to do with her following that membership meeting. "I'll have to see" was all she said, even though she thought it would be great fun to see him at the barn gathering.

"Well, I hope you'll be there." He put his hat back on. "Don't be a stranger, jah?"

She couldn't help smiling again.

When the van arrived at the Pucketts' house, she waited for Martin to open the van door to let her out. "Good-bye," she said to Yonnie. "Have a *gut* day."

"You too," he replied.

Walking to the house, she couldn't get over their many mutual interests . . . and the way they always found so much to talk about. But for the time being, Grace must set her mind on a layout for Janet Puckett's herb garden.

Heather checked her email and gulped when she saw a message from Devon Powers.

Hey, Heather!

How's life? I've been thinking about us lately. Really hope you'll overlook my stupidity.

I was wrong . . . can we talk? Write back when you can.

Missing you, babe —
Devon

She could hardly believe her eyes. "How dare you! You can*not* breeze in and out of my life," she whispered. Yet it was impossible not to remember the happy times they'd shared — biking along the Virginia Beach boardwalk, going to movies together — before he was shipped off to Iraq with his National Guard unit. And then the onslaught of the literally thousands of emails they'd exchanged over the months when he was so lonely and missing her. *Before my diagnosis.* She'd never told him about the cancer that propelled her to Amish country to see Dr. LaVyrle Marshall. *You bailed on me when I needed you most, Devon. . . .*

He'd dropped her like a stone for someone else, and now here he was, back in touch. The presumptuous correspondence triggered more queasiness in her, and just when she'd started to feel better, too: But *this* reaction had nothing to do with the cleanse. It was a knee-jerk response to a guy who hadn't a clue about women. *He needs to get a life . . . and without me!*

It was impossible not to compare his clueless email with the prayer Jim had sent. She'd read the prayer aloud so many times, Heather had made it her own, letting the words flow over her before she fell asleep the last two nights.

She felt the old anger rising and quickly deleted Devon's message. Then, going into Settings, she blocked his email address and felt instantly better. *There . . . no more weirdness,* she thought with a huge sigh.

She muttered to herself while she showered, refusing to let the unexpected email tamper with her emotions. Devon's wretched self-centeredness only made Jim's sweet-spirited correspondence all the more endearing.

CHAPTER THIRTY

Immediately upon stepping into the Pucketts' house that morning, Grace noticed how well organized Janet was — everything seemingly in its place. This being the first time she'd met their favorite driver's wife, Grace enjoyed getting acquainted.

After a glass of iced tea, Janet led her outside to the already-tilled rectangular plot — the location of the future herb garden. Grace would lay it out today and, next week, help plant it with Janet.

"How'd you know of my keen interest in herbs?"

Janet's eyes twinkled as she pushed her hair back. "Your father mentioned something to Martin a while back."

"Dat sure enjoys talkin' to him," Grace said. She stood beneath the shade of a sturdy maple and made a sketch of the projected garden. Front and center in the sunny plot was a spot for the sweet bay, as well as the garlic chive, American marigold, rosemary, and scarlet bee balm. She thought some plantings of butterfly milkweed would look pretty on either side of that midsection. There would be basil and oregano . . . and, of course, lavender. And to fill in the outer edges, Grace suggested chili pepper and English thyme, with cheddar pink, as well as teasel. Since mint was invasive, it would be confined to a second, much smaller plot in another corner of the yard. As would the dill weed, at the other end.

Janet asked where she'd learned about herbs, and Grace was quick to tell about Mammi Adah. "She's been sharing her knowledge of herbs and their healing properties with me ever since I was a little girl."

"She obviously taught you very well." Janet sounded pleased.

By the time Grace stepped out of the area, she felt as light as a hummingbird's wings. In the back of her mind, she thought of her ill friend and wondered if Martin might be willing to drop her off at the lodge for a visit.

I don't want to miss a single day!

Grace was surprised to see Heather strolling along the roadside when Martin let her out at the lodge after noon. "Hullo,

Heather," she called, climbing out of the van.

"Grace . . . hey!" Heather waved.

Martin reminded Grace she owed him nothing, saying he'd let her father know when they'd have to start paying for transportation again. "Janet's very happy with your work, Grace. We'll see you again on Tuesday."

"Glad I can help," she said, thanking him again. Then she hurried up the road to Heather. "How are you?"

"Doing a little better. Thankfully, I've been busy with classes on food selection and meal preparation. LaVyrle wants us to be able to continue a healing diet when we leave here. So it's crash course time for nutrition. I've still got lots to learn."

Grace could see how important that would be after Heather's struggles to get this far. She also sensed Heather wasn't as interested in discussing what she was learning as she was distracted by something else. "You sure you're all right?" she asked hesitantly.

Heather motioned for Grace to walk with her. "Yeah . . . I've just been thinking a lot about life lately. Mine's certainly had a few twists along the way. My dad told me something pretty mindboggling recently, and I've wanted to tell someone . . . especially someone here in Amish country." She frowned a little, then looked at Grace. "And, well, I'd like to tell you first."

Grace stiffened, wondering what Heather was about to say.

"I mentioned that I was adopted, but at that time I really didn't know a lot about it. Dad gave me more facts just last week." Heather went on to say her birth mother had been a teenager from Ohio. "She was Amish."

"Really?" Grace found this not only surprising but interesting. "And to think we were just there, too!"

"Right. And, while I knew it then, I didn't feel comfortable saying anything." Heather stopped walking. "After all, that trip was about your mom . . . and you."

"I wouldn't have minded, really."

"I know . . . which is what's so terrific about you."

Grace didn't know how to respond to that, unaccustomed as she was to receiving compliments.

"It's hard to understand how it happened . . . meeting a friend like you. I've never had much luck in that department." Heather picked up the pace, and Grace matched her stride. "By the way, Sally

Smucker said something about making strawberry jam at your grandmother's next week. Any chance I could crash the party?"

"Why, sure — come on over," Grace said, delighted, surprised at this — so out of character for Heather. "I'll be at Eli's, but don't let that discourage you from goin'. I'd like for you to have a chance to meet more of the folks round here, 'specially my sister, Mandy."

They talked awhile longer, then Heather looked at her watch. "I should head back soon for the next class."

"Are you still on the fast?"

Heather nodded. "But my cravings for solid foods are beginning to subside, so that's a big help, believe me."

Grace was cautious about asking which foods Heather would be permitted to eat come Wednesday. Her friend must've sensed the question and began to describe Tuesday afternoon's upcoming "break-the-fast feast," featuring a salad of greens and homemade vegetable soup. That evening, brown rice and black beans would be served, along with baked corn chips and salsa. And a dessert — whole-grain banana bread with pineapple glaze topping. "Right about now, that sounds like a real banquet," Heather admitted.

"I would guess so," Grace said.

"By the way, there's no need to keep to yourself what I told you about my Amish heritage. I'm proud of it . . . knowing you as I do, Grace."

Grace was relieved to hear it. After all, she'd seen firsthand the pitfalls of secret keeping.

When Heather had thanked her for stopping by and gone back to the lodge, Grace walked home. She was still pondering the interesting tidbit about her not-so-English friend when she was met by Adam in the backyard, where he was slowly walking Willow. "Come with us . . . Willow's been askin' for you." He smiled a sad sort of smile and patted the mare's shoulder.

"She's talkin' to you now?" she joked. "What's wrong with her?" She fell into step with her older brother and her favorite horse.

"Nothin's wrong with Willow."

She looked at him. "With you, then?"

He shrugged.

"Is this a guessing game?"

Adam wrinkled his nose. "Aw, Gracie, don't be lippy."

"Sorry, just thinking 'bout other things, I guess." It was no excuse to be flippant. "What's botherin' you?"

He shoved one hand into his pocket, keeping the other on Willow's lead. "Prissy's all ferhoodled."

"Again?" She tried not to laugh.

"Well . . . you know."

"Honestly, I don't. I ran into her at Eli's recently, but she seemed herself — just fishin' for information."

He kicked a pebble aside as they walked to the stable. "She's just so sure Mamma's confession is goin' to upset the fruit basket for us all."

"She means it'll upset it for *you* . . . for the two of you."

"Could be."

"Is her family puttin' pressure on her to break things off with you?"

He turned swiftly. "Puh! Why would you say such a thing?"

"Because that's what I think."

"But, Gracie . . ."

"Since when can't we speak frankly? We've always talked openly before."

"Jah, before our mother ran off into the night. She never once stopped to think how all this would affect us, did she?"

She could see Adam was upset. "Maybe not. But how is any of what's happened Prissy's concern?"

Adam fell silent for a time as they approached Willow's stall.

Then Grace asked, "Prissy doesn't know 'bout . . . Mamma's past, does she?"

He blew air out of his mouth. "Not from me, no. But she will soon enough — from Mamma, if she confesses." He turned and stared at her, incredulous. "You must not understand what could happen a week from tomorrow, sister." He frowned severely. "Do ya?"

"It's my first members' meeting for a kneeling confession . . . so, no." She stiffened. What on earth did he mean?

"Our mother could be shunned if the membership doesn't accept her confession — the worst thing that can happen to a church member." Adam wore agonizing worry on his face.

She winced. Enough bad things had happened to their family already.

"And if Priscilla's parents decide they don't approve of her in-laws — Mamma, especially — they could step in."

"And do what?"

"End the engagement," he said flatly. He reached to open the stall, ushering Willow inside.

"Well . . . this isn't an arranged marriage, is it?"

"Don't be *lecherich* — ridiculous." Bowing his head, he added, "Maybe this is why some couples run off to get married."

"Elope?" Grace stroked the mare, who had turned and was looking right at them.

"Maybe so." He reached for Willow's mane.

"Ever think you could do better than Prissy Stahl?"

Adam gave her a glaring look. "Ever think of standin' by your word?"

She cringed, knowing he meant Henry, but ignored Adam's response. "Prissy will rule the roost, for sure. *Your* roost."

"But that doesn't merit a breakup, 'least not on my part. My word is *gut.*"

They were quiet for a time. Then Grace said, "Guess I spoke out of turn."

"You don't give her enough credit," he said. "There's a whole other side to Prissy that you don't know."

Grace didn't know what to say to that.

Just then, she saw Dat and Mamma walking toward the meadow, hand in hand. "Lookee there," she said, feeling suddenly warm inside. "Did ya ever think you'd see that?"

Adam shook his head.

"Appears to me like they're fallin' for each other — 'least deeper than they ever were before."

"A long time comin'," he said.

Grace kept watching their parents. "Don't know what to make of it," she admitted.

"Something happened to them while Mamma was gone," Adam said, petting Willow gently.

"Maybe they're tending to what they have, instead of wishin' for what they don't."

"Mamma's heart's softer, that's for certain," Adam said.

"And Dat's more talkative than ever . . . even affectionate. Both of them are ever so different." She watched Dat slip his arm around Mamma and had to look away, lest she cry. "Whatever comes of the confession next week, I guess it's not anything you can help, jah?"

"I sure don't want to have to run away to get hitched with Prissy."

"Then don't." The thought of missing out on her favorite brother's wedding made her grit her teeth. "It's a family day. We'll all want to be there."

Her brother's face was set and hard. She thought she saw his chin quiver and realized Adam cared as much for Prissy as Dat loved Mamma. "Adam . . . no need to borrow trouble," she said.

"Well, I can tell ya . . . there's no way Mamma's going to back down and not kneel before the congregation." He left the stable, stepping into the brilliant sunshine. "That type of sin requires it."

Grace understood something of Adam's fear. She had been concerned over what might happen to her friendship with Yonnie, and he wasn't even her beau.

Looking up at her brother, she slipped her arm through his and walked beside him, helping to bear the immensity of his burden.

Heather really did feel some better today. According to LaVyrle, her body was already well into the detox mode by this sixth day, sloughing off diseased cells. Only once that process came to an end could it replace the cancerous tissue with healthy new tissue.

Eager to document the day, she opened her laptop to her daily journal.

Day 6 of the Wellness Lodge

I'm more than halfway into my juice fast and feeling better than I'd ever thought possible, especially after my "near-death" day. My sleep is deeper and I have increased energy, even without eating solids!

Dad dropped by again tonight and showed me some digital pictures of the housing site. My outlook on the new home seems more positive, now that I'm over the worst of the detox. I don't know why exactly, but I'm excited about seeing the house all framed in and the interior starting to take shape. With so many Amish workers swarming over the place, it might look like an ant colony. If I can finish my thesis in time, maybe I'll drive back up here and check it out.

Dad stayed around for quite a while to talk with LaVyrle and me. I've agreed to caravan home with him a week from tomorrow, since his realtor wants to discuss staging the house so it will sell more quickly. That means I'll get to stay at Sally Smucker's from only next Wednesday through Saturday before heading home . . . but what a great add-on to what I've learned here!

It'll be hard saying good-bye to LaVyrle — I expect Dad will be counting the days till his return. And by the way she hangs on his every word, I'm pretty sure she'll be looking forward to seeing him again, too.

On top of everything else, Jim sent me an email asking if he could call me sometime. After some careful thought, I've decided to go out on a limb and say yes. I hope I don't regret it. . . .

I certainly don't want to regret starting a

search for my birth parents. Such a move might put a wrench in Dad's happiness. I wonder what Grace would advise — she has such insight into other people, something I've always lacked. I really missed her after today's short visit. Is this part of the detox process, too — desiring to connect with the human race . . . to make friends?

And why am I so taken with Grace, so totally unlike anyone I've ever known? Unless . . . is it possible I'm catching up for all the years I was never aware of my genetic roots? Maybe she's exactly the sort of friend my first mom would wish for me. . . .

CHAPTER THIRTY-ONE

That evening, instead of heading upstairs to her room after family Bible reading and prayer, Grace wandered over to her grand-parents' kitchen. Dat and Mamma had gone riding alone in the family buggy, of all things, like they were courting again. *Making up for lost time.*

Dawdi Jakob was holding a pack of Uno cards when she stepped into the kitchen. He looked like he was itching to get started. "We've got us another player, Adah." He gave Grace a lazy grin.

"Come join us." Mammi waved her into the room.

Grace slid in next to her grandmother at the table and picked up the cards to shuffle them.

"Uno all right with you?" Mammi asked.

"Better than Old Maid," Grace was quick to say.

Dawdi chuckled, a sparkle in his bluish

gray eyes. Then he said, "How was your mornin' over at Pucketts'?" He folded his wrinkled hands, the veins on the back of his hands evident through the onion-thin skin.

Grace described Janet's herb garden, with its decorative floral elements. "Anything to do with herbs and gardens, I love. Much like someone I know."

Mammi smiled sweetly.

They drew cards to see who would deal, and Grace got the highest number. "Heather seems to be feelin' better," she said, making small talk.

Mammi flipped the top card over and placed it on the stack. "Poor girl. To think she's fighting such a serious disease at her age. I wish Marian and I would've known sooner."

Grace murmured her own concern, then looked at her cards and found a match.

"I hope she responds to whatever they're doin' for her over yonder," Mammi said.

"Me too." Grace thought again of Heather's surprising news that she had Amish kin living somewhere in Ohio.

Mammi drew a card, and the game went on amidst a running commentary from Dawdi, who made Grace laugh repeatedly. Then, when she was down to a single card, she called out, "Uno," and on the next play, she won the game.

Dawdi insisted they play a second game, so they reshuffled and started again. Before long, Dawdi triumphed over the second game with great glee.

Mammi rose and filled the teakettle with water. "Will you stay for some tea?"

Grace looked at the day clock. "Oh, I shouldn't. I was up so early this morning."

Mammi's eyes pleaded. "Aw, just one cup, Gracie?"

Dawdi nodded as though she should stay.

"All right, then. Only one cup, though." Grace gathered up the cards and put them away, then went to get three pretty cups and matching saucers from the china hutch. "Do you want the everyday ones?" she asked over her shoulder.

"Sure . . . fine." Mammi Adah carried the sugar bowl to the table.

"Why not use the best cups?" Dawdi piped up.

Mammi agreed. "No need savin' them for a special gathering, I guess."

"This is about as good as it gets," Dawdi said, grinning at them.

When the water was poured and tea bags and sugar set in, Grace noticed Dawdi begin to nod off. "Looks like someone's as tired as I am."

"I think all of us should call it a night soon," Mammi said, stirring in some extra sugar.

Grace raised her dainty cup and took a sip. "Ah, this is nice."

"Glad you stayed, Gracie."

They looked over at Dawdi, whose beard was crushed against his chest. He'd fallen sound asleep right where he sat, waiting for his tea. They exchanged silent smiles.

"Your Dawdi didn't need tea to relax him," Mammi said softly. "He's ever so relieved your Mamma's home, I'll say." She remarked on how well Dat and Mamma were getting along.

Grace thought it awkward that her grandmother should comment on that. "Mamma seems so happy" was all she said, wondering if they shouldn't retire for the night. With tomorrow a no-Preaching Sunday, they could take the day a little more slowly than usual. *Unlike Heather,* she thought, *who won't be getting a break from her new routine.* It was still hard to believe the Virginia girl was part Amish.

Mammi Adah'd never guess.

A warm breeze came in through the open back door as Grace said quietly, "My friend Heather told me something fascinating today." She paused. "Hard to believe, really . . ."

"What is?"

"Well, she says she's part Amish."

Mammi's eyebrows rose at that. "How do ya mean?"

"I've known for a while Heather was adopted," Grace said. "I just didn't know till today she had an Amish mother."

"Well, for goodness' sake!"

Grace told how both girls had felt drawn to friendship — "from our first meeting over at Eli's Natural Foods. It seemed peculiar to me at the time, but now, knowing this . . . well, it might make more sense. Just think: We could even be cousins — who's to know?"

Mammi's face had turned as red as the hummingbird feeders. "Where . . . was Heather born, do you know?"

"Ohio somewhere."

Mammi grew quiet and stared for the longest time at the remaining tea in her cup. Dawdi, meanwhile, was beginning to snore. "Are ya sure?" Mammi seemed to look right through Grace, as if staring at something beyond.

"All I know is her mother came from a town in Ohio."

"And you said the other day she has an April birthday, ain't?" Mammi Adah asked.

"Jah, just six days after mine — April twenty-ninth."

Her grandmother rose from her chair, then wavered a bit, putting her hands out to steady herself as she headed for the sink.

"You all right?" Grace called to her.

"Ever so tired," Mammi muttered. "Not to worry."

By now, Dawdi Jakob was tilting so far forward in sleep that Grace was afraid he might fall face-first on the table. She got up and stood behind him, placed her hands on each side of his whiskered face, and gently raised his head. He awakened with a great sputter, knocking the pretty teacup with his hand and accidently spilling the now-tepid water.

Abruptly, Mammi turned and dried her face on her apron. She spied Grace mopping up the water and came over to help Dawdi out of his chair. "Ach, should've put you to bed earlier," she said, helping him as they both hobbled toward the stairs.

Grace watched to make sure they made it safely up the back steps, then went to her room to slip into her own bed. Yet long into the night, Grace couldn't help wondering about Heather's Ohio Amish origins. *Such a peculiar surprise!*

CHAPTER THIRTY-TWO

Before Sunday breakfast, Grace meandered outside to watch the many birds. The jays pranced about, pecking at hulls as if they owned the place, while the songbirds fluttered gracefully to the feeders, flying off to deposit seeds elsewhere before coming back for more.

This being the first day of June, Grace expected it would be warm and humid, if not downright hot. She would go barefoot to visit first Becky, then over to see Heather later in the afternoon. A no-Preaching Sunday meant cold cuts and pie at the noon meal and suppertime, allowing ample time to read the Good Book and visit family and friends. *Such a relaxing day.*

Grace wanted to take along the Cape May diamond to show Heather. She might take the Uno cards, too, hoping to teach her friend how to play, if she didn't already know. Sure, they were both excuses to see her yet again, but now that she knew Heather had some Amish roots, it made her feel closer to her than ever.

Between breakfast and the noon meal, Lettie read four chapters from the old German Bible and four from a Pennsylvania Dutch version of the New Testament that had been translated from the King James. Later, she wrote a letter to Susan Kempf, added several paragraphs to a circle letter from New Holland, and took a long walk with Judah out on the mule trails that led to the hayfield. Never before had she felt such peace. She wholeheartedly believed she and her husband had turned a corner, and even their children were taking notice. So were her parents. By turning over the search for her child to the Lord, Lettie had settled the angst that had plagued her life for so long.

She believed God was calling her to fast one meal each day, for several days prior to her confession next Sunday. Judah had agreed, and it felt good to be in one accord with him. The barrier of more than two decades was beginning to crumble.

Yet despite the strides she'd made since coming home, Lettie still longed for the child she'd given up — missed her as much as when Mamm and the midwife had taken her away.

Each day now required a purposeful extending of mercy to Mamm — a conscious act of forgiving so that she, too, could receive God's forgiveness. The Lord's cherished words from the Sermon on the Mount came to mind: *Blessed are the merciful: for they shall obtain mercy.*

Lettie prayed that not even the coming confession could disrupt this sweet tranquility.

Heather strolled down to Mill Creek with her phone to find the spot where Sally Smucker had gone to pray during her stay at the lodge. She knew she was becoming stronger. Even her breath was sweeter, one of the significant signs pointing to improved health.

She liked the sheltered feeling inside this little grove of trees, where green branches and vines enclosed her and the wide creek rushed past. Sally had said it was an ideal spot to commune with God. So there Heather was, offering her private thoughts to the Creator. Nearly everything else in this life could be laughed away, but her struggle — this was for real. She'd found herself pondering hard her purpose for being, the twists her life had taken. It didn't seem fair that she'd never known her original parents. But hadn't she enjoyed the flip side of that? The truth was, her adoptive parents had been more than enough.

She sat cross-legged in the grassy spot and silently prayed a prayer of broken hearts and broken wings . . . of being small in an enormous universe, and of feeling so utterly alone at times. Oh, how she missed the person she'd been closest to! "My mom," she whispered. "Of all people, why'd you choose to take her?" The question needed to be spoken.

When she finished her solitary time, her phone vibrated, signaling a call. She did not recognize the number or the last name — *Lang* — but she answered. "Hello?"

"Is this Heather?" a man asked.

"Who's this?"

"Wannalive . . . Jim, remember?"

She smiled. How cool was this? "Of course I do. Hi, Jim!"

His voice was pleasantly mellow and deep as he asked how she was doing, sounding glad *and* relieved when she told him the positives that indicated progress. They talked about the day — what the weather was like in Virginia, where he lived — a tidbit she hadn't known before. And what she was experiencing there in "Amish country." He chuckled easily.

She embraced the sound and felt comfortable telling him about this wonderful lodge . . . and its location.

"Hey, I'm only a few hours away."

Her heart flipped. What was he saying? She waited, not daring to jump to conclusions.

"When will you be dismissed?" he asked.

"Wednesday after lunch."

"Mind if I drive up?"

"Well, I'll be heading home on Sunday," she told him. "A change of plans." She mentioned she would be staying with a local family until then.

"I have the day off on Wednesday, and I'd really like to see you, Heather."

He was persistent, that was certain.

"All right, sounds good," she said. "Thanks, Jim."

He said he'd MapQuest the location, so not to bother with directions. He seemed reluctant to say good-bye. The warmth in his voice was contagious.

When they'd hung up, she looked at his last name and phone number again. "Jim Lang," she murmured as she headed back to the lodge for the late-morning class. Knowing his full name — and the sound of his voice — made him seem that much more real. Never would Heather have thought she'd connect with a guy she'd met online, or that she'd allow their friendship to progress this far.

Chapter Thirty-Three

While Heather was saying good-bye to Arielle and LaVyrle and other lodge staff members the following Wednesday, there was a knock at the front door. She had just jotted down an email address from one of the other patients when she looked across the foyer and saw a tall, auburn-haired man standing on the other side of the screen door.

Curious, she excused herself and went to the door. She caught the pleasing scent of his cologne. "Are you Jim?"

"I am." There was a flicker of recognition in his warm green eyes. "You must be Heather."

She opened the door and stepped out onto the porch. "Nice to meet you, Jim."

"It's great to put a face to an online presence." He reached to shake her hand. "Do you have time for a walk?"

"Sure," she said, then wanted to kick

herself for the almost too-casual reply. After all, Jim had driven five hours one way to meet her. She followed him down the wide steps and over the rolling lawn, toward the formal gardens.

He remarked about the tranquil landscape surrounding the lodge, comparing it to the midwest location where he'd had his cleanse. She felt a little nervous at actually being with him, yet she quickly became engrossed in their conversation. *He seems so normal — not at all saintly,* she thought as they turned toward Mill Creek. *And very good-looking.*

"I wanted to tell you my news in person," he said as they walked beneath the willows.

Her heart stilled.

"My latest blood tests came back normal — I've been given a clean bill of health." He was grinning now. "I've waited a long time for this news."

"How wonderful, Jim. I'm so happy for you!"

"I hoped it might encourage you to follow through with a mostly raw food diet . . . now that you're leaving here."

She assured him that she would need some help with that. "I've been invited to stay for a few days with an Amish preacher's wife who nearly lost her life to cancer, before coming to the lodge. She changed her diet radically, and she's stuck with it." Heather looked back at the grand old house. "Sally's offered to help me stay on track with an 80/20 raw-to-cooked-food ratio. That should get me into a routine before I head home."

"Sounds terrific."

"Dr. Marshall recommends doing a juice cleanse two weeks per month for aggressive cancers. I'll know better where things stand for me when I have another blood draw at my oncologist's in Virginia."

He seemed to perk up at the mention of Virginia. "Where's home for you?" he asked.

"Outskirts of Williamsburg. How about you?"

"Within walking distance of the College of William and Mary," he said.

"Are you serious? I did my graduate work there — American Studies."

"Really?" He chuckled. "I considered going there but wound up at MIT for my undergraduate degree in architecture. It proved to be an incredible choice. They have the oldest department of architecture in the country."

We both chose older schools, she thought, amazed that he lived practically in the same neighborhood as her alma mater.

She asked if he'd ever gone to Busch Gardens, and he said he'd worked there several summers in a row during high school and college. "I also did short stints during spring break."

"So maybe we've met before. . . ."

"You know, when you first came to the door, I thought I'd seen you somewhere. Did you go to Busch Gardens a lot?"

"Actually, my dad still has a season pass — we go all the time." She didn't say that she and her one-time fiancé had also gone there together.

"Small world, eh?"

"It is." She smiled back at him. "I just can't get over the great news about your blood work, Jim."

"I've been waiting to post it on my blog until I could see you in person," he admitted.

"I haven't read the last couple of entries. I'll have to catch up as soon as I get settled in at Sally's." Then she realized what she'd said and couldn't help laughing.

"What's funny?" He touched her arm lightly.

"Oh, just thinking." She was, after all, catching up with him in *person,* wasn't she? And they related so well to each other in the here and now. *Not only online.*

They walked in silence for a time, enjoying the breeze. He pointed out a few birds perched on the rocks in the creek below, preening their feathers. Then he glanced at her, smiling thoughtfully. "I knew you'd be this pretty, Heather. From the way you expressed yourself . . . I knew."

"Thanks." Her face felt warm, but she wouldn't let herself be fooled. And while Jim was probably the most attractive — and most affirming — guy she'd ever encountered, she was already shielding her heart.

"Would you like to go out with me sometime?" he asked as they turned toward the road.

"Um . . . can I get back to you on that?" Immediately she felt horrible. *What did I just do? He drove all this way for just a short walk?*

They parted soon after, with Jim asking if they could keep in touch. She agreed before watching him drive out of the lane and onto the road. He waved and gave her a big smile — anyone observing would have thought she'd said yes to seeing him again.

Will I lie awake tonight regretting my response? The answer entwined itself with her heart. Sighing, Heather turned and walked slowly back toward the lodge, having a *listen here, Heather,* heart-to-heart talk with herself. She wondered when and where the pattern of rejection she was so comfortable dishing out had begun. Something was, and always had been, eating away at her. *All of my life!*

Heather had to address it — deal with the elephant in the room. She needed closure, one way or another. Had her adoption somehow played a role in her pattern of making friends and rejecting them? If so, maybe finding her birth parents would make some sense of this . . . even put an end to it.

Heather's dad was sitting on the porch talking with LaVyrle when Heather returned. "New guy?" Dad wore a quizzical look.

She shrugged. "A friend."

LaVyrle squeezed her lips together, repressing a smile. She glanced at Heather. "You and your dad are always welcome to visit here. I'm also available for follow-ups and counsel, too. Whatever you need."

"Thanks so much . . . for everything." Heather let her eyes sweep the beauty of the landscape before looking again at LaVyrle. "We'll definitely be in touch."

Later, with her dad's help, she loaded the car and bid another round of farewells to the naturopath and her terrific staff. Each patient had been given a large container of chopped raw veggies for the afternoon, as some were traveling long distances by air or car. Heather was thankful she had only a short drive to Sally's, though she wanted to stop to see Grace en route.

"I'll be over at the house site most of the rest of this week, but I'll drop by the Smuckers' a couple of times," Dad said, giving her a bear hug.

"I love you, Dad," she whispered.

His eyes were bright as they parted. "What you've gone through here, kiddo . . . I hope and pray it works."

"Me too."

He walked with her down to the car, then followed alongside the vehicle until she waved one last time. "The new house is going to be great," she called over her shoulder through the open window.

He popped a thumb up, smiling now. "See you, kiddo!"

Heather waved and smiled in return, delighted her father looked so happy.

At the Bylers', Heather enjoyed seeing Willow and also meeting Adam and Joe, who took time from their work to show off the youngest lambs of the season, now a few days old.

"They're adorable." Heather touched the

fluffy fleece.

"You wouldn't think that if you could see beneath all that wool," Joe said, explaining how a good shepherd monitors the condition of the skin.

"So they're vulnerable to disease or wounds under there?" she asked.

"Oh, constantly," Adam put in. He ran his strong hand through the fleece to demonstrate how they checked the skin, wool, and body.

She thanked Grace's brothers, who were dressed identically in black work pants and short-sleeved green shirts with tan suspenders. Their long bangs were cut straight across, nearly touching their eyebrows. Even their straw hats matched. She found it remarkable that they were so polite to a total stranger.

After a tour of the mule and horse stable, Grace again took Heather to her beloved garden to point out the cleansing herbs. "I planted one similar to this for an Englischer yesterday," Grace said. She pointed out the blue blossoms of the gentian, also known as bitterroot, as well as the senna herb, then showed Heather the white-flowering chickweed. "Some folk mistake this for a weed, but it's delicious in salads — tastes like spinach — and is *gut* for whatever might ail a person." She explained it was a natural diuretic and laxative. "But no doubt Dr. Marshall's taught you some about the value of herbs," she said, suddenly seeming a little wistful. "Ah, Heather . . . I wish you could stay longer than just till Sunday. You could help me tend my herb garden."

"Sounds like fun, but I really need to buckle down and finish my thesis, and Dad needs some help getting the house ready to sell back home."

"Where will *you* live after the house is sold . . . and your dad moves into his new place?" Grace looked concerned.

"Not sure yet — I must get busy submitting my resumé. Once I land a job, I'll lease a condo or something small. But I'll visit Dad here, too."

"What 'bout workin' at the Wellness Lodge?" Grace smiled mischievously. "Just maybe?"

"You know, I hadn't given that any thought — but I certainly like the people there." Now that Grace had mentioned it, the idea seemed quite appealing.

"Well, anyway, we have a few more days before you must go, jah?"

Heather assured her they'd see each other again before her trip home. Grace said good-bye and headed toward the stable while Heather made her way back to the car. As she opened the driver's-side door, she spotted Adah Esh coming out of her side of the large farmhouse, waving.

"Do ya have time for a cup of tea?" Adah called, but Heather declined, saying she was very tired. Yet she was surprised at Adah's invitation.

"I'll see you in two days — at the jam session," she said, laughing at her own joke. "Rain check?"

"Des *gut.* You get some rest, dear. I'll look forward to Friday." Adah nodded, and although she smiled pleasantly, Heather could not mistake the disappointment in the elderly woman's tone.

Anxious to get settled in at Sally's, she backed up to the road. Grace waved to her, standing near the stable now with beautiful Willow, sporting a big smile. Her free arm was draped around the mare's neck. *A real live country girl!*

The day was balmy, and Heather was keenly aware of the high dew point. She wished she'd put her hair up this morning. Later, once she unpacked and found her hair ties, she would.

When she arrived at Sally's, the kindly woman put her rolling pin down to greet her at the screen door. "There you are,

Heather. Oh, it's so *gut* to see you again!" She led her through the kitchen and out toward the front room, then to a small bedroom on the main floor where she would stay. "Once you're settled, feel free to come and meet the children . . . if you'd like." Sally explained that she needed to finish rolling out her piecrusts. "Before they dry out."

Heather sat on the bed and ran her hands over the colorful quilt, amazed at the workmanship, all of it hand sewn. She let her gaze drift over the room; in spite of its meager furnishings, it was as tranquil a place as she'd ever stayed . . . having never actually slept in a bona fide Amish bedroom. Marian's upstairs guest rooms had been decidedly less spartan, designated as they were for outsiders. She was excited to try the real thing for a few days.

She took her time unpacking and putting things away. Her laptop, where she'd kept a running journal of each day at the lodge, lay on the bed in the corner. She would continue to add entries, as well as begin work again on her thesis. She didn't exactly trust how good she was feeling physically. *Am I already on the way to health?*

When Heather was settled, she returned to the kitchen as Sally had suggested and met the Smucker children, six in total. Three were school-age boys — Josiah, nearly eleven, named for his preacher father; Isaac Eli, nine and a half, he emphasized with a playful grin; and Danny, just turned seven. The three youngest Smuckers were girls. Katie, the oldest daughter at six, was the only child Heather had met previously. The blondest of Katie's little sisters — baby Esther — was still crawling, and the other girl, named for her mother, Sally, was toddling and jabbering as she went.

"This is Heather Nelson." Sally wiped her brow and smiled sweetly at her brood.

Little Sally stuck her chubby finger into her loose golden braid and twisted it until it fell completely out. She didn't seem to mind as she stared at her dirty bare feet, transfixed. *Dreckich,* she kept saying and pointing to her toes. Heather guessed from their condition that she meant "dirty."

She couldn't ignore the white splotches of dough on Sally's long black apron and on her forearms and hands. *This is what Amish mothers do all day. Cook and clean, and take care of kids . . . and start all over again the next day.* She tried hard to picture herself as a young Amishwoman, married to a nice Amish boy . . . and having one baby after another. The idea was hard to wrap her mind around.

When Sally gave a slight nod to her sons, they wiggled their fingers to Heather in a farewell gesture that instantly endeared them to her, then headed outside. "Returning to help their father make hay," Sally said. The littlest girls played at their mother's bare feet as she finished making pies, Katie standing on a stool to help.

Heather turned to sit at the table, watching the little ones and wondering if her somewhat letdown feeling was normal for post-lodge patients. The events of the day — leaving the atmosphere of the Wellness Lodge and its very caring staff behind and meeting handsome Jim Lang — all of it had caught up with her.

If Jim's blood tests came back normal, why can't mine?

She yearned to slip away to her little room at the end of the house and close the door for some downtime, but Heather didn't want to closet herself away when she'd just arrived, so she remained where she was.

Once Sally's trademark "healthy pies" were in the oven, Sally asked if she'd mind bathing the two youngest children.

"Of course not." Heather had willingly agreed to help out occasionally with the children in exchange for a few days of room and board, but as she hadn't actually babysat before, this might prove to be interesting. *Sally wants* both *girls in the tub at the same time?*

She had her work cut out for her getting the girls washed without getting their mother's homemade soap in their sensitive eyes or the soapy bathwater splashed onto the bathroom floor. But eventually the task was done.

The girls were still wrapped in their towels when Sally came. She said in passing that it was their turn to host Preaching service this coming Lord's Day. "Do ya think you could keep an eye on the girls for a few hours while some of the womenfolk help me scrub down the house on Saturday?"

"Sure," she said, relieved to hear that tiny Sally and Esther were "good little nappers."

Sally leaned down and patted her namesake's head, smiling sweetly.

At the tender sight, Heather thought again of her birth mother. *Does she ever think of me?*

The curiosity had become incessant. What had begun as an impulsive need to connect with her first mother now persisted stronger than ever. It wasn't just a weird *I-think-I'm-dying* fluke, but a very real desire that had been submerged in her until her ten-day lodge stay had revealed it for what it was.

The very first minute Heather could politely get away — perhaps tomorrow morning — she'd print out the request form from the adoption registry and send it off to the proper department in Columbus, Ohio. She needed to at least know the identity of the Amishwoman, assuming the woman had authorized its release. She didn't want to consider that the file might be closed to her.

Supper that evening for her and Sally consisted of a vegetable broth similar to that served at the lodge and a large salad of baby greens, spinach leaves, tomatoes, cucumbers, and alfalfa sprouts. She was surprised at how well behaved the older four children were during the meal, but the two little ones . . . they were a different story. She'd heard once, maybe from her own mom, that Amishwomen doted on their children until they were two years old, after which time the obedience training began in earnest. Little Sally's antics had Heather guessing she had not yet reached that mark, although she couldn't be sure. What did a two-year-old look and act like, anyway?

How will I work on my thesis here with such cuties around? she wondered while Sally washed dishes. Suddenly Heather realized she'd already lost track of the talkative miniature Sally.

Stifling a laugh, she headed out to the soap and sundries boutique on the back porch. There she found the blondie reaching for some sweet-smelling potpourri.

"No, honey," she said, lifting her up.

"Nee?" little Sally asked in Heather's ear. She was so soft and cuddly, Heather was actually reluctant to set her down on the floor next to baby Esther. Holding the precious child close for a moment longer, she felt like crying.

My first mother missed out on everything about me!

After supper dishes were done, Lettie walked out to the barn. She'd come to see all the feeder lambs her husband had pegged for market in mid-September. She found him and the boys in the process of checking for any winged parasites. Due to their restlessness and lack of appetite, afflicted sheep were easy to spot.

"How's our Willow today?" Lettie moved in the direction of the elderly mare's stall, surprised when Judah followed. Since she'd come home, he was more attentive than she'd ever remembered, even back when they were newly married.

The earthy smell of the bedding straw and feed was familiar and even comforting as she and Judah stood stroking Willow's mane and nose.

"A *gut* thing you were spared seein' her so bad off." Judah told how Ephram Bontrager's boy Yonnie had helped the rest of them nurse her back to health.

"You had a real fright, then."

Judah nodded and rubbed Willow's shoulder. "You're mighty treasured, old girl."

They stayed with the mare for a while, and Judah said he was going to allow Willow to spend a few hours at a time in the pasture each day. "Now that her buggy-pulling days are most likely past."

Lettie was quiet for a bit, then mentioned being concerned for her father. "Seems he's gone downhill some."

"Jakob became feeble while you were gone." He bowed his head. "None of us did so *gut* without ya, Lettie."

She reached for his hand. "I'm so sorry, Judah. Every single day I am."

"All's forgiven," he whispered.

"That night you left me to go help with Adam — my last night home," she said, swallowing the lump in her throat. "What if I *had* managed to say what was on my heart? Would you have understood then — shown me mercy — as now?"

He slipped his arm around her as Willow nuzzled her shoulder. "How can anyone know what they'd say or do, Lettie?"

"Jah, ain't fair to ask."

Judah nodded his head. "Might've spared us the pain of your goin', though," he admitted.

Willow pushed her nose against Judah's straw hat, knocking it off. This brought a chuckle and — "Now, you watch it, ol' girl!" from her husband, who suddenly looked ever so lively, all but his flattened hair.

Lettie picked up his old work hat and gave it to him.

Judah planted it on his head and glanced over his shoulder, looking back at the sheep barn. Then he leaned over and kissed her full on the lips. "God answered my prayers for you, Lettie."

The evening sun broke through the rain clouds at that moment, creating a streaming shaft of light over the house and property. Was it an omen of good things to come?

Chapter Thirty-Four

Heather stood outside Adah's on Friday morning, watching the red-throated hummingbirds at the various feeders. She waited there with Adah for Sally Smucker to arrive, since the preacher's wife had insisted on coming later by horse and buggy.

Presently, she noticed one of the hummingbirds flying in an aerobatic U-shaped pattern. "Look at that!" She pointed out its sharp ascent, then the dive straight down.

" 'Tis a mating ritual," Adah explained. "If ya listen close, ya might hear some buzzing and popping sounds, too . . . sometimes even whistlin'."

"I've never noticed this before," Heather replied.

"Well, the expert on hummers is my daughter Lettie . . . and she'll be comin' over soon to help make jam."

Grace's mom — the woman who caused Grace and her family so much sorrow. "You know, I saw a list of bird sightings she made while staying in Baltic. Lettie must be a serious bird-watcher."

Adah laughed softly. "Oh, I should say so. We Eshes *all* are."

A few minutes later, a plump but pretty girl stepped out from the opposite side of the house, looking fresh in a blue cape dress and matching apron. Her strawberry blond hair was combed neatly into a bun, but instead of the traditional Kapp, she wore a blue-and-white-checked kerchief tied behind her head. "You must be Heather," the girl said, her smile revealing deep dimples.

"And you're Mandy, right?"

"Jah, Grace's sister."

"Very nice to meet you." Heather mentioned that Grace had talked about introducing them a couple weeks ago, when she'd first given her a tour of the herb garden. Heather bobbed her head toward the colorful plot beyond the backyard.

"Grace felt awful bad that she had to work today," Mandy said. "She really wanted to be here."

Heather didn't let on to having seen Grace each of the ten days she'd spent at the lodge.

Just then, Adah suggested they head inside to begin washing the freshly picked strawberries. Heather was glad to sit down as

Adah showed her how to rinse off the berries and instructed her to set aside those that had any mushy spots. "All right?"

Heather laughed. "Nothing to it, jah?"

Adah gave a hearty chuckle as Heather reached into the big pail and gently pulled out her first batch. She enjoyed the feel of the strawberries, some of them still slightly warm.

In a short time, Marian Riehl arrived from across the cow pasture. When she noticed Heather, she greeted her warmly. "Well, hullo there! Good seein' you again, Heather."

"You too." She smiled, remembering how she'd arrived in this neighborhood as a complete stranger.

Marian pulled out a chair and sat across from her, then got right to work trimming off the stems. She, too, had worn a blue cape dress and apron in the exact style of Mandy's.

After a time, Marian leaned forward and said, "You doin' all right, Heather?"

"Better than last week, thanks," Heather replied, grateful to be on this side of her cleanse.

Soon thereafter, Sally Smucker arrived by horse and buggy and hurried inside to greet everyone. She clapped her hands when she spied Heather. “This’ll be such fun, ain’t?”

Marian’s eyes shone. “Heather’s learnin’ how to make jam.”

“I daresay she’s come to the right house!” Adah declared.

Heather watched Sally get busy preparing the fruit pectin and natural sweeteners for those who wanted to use them instead of what she explained was the typical refined sugar. *So diligent about her strict diet. Will I be the same for the long haul?*

Hearing footsteps in the hallway, she looked up to see Adah welcoming Grace’s mother into the kitchen. *This is the elusive woman!*

Lettie Byler was plumper than she’d expected and bore a strong resemblance to Mandy. Lettie wore an engaging smile as she breezed into the room, greeting everyone at the table just as Sally Smucker had, going around and touching shoulders . . . pecking cheeks.

Adah motioned to Heather. “I’d like you to meet my daughter, Lettie Byler.” Adah turned back to Lettie. “And, Lettie, this is Heather Nelson, Gracie’s friend.”

“Hullo.” Lettie offered a somewhat shy smile.

“Glad to meet you.” Heather could’ve added *finally,* but that wouldn’t be appropriate. Lettie's blue eyes were captivating — stunningly so. They drew Heather in . . . made her want to know this mysterious woman. She wondered if others had the same reaction when first meeting her. "It must be nice to be home," Heather said without thinking.

"Surely is." Lettie smiled again and cast a careful look her way, as if curious about Grace's fancy friend.

She's not too thrilled with me — worried I'm a bad influence on her daughter.

She gulped, remembering she'd worn her denim capris. Thankfully they were well hidden beneath the table. Groaning inwardly, she thought, *What was I thinking?*

"Lettie, why don't you sit next to Heather?" Adah suggested, moving with Lettie toward Heather's side of the table. "We're nearly ready to remove any of the rotten or mushy spots. Marian's already cutting out the stems."

Heather figured the perfunctory explanation was for her benefit, since everyone else knew the ropes. *I'm the newcomer here.*

While she worked, it was hard not to observe the uncomplicated surroundings, so reminiscent of Marian's own kitchen, where Heather had enjoyed numerous rich breakfasts. *A lot like Sally's, too.* She wondered if every Amishwoman in the area had a similar setup.

She surveyed the shining Ball jars lined up on the counter behind them. The women were all chattering now — *like manicurists at a nail salon,* she thought wryly.

This, then, was the life she'd never lived. These devout and talkative women, with upswept and veiled hair, picking the firmest red berries out of the pails for pies and strawberry shortcake, setting them aside — had no idea she, too, could very well have been raised Plain.

My birth mother must've panicked when she discovered she was pregnant with me. Would it unnerve her to meet me now?

Working beside her friends and family to fill the canning jars with the boiled strawberries, Adah felt all on edge. She stood at the gas stove, waiting for the water to heat for the strawberries, and recalled Grace's strange declaration last Saturday. To think Heather had been adopted from an Amish mother . . . and had the same birthdate as Lettie's first child!

She observed Lettie sitting next to Heather, mesmerized by the sight. *Could it be?*

She found herself staring at Heather,

noticing the heart-shaped face. Who in the family, or amongst the People, had such a pronounced widow's peak?

No one that I know of, she was certain, resuming her attention to adding more sugar to the next batch of boiling berries. In hardly any time at all, or so it seemed in the midst of her musing, the kettle of water came to a rolling boil.

Plenty of folks share the same birthday. Adah dismissed her thoughts as utterly ridiculous. Surely Heather could not be Lettie's child. *Besides, Grace said her birth mother was an Ohio girl!*

Friday, June 6

I helped put up strawberry jam today with one of the most entertaining women I've ever met. Adah Esh, Grace Byler's maternal grandmother, is a wealth of knowledge about anything kitchen related, and it was fun to be there with so many Amishwomen, all of them delighted to show me the ropes of jam making. Thanks to Sally's more healthful modifications, I might give it a try someday. What would Dad say to that?

I wonder what he'll say when I tell him I sent in the paper work yesterday to request information on my birth parents. I second-guessed the idea, wondering if I was merely considering a search because of the real possibility that I might die soon.

But now I realize I was wrong about my motivation: It wasn't only the fear of dying without knowing her that compelled me to think of contacting the Ohio Adoption Registry. It's about far more than that.

Maybe it's seeing that Dad may have someone to love. Or maybe it's being among these lovely people, so ready to open their hearts and give of themselves. The lack of pretense is refreshing, and I can't help but wonder if my birth mom is anything like them. Oh, I hope so!

Well, I've sent in my request . . . now to see what comes of it.

Immediately following breakfast on Saturday, Adah Esh and Sally Smucker's older sisters showed up with mops and buckets and dustcloths — a veritable bunch of housekeepers. Heather had never seen walls being swept down or washed that way. Humming and chattering abounded, as though the enormous chore was merely a game. Even young Katie joined in the fun, grabbing a rag and taking her place next to her aunts.

"We view work as play," Sally explained

later in the morning when she helped Heather put little Sally and baby Esther down for a nap. "Not 'we'll play once the chores are done.' "

"Like Englischers say," Sally's oldest sister, Ruthanne, observed, then clapped her hand over her mouth, looking with wide, embarrassed eyes at Heather. "Ach, I almost forgot . . ."

Heather was not at all offended. She laughed merrily, and soon both Sally and Ruthanne joined in.

Later, little Sally and Esther were sound asleep in their small bedroom when Heather checked on them. When she turned to leave, she nearly bumped into Adah in the hallway.

"Can we talk privately?" Adah's eyes probed Heather's.

She wondered why but said, "Sure . . . where?"

Adah motioned to a vacant bedroom at the far end of the hall. "We're finished cleaning up here," she said, leading the way. Adah closed the door with a *click* behind them, then walked to the window and turned to face her.

Heather had the distinct impression that whatever was on Adah's mind was an uncomfortable topic, because the older woman wore a sudden grimace. "Are you all right?"

she asked from where she stood near the foot of the bed.

"Well . . . I'm not sure." Adah sighed, her bosom rising and falling. "What I have to say may upset you, but that's certainly not my intention."

"Okay." Heather wondered if it had been such a good idea to let Adah corner her in this way.

"Grace says you were born to a young Amishwoman in Ohio." Her eyes held Heather's. "Is that right?"

"That's what my father told me, and I hope to know more about it very soon." She told Adah about sending in the form to obtain the court-sealed information regarding her adoption. "I felt a need to meet my biological parents — particularly my mother — before I die." She laughed softly. "Of course, I do hope to stick around a lot longer."

Now it was Adah who looked shaken. "Ach, but Dr. Marshall seems to have helped many patients."

"Yes, I've heard that."

"Let's pray you're one of them. . . ."

Heather made an attempt to explain how she had felt as if she were dying during her cleanse. "It was then I became literally consumed with getting in touch with my birth mom, wherever she is."

Adah's eyes were solemn and downcast as she nodded. "I hope you *do* live to meet her. In fact, I hope you live to a ripe old age, Heather dear."

"Thank you. You're very kind."

"I don't know 'bout that." Adah looked out the window without saying more for a time. Then, almost as though reluctantly, she asked, "Do you happen to know the name of the place in Ohio where you were born?"

There was a sad, almost lost expression on the woman's wrinkled face, and Heather wondered why she was asking.

At that moment, there was a knock and the door cracked open. Grace peeked in. "So sorry . . . I just got here and was lookin' for ya, Mammi." She smiled instantly when her eyes caught Heather's. "You want this door closed again?"

"Nee . . . no, that's all right." Adah removed a handkerchief from beneath her sleeve and fanned her too-rosy face. "I must be ferhoodled," she muttered. "Wishful thinkin'."

"Sorry?" Heather said.

"Nothin'." Adah motioned for her to go on ahead with Grace. "Let's see what Sally wants done yet for Preaching tomorrow."

The woman's eyes looked dazed.

Heather walked down the hall with Grace and stopped to peek in again at the youngest Smucker girls. When she saw they were still sleeping, she gently closed the door and joined Grace on the stairs.

Chapter Thirty-Five

Es schwere Deel — the main sermon — was longer than customary that Preaching Sunday. Lettie sat between Grace and Mandy on the women's and children's side of Preacher Josiah's front room for the three-and-a-half-hour service. She folded her trembling hands and looked over at Judah, Adam, and Joe, sitting together in a row with her father and Andy Riehl and his teenage sons. Breathing a prayer for peace, she silently called upon the name of the Lord.

More people had crowded into the house of worship than was typical. Or was she imagining this because she felt so ill at ease? The ministers had already discussed the gravity of her sins with her in private, preceding the start of the service today. The bishop had been the one to lay out the situation: Since she'd offered to own up to her wrongdoings publicly, without being approached by the ministers first, the only thing left — apart from the confession itself — was the vote of the People. They alone would decide whether or not to accept her back into the membership. This would follow directly after Lettie's admission of sin.

She clenched her teeth as she contemplated her name being called out by the bishop for the hearing less than one hour from now. After her confession, she would rise to walk the long aisle that separated the men and teenage boys from the women and children, making her way slowly and reverently toward the back of the house. She would be expected to wait prayerfully outdoors for the verdict. If the membership agreed not to shun her for the sins of her youth, as well as her more recent transgression in abandoning her family, then she would not be excommunicated.

Lord, you alone know my heart fully. . . .

Her breath caught in her throat, and Lettie pressed her hand to her lips.

Gelassenheit, she thought. She must embrace an attitude of submission, just as she had been taught: giving up her will to God first, the ministerial brethren second, then down the order of command to her father, husband, and older brothers. The length of the worship service alone pointed to the importance of the act of waiting, of the need for meekness and unity and compliance evidenced each time the People gathered. Such was the age-old reenactment of surrender required by the revered ordinance.

This is the path I chose to walk, as I promised at the time of my baptism. She gripped her hankie with one hand, and Grace's hand with the other.

When the final points of the second sermon had at last been made by the older of the two preachers, Lettie felt not only contrite but fatigued by the steady stream of her thoughts. *If only Judah might be permitted to give me a word of comfort!*

She closed her eyes and recalled their tender moments in the stable last week. Other precious times since her return came to mind. Formerly a man of few words, her husband's kindhearted remarks encouraged her even now.

To this very hour!

Judah hankered to see how Lettie was holding up, yet he didn't dare move his head so much as an inch. The main sermon had focused solely on the need for holy living and walking uprightly, avoiding fornication and adultery and all manner of evil — and, as a member of the "true Christian faith," being willing to repent wholeheartedly when a breach of the baptismal vow might occur.

Without a doubt, the second sermon was meant primarily for Lettie. He'd heard similar sermons through the years, prior to a hearing of the People . . . before an errant member was put to a kneeling shame. The brethren felt the need to make a point of the person's particular sin during that sermon.

Knowing his wife, Judah was confident she was presently in need of reassurance. He bowed his head slowly, discreetly, and clasped his hands in sincere prayer, hoping that by this act she might know that he was truly joined with her in spirit.

While Mamma clutched her hand, Grace offered her earnest, silent prayer: *O Lord, please help my dear mother. She needs your mercy and grace. Will you give her the strength to bear whatever may come? May she be comforted and find peace here, in this fellowship of believers. In Jesus' name, amen.*

Lettie was heartened by Judah's quick look of loving concern when their eyes met briefly during the final testimonies — *Zeugniss* — associated with the main sermon. They were offered by several visiting ministers, as well as a few men specifically appointed by the preacher, including Lettie's own father and her former brother-in-law, Ike Peachey. *All of them relate to iniquity in our lives.*

The final piercing remarks intended to underscore the theme of his sermon were offered by the minister himself. Then the entire membership, cramped as they were, turned and knelt at their seats while the traditional prayer was read from *Die Ernsthafte Christenpflicht.*

Soon the People stood and the benediction was given. Deacon Amos made the formal announcement that all members were to stay for "an important meeting" after the dismissal. The unbaptized youth, her young Joe included, and visiting nonmembers were released to go quietly from the house of worship.

The room was quiet enough to hear the People's collective breath when Lettie's name was finally called. She rose and went to kneel before the ministers at the front of the room. Closing her eyes, she bowed her head as the bishop stood to his feet.

"Do you, Lettie Byler, our sister in the Lord, promise to work with the church to be reinstated as a member in good standing?" the bishop asked.

"Jah."

"Do you have a confession to make before the Lord God heavenly Father and your brothers and sisters gathered here?" he asked. "Do you?"

"With God's help."

"Are you ready now to reveal your sins to the membership?"

"Jah." She did not lift her eyes to the bishop as she'd sometimes seen others do in a similar confessional position. She could not bear to catch Judah's sad eyes in the background as she told of her immorality with Samuel Graber. Nor did she want to see the dear faces of her parents or her many siblings. And her children — oh, her precious children, having to witness this! No, Lettie would keep her eyes tightly closed.

"What sins did you, our sister, commit as a youth?" the bishop asked.

She breathed a prayer. *Dear Lord, be near to Adam, Grace, Mandy, and Joe. . . .* "I entered into sin with my first beau when I was sixteen years old."

"Was the transgression repeated with this man?"

She nodded her head, unable to speak for her humiliation.

"Our sister will answer audibly."

After taking a short breath, she managed to speak. "It was."

"And did this man lead you away from God and the church by your own volition?" came the bishop's harsh question.

"Jah."

"Did our sister express a rebellious spirit toward God and the church at that time?"

"Jah . . . and toward my parents, too." She began to weep, thinking of the heartache she'd brought her family. "Father in heaven, forgive me!" she cried, covering her wet face with her hands and bowing low.

A collective sigh spread through the congregation.

After a time, the room was still once again and deathly silent.

Then the bishop spoke again. "Did our sister enter into an unholy agreement, though undeclared, with her parents and thus deceive the church and her own family?"

She wanted to be completely obedient, yet the weight of the question bore down on her. "I did," she answered after a painful moment.

"And did you further deceive your own husband, Judah Byler, by keeping any knowledge of your sins from him these many years?" The bishop's voice cracked unexpectedly.

"Jah."

"Did our sister also birth a child from this forbidden union?"

Another wave of tears made her mute. *O Lord Jesus, will you lift this disgrace from your faithless child . . . your little lamb?* She prayed, using the name her father had given her as a child. "Jah, I birthed a daughter, a secret I kept with my parents."

A hushed gasp rose from the large room.

"Did our sister leave behind her husband and family to search for this child . . . and her father, without permission from the ministers or Judah Byler?"

"I did."

"And was our sister gone for weeks without the consent of her husband?"

If I can just persevere to the end . . . Lettie thought, weeping. Her answer mixed with great sobs. "Jah, I did sin these . . . many transgressions."

"Does our sister now believe that her sins are covered and forgiven by the blood of Jesus Christ?"

"That, I do . . . jah."

"Are you, our sister, willing to submit to the order of this church?"

"Jah."

"Lettie Byler, our sister, you may rise."

She tried, but she could not get up. Her legs were limp. Falling slightly forward, she felt as if she might faint. And just when she felt the weakest, she was caught, suddenly, by strong hands . . . arms.

Looking up into the confident face of her husband, she gripped his hand and stood with his help.

Judah led her down the long aisle, toward the back porch of the house. "You endured to the end," he whispered when they were alone.

She leaned on his arm, sobbing.

"The worst is over." He gave her a peck on the cheek and turned to leave. "I must go inside now for the vote."

Too weak to stand alone, Lettie lowered herself to sit on the back step, concealing her tear-stained face in her hands.

CHAPTER THIRTY-SIX

Heather had agreed to help Sally Smucker with her six children during the special members' meeting following the church service. During the long morning gathering, however, she'd relished her time alone, even making some strides on her thesis work . . . having the largest Dawdi Haus all to herself. She'd occasionally heard singing — what sounded like Gregorian chant, except for the female voices mingled in. But she didn't pay much attention after that as she reread and edited the many pages she'd written before coming here at the end of April. *On my birthday . . .*

Presently she sat on a blanket under a giant oak tree, up near the barnyard and well removed from the house, with not only the Smucker kids, but Becky Riehl's younger sisters, Rachel and Sarah. The Riehl girls had spotted her and offered to help entertain little Sally and baby Esther, so there they all sat, playing every imaginable game. Rachel and Sarah had even used the white hankies they had in their pockets to make little mice in cradles and other things Heather had never seen. She thought of her dad's lively black Persian cats, Igor and Moe, and missed them. She told the children about the adorable pair.

After a time, the breeze carried the sound of an opening screen door, and she looked up to see Grace's parents coming outside, just the two of them. Lettie Byler reached for her husband, crying on his arm. Thankfully, the children weren't paying attention, but Heather was riveted to the scene unfolding on the back porch.

What could've happened to Lettie in there?

Her heart went out to them, especially to Lettie, when Judah left her to sit alone on the back steps and weep.

Adah was all in. Not only had the bishop put Lettie through the wringer, but Adah herself felt further implicated, even though she'd already offered her own private confession to the deacon.

Momentarily, the vote would be cast, and Lettie would be called back to hear the decision. Adah felt as wilted as her daughter had looked up there. She had been quite astonished to see Judah get up from his seat to walk to the front to help poor Lettie up.

Covering her mouth, Adah refused to weep, though she wanted to with all of her heart. This had been the most wrenching confession she'd witnessed in all her years. The man of God had set her daughter up as an example to the membership, especially to the young people who'd most recently joined church.

But it was while Lettie had answered the final difficult questions that Adah experienced a new wave of responsibility for Lettie's leaving her family. She asked for God's mercy to rest upon Lettie as she waited for the membership vote.

Grace's eyes were riveted to the bishop as he rose to give the announcement. Heart in her throat, she waited for her mother to return to the meeting, and when Mamma walked down the middle aisle to the front, Grace caught Yonnie's eye. For a moment, she felt terribly conflicted, uncertain if his glance meant he was hopeful . . . or mighty worried.

The bishop was speaking now, reporting the vote as unanimous "to restore our sister, Lettie Byler, as a member in good standing."

Oh, thank the dear Lord! Tears of joy rose up in her eyes as Grace stood quickly with all the others. She looked at Dat and Adam — and Dawdi Jakob, too — all of them waiting for the line to form to welcome Mamma back.

The atmosphere was charged with relief and gladness; the People were clearly rejoicing. Nary a word was exchanged between herself and Mandy or Mammi Adah, but their sparkling eyes and smiling faces spoke volumes.

Grace could hardly wait to greet her mother. The long night of fear and sadness was behind them. God had heard their prayers!

Strangely, though, when she looked back for Yonnie, he had disappeared.

Minutes later, Adah stood in the line to welcome Lettie back into fellowship with a customary handshake. She'd much rather have embraced her, but she'd do that privately, once they were home. Remarkably, the membership had, in one accord, restored her daughter to the church.

Making her way through the packed room, Adah went outside for some fresh air before the light meal was served. She sighed, enjoying the warmth of the day and trying to compose herself after the morning's somber service. It was then she saw Heather Nelson sitting under the big tree with the Smucker children and two of Marian's girls. She observed the way Heather interacted so lovingly with Sally's two little ones.

She pondered the suspicion — foolish as it was — that Heather could be Lettie's daughter. She rehearsed what she knew: *born April twenty-ninth in Ohio . . . to an Amish mother . . .*

Watching Heather from afar, she realized that no matter how outlandish it seemed, she simply could not dismiss what she suspected. *I've got to deal with this once and for all. That'll bury it for good.*

The best way to do that was to finally confirm that Heather was *not* Lettie's child. *Find out what city she was born in . . . and what year. . . .*

Sighing, Adah wondered how she might go about obtaining the information without seeming overly intrusive, especially since she'd tried asking once already.

She began to walk toward the children and Heather, focused again on the young woman's prominent hairline. Something clicked and it dawned on her that she *had* once known a person with such a well-defined widow's peak.

Her memory flew back to one summer day — oh, so many years ago. She'd seen Lettie's beau, young and wiry, with his straw hat off, his wet hair slicked straight back as he and Lettie ran up the road together, holding hands. Lettie had explained later, when Adah had pressed her, that her *"ornery friend"* had purposely dunked his head into Mill Creek on a double dare. The very notion had made Adah dislike the fellow all the more.

But now, studying Heather's face, she was reminded again of Samuel . . . and that day. *And Samuel's twin, Sarah, as well!* Now it was all coming back to her. She moved closer to the happy group of children surrounding the girl, desperate to know the truth. If the pretty Englischer was to name a different city as her place of birth, then and only then could Adah finally dismiss her hunch as wishful thinking.

"Hullo, Heather," she called in her most cheerful voice.

Heather looked up. "Oh, Adah . . . I wasn't sure if I'd see you before I leave today." She set little Esther in Josiah Jr.'s lap, then stood up.

"Today?"

"My father needs my help to get our family home ready to sell."

Adah struggled to compose her rising emotions. "We'll miss seein' you round here."

"I'll miss all of you, too, Adah."

"Come visit anytime, all right?"

With a smile, Heather agreed. "Oh, and before you go, I should answer the question you asked yesterday."

Adah held her breath.

"I was born twenty-four years ago in Kidron," Heather said. "Kidron, Ohio."

Kidron! The town forever embroidered on her heart. Oh, goodness! She started to speak, but Heather had quickly excused herself and was already running over the lawn toward a car that was carefully navigating its way amidst the narrow maze of buggies parked on either side of the driveway.

Adah's lungs ached for air. Heather Nelson, a fancy Englischer, *had* to be Lettie's daughter! Oh, she was tempted to run after her, exclaim what she knew. But not yet.

I still don't have enough proof, do I? Her mind raced. She couldn't let Heather leave now, not when Adah was this close to knowing for sure . . . and for certain.

She turned to look across the spacious lawn and saw Heather waving, motioning her over to the car and the man who was getting out. "Come meet my father,"

Heather's youthful voice rang out.

Adah glanced at the children still clustered at play on the blanket and made her way toward Heather and a tall man with deep-set eyes.

Heather seemed eager to introduce her. "Dad, this is my friend, Adah Esh . . . you remember Grace? Well, Adah's her grandmother." Heather's blue eyes twinkled.

Eyes nearly as blue as Lettie's . . .

Heather introduced her father to Adah, saying his name, "Roan Nelson."

"It's nice to meet you, Mrs. Esh," he said, smiling as he took in the scene. School-age children were scampering about and young people were mingling near the stable as the church members continued to pour out of the house. Amongst them was Grace, who called to Heather.

"Oh, just a sec. Excuse me, Dad . . . and Adah." With that, Heather rushed off, leaving Adah standing there awkwardly with her father. The sky seemed to descend upon her. She looked down, not knowing what to do. And poor Mr. Nelson, he must've felt like a stalk of corn growing in a lettuce patch.

What if I'm wrong? thought Adah. *I can't announce my suspicions to this man without being certain. But* how *to be sure?*

Suddenly it occurred to her what to say — a way to know beyond a shadow of doubt. She'd never forgotten the name of the doctor who had assisted Minnie Keim — who'd lined up the Kidron attorney, too. She'd literally memorized the letter Minnie had written, the one she'd recently given to Lettie.

"You may think this a strange question, Mr. Nelson, and, well, I s'pose it is," she began, feeling peculiar speaking alone to an English man, of all people.

His cordial laugh helped set her at ease. He shrugged. "Anymore, my life is an open book. What would you like to know, Mrs. Esh?"

She briefly shared that her daughter had been searching for her first child. "A daughter given up for adoption twenty-four years ago. Oddly enough, the child shares the same birthday as Heather."

His eyebrows rose. "Is that right?"

Adah paused for a moment, then blazed ahead, not caring now how nosy she might sound. "Do you, by any chance, recall the name of the doctor who arranged Heather's adoption?" She wrung her hands.

He stared off into space for a moment, clearly pondering the question. "Not offhand . . . I'm sorry."

Adah's hopes were dashed. She didn't want to reveal the doctor's name — wanted it to come from Roan Nelson first. She turned to look back at the house, but Heather and Grace had gone up to the oak tree to sit with the children, and it looked as though even more little ones had gathered there to play hand-clapping games.

"Wait a minute," Roan said. "I remember thinking the name had something to do with an ax . . . or a hatchet. For several years, that's how I remembered it, actually." He shook his head. "This must sound ludicrous to you."

Her heart was in her throat. "No . . . no, that's quite all right. What do you remember?"

"What sort of doctor has a hatchet in his name?" His laughter carried on the wind, and Jakob, who was coming out of the house with the help of his cane, gave her a narrowed-eyed look. "Hatch . . . Hack . . ." said Mr. Nelson, muttering to himself, though Adah's hopes hung on each faltering syllable.

At last, Roan said it right out. "Hackman . . . I think the name was Dr. Hackman," he said as Lettie stepped out of the house with Judah by her side.

"The good doctor sometimes went by the

name Dr. Josh, as well," she said softly, more to herself than to him.

"Do you know him, Mrs. Esh?"

She nodded her head, but she had to turn away as the confirmation she'd sought sank in. "Ach, so sorry, Mr. Nelson . . . will ya please excuse me?"

Making her way up the sloping lawn, hurrying as best she could — away from Jakob, who looked befuddled and alone over on the walkway — Adah made a beeline toward Heather.

"Adah, you're crying," Heather said as Adah approached her.

"Will ya come with me, my lamb?" she asked. The endearing name was the very one she and Jakob had always called young Lettie . . . so long ago.

Heather rose to meet her and touched her arm. "What is it? What's happened?"

"Oh, my dear, dear girl, somethin' ever so wonderful." She brushed away her tears, wanting to see clearly Heather's face. "You told me yesterday that you'd like to someday meet your birth mother. Are you still serious 'bout that?"

Heather's face froze in astonishment. She looked over Adah's head at the crowd gathering around the yard and spilling up along the lane that led to the corncrib and woodshed. "Adah, why? Do you know someone in Ohio searching for me?" Her lips quivered.

"No, not in Ohio. *Here.* Your first mother is here."

Heather searched her face silently, tears welling up. "Does she know *I'm* here, too? Does she want to meet me?"

"Come along, child," Adah said, walking with her toward the back of the barn. "I have a surprising tale to tell you . . . about the very first person who ever held you . . . twenty-four years ago on a lovely April afternoon, in Kidron, Ohio. . . ."

Chapter Thirty-Seven

Depleted of energy but filled with peace, Lettie was thankful for Judah's presence as they waited to be called inside for the common meal of cold cuts. She was aware of a yellow warbler in a tree up the slope, calling a rapid and musical song to its mate: *sweet-sweet-sweet.* Over in the meadow, teeming clusters of pink cup-shaped mountain laurel flourished. The world struck her as incredibly beautiful.

Judah said not a word to her, but his being there was a comfort. Had he not come for her following her confession, she might still be kneeling on the floor. Such a brave gesture; she'd never known any man to assist a wayward wife in such a manner. Thinking of it even now made a lump in her throat. *I am so blessed to have my husband standing by me . . . despite our past problems.*

Preacher Josiah called to Judah. "Mind

helpin' fold down the benches?"

Judah glanced at her, as if to ask whether she'd be all right. She nodded her consent. "I'll be fine here."

He seemed reluctant to go, but headed off toward the house to do the preacher's bidding.

Still hearing the warbler's pretty song, Lettie wondered where her mother had disappeared to, not having seen her since clasping her hand after the amazing verdict.

Lettie began to walk toward the barnyard, thinking it might help to steady her legs. She felt as if she'd survived a fiery trial, and she raised her face to the sky and thanked God. This was the first day of her new life as a woman cleansed and made whole . . . and fully accepted. *I will be ever grateful to you, Lord.*

Enjoying the sunshine and the summer-like aroma in the noonday air, she noticed her mother coming around the side of the barn with Heather Nelson, the young woman who had made jam with them. "Gracie's friend," she whispered, wondering why Mamm was talking with her. "What on earth?"

She caught her mother's eye just then, and Mamm and Heather hurried toward her. Their eyes were puffy and red, and they both appeared to be somewhat dazed. None of what she saw made one whit of sense.

"Mamm?" she called.

Her mother reached for Heather's hand, of all things, and led her over the grassy area. "Oh, praise be . . . you're here, Lettie."

"Is everything all right?" she asked.

Mamm and Heather stood there, shoulders nearly touching. "Lettie," her mother began, the words coming quietly at first. "Years ago, I took something very dear from you — twenty-four years ago, in fact. And now . . . *now* . . . I want to . . ." Adah stopped, her chin quivering uncontrollably. "I want to give . . . her back."

Lettie started, her eyes searching Mamm's. "What are you saying?" She looked into Heather's face.

Mamm stepped back, folding her hands in front of her. "Heather wants to tell you all about it." Just that quick, her mother left them alone.

Twenty-four years ago, Mamm took away my firstborn. . . .

Lettie stared in disbelief at the pretty young woman. *Does Mamm mean to say Grace's friend is* my *daughter? How is that possible?*

"Lettie . . . I don't know what to say,"

Heather stumbled. "It never occurred to me that . . . I mean, I never thought —"

It was impossible not to stare at Heather's face — the way her hairline formed to top off a near perfect heart. She'd never paid much attention to the shape of the girl's face before now. And there was something about the set of her eyes.

Lettie trembled. *Samuel's hairline . . . his eyes. Why didn't I notice before?*

Yet, in spite of these resemblances, Lettie felt herself backing away, struggling to acknowledge what was implied here. After the years of yearning and her weeks of searching, had God actually brought her lost daughter into Lettie's own neighborhood?

Heather's voice quavered as she shared what she knew about the date and location of her birth — and the fact she had been born of a young Amishwoman. "Initially I thought my biological mother was from Ohio . . . but it turns out she was only visiting there. . . ."

Lettie soaked in every detail, unable to take her eyes off the girl. Their surroundings seemed to fall away as the two of them became oblivious to anything but each other. "It's so hard to believe," she whispered.

"I know what you mean — it's a little crazy, isn't it?" Heather broke into a wide smile. "But everything matches up, at least according to what I know . . . and what your mother says. Right down to the name of the doctor: Joshua Hackman."

Lettie's hand flew to her lips as tears sprang to her eyes. She swallowed hard.

"Lettie . . . I never thought I'd know you," Heather said, eyes bright. She frowned. "I didn't think —"

"How can this be?" Lettie whispered, shaking her head as the truth began to sink in.

"Solid proof is coming by mail," Heather said. "In a few weeks."

Lettie barely heard her. Without thinking, she opened her arms to her. "Oh, my darling girl, I'm so sorry."

Heather stepped into her embrace. "Please, don't be —"

"I missed you . . . all these years." Lettie was unable to maintain her composure. Then, lest anyone witness their tender exchange, she pulled away. Holding Heather at arm's length, she looked into her lovely face again.

Together, they fell into step, walking toward the meadow and momentarily abandoning all thoughts of eating or that

Heather's father was waiting to lead her home. Heather told Lettie about the letter she was expecting from Ohio.

"So, then, all that time I was off lookin' for you," Lettie said, "you must've been searchin' for me."

"Not the entire time." Heather explained how very sick she'd felt during her lowest point at the lodge. "That was the day I decided to contact the Ohio authorities about my adoption."

Lettie's heart dropped. "You'll be all right, won't you? You *will* get well?"

"I'm hopeful, but it may take some time. I'll know better after more tests."

They talked about Heather's loving adoptive parents and their interest in Amish country. "We came here together every summer for as long as I can remember. But I never knew until recently that I was of Amish heritage. It's one of the reasons my dad's building a house here."

Lettie was helpless to hold back her tears. "I've waited so long for this day." Deep sobs escaped her chest in waves as she reached again for Heather, closing her eyes as she cradled Heather's head against her own. "Oh, my dear daughter, I've found you at last."

The Lord giveth and taketh away; blessed

be the name of the Lord, she thought, thanking God for His great goodness and mercy.

Grace straightened her long white apron as she watched her mother and Heather make their way through Preacher Josiah's meadow. She stood near Becky while waiting for the common meal, quite puzzled by what she saw.

Mamma scarcely knows Heather. . . .

She glanced across the yard at Roan Nelson, who was still leaning against his car while talking with Adam and Joe. Unable to dismiss the fact that her mother and Heather seemed surprisingly familiar with each other, Grace shifted her Kapp, helpless to comprehend the scene. It was reassuring to have such a good friend as Becky by her side.

"Your Mamma looks mighty happy," Becky remarked quietly.

"I'd say she's joyful, knowin' she won't be shunned." Yet Grace wondered if that was the reason for her mother's blissful expression.

"Will you be at Singing tonight?" Becky asked. "No need being shy 'bout it, ya know."

Grace knew exactly what Becky meant. "I prob'ly won't go," she said, not trusting herself to attend the social gathering. Not after the revelations that had come forth during Mamma's very public confession. She couldn't help wondering if Adam and Mandy would attend the Singing tonight, either. The day had been jolting in so many ways.

"Well, I wouldn't miss it," Becky told her. "I'll even come and sit with you, if that'd make ya feel better."

"It's best I stay home, considering . . ."

Becky's eyes were suddenly downcast. "Whatever you think."

Priscilla Stahl strolled up to them, a warm smile on her face. "Grace . . . just wanted to say how glad I am your Mamma's a member in good standing yet again."

Well, *this* was unexpected. "Denki," she said, wondering what more Prissy might say.

"I admire her for owning up to her sins thataway. Sure says a lot 'bout her." With those words, Prissy looked prettier than Grace had ever noticed before.

"The kind of woman you might want for a mother-in-law, maybe?" Grace teased.

Prissy laughed outright. "I just might . . . but don't yous go tellin' anyone I said so." With that, Prissy waved and turned back toward the house.

"Ach, what do you make of that?" Grace

whispered to Becky.

"Mighty surprising, that one." Becky poked Grace's arm and put her hand over her mouth.

The sun peeked out from behind a cloud and shone down on their faces. "Would be a *gut* time for a sun hat, jah?" Grace looked toward the meadow again, bewildered that Heather and Mamma were still out there.

"Gracie," Mammi Adah called from near the barn, "come . . . I need to talk to you."

"I'll see ya later, Grace — at Singing, I hope." Becky left to collect her younger sisters.

Mammi Adah's face beamed as Grace asked about her mother and Heather.

Mammi patted her hand. "Gracie, you may have a hard time believin' what I have to tell ya. . . ." She explained ever so slowly the mighty convincing connections she had made between Heather and Mamma. "I didn't dare believe it at first, but the puzzle pieces all fit," she concluded. "Heather is surely your mother's first child!"

Goodness! Grace stared at her grandmother. "What?"

"Are you all right, dear?"

She shook her head. "I honestly don't . . . know." Grace contemplated the many hours she and Heather had shared on their trip —

their curious bond from the start: Heather's willingness to drive her to Ohio, her eagerness to help look for Mamma. The times they'd talked confidentially about their broken engagements, and Heather's online friend Jim. *Even Yonnie.*

As she considered these things, the astounding reality dawned on her, like a daybreak with clouds, diminishing one by one. "Oh, such strange yet happy news!"

Her grandmother's lips quivered and her head nodded — no longer could she speak.

"Prayer surely brought this gift to Mamma. To us all." Grace looked over to see her mother giving Heather a welcoming hug, and she felt she was witnessing something almost too personal. *Too dear.*

Her grandmother's eyes followed hers and gazed with love at Mamma and her newfound daughter. Then Mammi Adah turned and regarded Grace again. And there, before her, Grace saw a depth of affection in her grandmother's blue-gray eyes she'd never observed before. It nearly took her breath away.

Grace looked to the meadow once more, joy for her mother and for her English friend — *my sister!* — flowing through her. How long had she yearned for her mother to be this happy . . . to find a balm for the ache in her too-fragile heart?

The sweet smell of hay wafted out from the Smuckers' barn as Heather walked past the wide door and toward the farmhouse with Lettie Byler. She could hardly fathom the remarkable things that had transpired here in the past hour. Her mind reeled, but her heart believed — in every way — that Grace's mother was also her own.

She smiled now at Lettie, who walked with great confidence — this courageous woman who'd shared about having just offered a confession to the church membership, the reason for her weeping earlier. But Heather did not care to contemplate that, because what the Amish required of their members was their business. She was, on the other hand, incredibly touched by Lettie's contagious excitement at discovering their relationship on the very day of her repentance.

As they walked, Heather looked at the sky, knowing how pleased her adoptive mother would be to hear this if she were alive. *Do you know, Mom? Do you see how overjoyed I am?*

"Can ya stay over another day?" Lettie asked, eyes smiling.

She considered it, knowing she'd have to

fill her dad in quickly. "I'd like to . . . but I want to check with my dad first."

Lettie appeared to be holding her breath. "I'm sure there's more than a day's worth of catchin' up between us," she added.

Heather smiled. "Remember, I'll be back to visit my dad here, once his house and my thesis are finished," she said. "The first of many visits, I hope."

That seemed to satisfy Lettie. "Wonderful-*gut,* then."

Heather searched the backyard for any sign of Grace. *To think we're half sisters and didn't know it!*

"If you do stay longer, I hope you'll spend the night with us," Lettie said, her voice hopeful.

There was something about the way the woman's face exuded happiness that tugged at Heather's heart. "You know what? I'm going to stay — I just am. Thanks." She spotted her father walking toward the barn with Grace's brothers, well occupied for the moment.

Her eyes continued to scan the yard. It was Grace, after all, whom Heather most wanted to seek out in the throng of Plain young people now. *What will she think of all this?*

CHAPTER THIRTY-EIGHT

Grace never would have considered attending the Singing at Preacher Smucker's that night — not with Mamma's staggering confession still lingering in her mind. But Heather had come to stay and visit with Mamma, so Grace decided to go.

Mamma's heartfelt confession had shaken Grace . . . and the whole family. But there was a sense of good things ahead, especially with the news of Heather's belonging to them. Even Dat had offered Heather a warm handshake and a welcoming smile, treating her as if she were his *own* lost daughter when Mamma introduced them during the common meal.

Grace had hugged Heather after her long walk with Mamma and looked into her face, knowing why they'd felt such a companionable — no, *sisterly* — bond, right from the start. Oh, the *miracle* of God — *His ways are past finding out!*

Presently, Grace made space for Heather to spend the night in her room, offering two wooden pegs on the wall to hang her bathrobe and anything else. "Feel free to pick your side of the bed," Grace told Heather, still getting used to their kinship.

"I'll be fine wherever." Heather went to sit on the bed, seemingly cautious. Was she a little uneasy about sharing the room? Although when Mamma appeared in the doorway, Heather's face lit up bright as a full moon.

"I have something for you, Heather . . . if you'd like to have it." Mamma glanced at Grace and held out a book. "It's poetry — your biological father loved to read and write it. This book was a birthday present from him to me . . . the year you were born."

"Really?" Heather's mouth dropped open and she rose. "You saved it all this time . . . for me?"

Mamma fell silent for a moment; then she handed the book to Heather. "You'll see the inscription inside."

Carefully, Heather opened the book of poems, slowly turning the pages as if they were somehow priceless. "My father liked poetry?" Heather drew Mamma inside the room, and they sat together on the edge of the bed.

Grace moved toward the doorway. "I'll be goin' now, Mamma. Adam's takin' Mandy and me to the Singing," she said.

"You won't be too late, will ya?" Mamma looked up.

"No need to fret," she replied, fairly certain she'd return as soon as the actual singing portion of the evening was over. Then, to Heather, she waved. "Welcome to our family," she said. "I'm so glad to have a big sister."

Getting up, Heather gave her a hug. "I can't wait to get acquainted with my entire extended family, too."

"That could take some doin'!" Grace looked at Mamma, whose eyes brimmed with joyful tears.

"Well, I'm up for it, however long it takes." Heather gave a quick laugh. "Ain't so?"

At this, Mamma's lips spread into a smile. And Grace headed downstairs, her heart torn between Heather — here with Mamma — and seeing Yonnie.

Grace slipped into Preacher Smucker's big barn unnoticed and went to stand next to the bales of hay. Not seeing Becky yet, she almost wished she'd stayed put at home with her newfound sister.

Across the haymow, Yonnie was talking

with several other young men, all of them still wearing their Sunday best — white shirt-sleeves rolled up to the elbows, black trousers, suspenders, and their best straw hats. If she hadn't known precisely who was who amongst them, she might've thought they all looked alike in the dim light of the few lanterns scattered around.

True to her promise, Becky hurried to her side, and they went to sit together on the girls' side of the long table. Soon the singing began, nearly the same as always, except the songs were a bit faster tonight, with some more "progressive." *Songs Yonnie's church youth might've sung in Indiana.*

She noticed her older brother's position directly across the table from Priscilla Stahl, like always. But tonight, Grace observed a particular fondness between Adam and Prissy. *Does he know what Prissy thinks of Mamma now?*

Much later, when the songs were done, Grace noticed Henry Stahl amble over to Yonnie, and the two of them talked head to head, Henry's straw hat hiding their faces.

She stiffened as she watched them across the haymow. *What's Henry telling him?* She could only imagine, given that both fellows and their families had been in attendance at the members' meeting today.

But the vote was unanimous. . . .

Sighing, she turned to leave, trudging down the grassy barn ramp to the pasture. The moon was scarcely visible now. *Close to the dark side of the month,* she thought. Her friendship with Yonnie was finished — how could it not be? And what about Henry? What concern was it of *his* that Mamma had committed such sin when she was young?

Drawing a long breath, Grace felt nearly too frail to shield herself against the possible ongoing talk.

She walked clear out to the perimeter of Preacher Josiah's field. The sky had turned completely dark. For a moment, she wished she'd brought along a flashlight.

"Lord, you see me," she whispered. "You see Mamma, too . . . and Heather. Thank you for their precious reunion. May it be blessed with understanding and tender mercy." She still could hardly grasp her family's new reality.

In the distance, near the barn, she saw a glimmer of light dance back and forth — like a lantern swinging gently. Following the light, she walked in a straight line toward it, keeping her eyes on the mysterious golden glow.

Soon, she realized someone was coming

this way, though he or she couldn't possibly see very far in the pitch-blackness. She wondered if it might be Adam, hoping to find her, worried as he sometimes was.

Now she was within several yards of the light and the person carrying it. Goodness, but she recognized it was Yonnie who carried the lantern. *Looking for me?*

Sensing what was surely ahead, she stiffened. Then she heard Yonnie's voice, pleasant as always. "Gracie . . . what're you doin' out here alone?"

"Just walkin'."

"Could ya use some light, maybe?" He paused for a moment, then fell into step with her. "Some company, too?"

She laughed a little. He sounded so jovial, but that was Yonnie.

"Your mother's a mighty brave woman," he said.

She agreed.

"I wasn't surprised she was voted back in without a shunning," he admitted.

A little startled at that, she replied, "Truth be told, I wasn't sure what would happen."

"The People here aren't unreasonable," he said. "A mighty nice thing." He added that he had been glad to see her father go to the front to help her mother up. "Somethin' my own Daed might've done."

His words moved her deeply. "Denki . . . for that."

He stopped walking and faced her, the golden circle from his lantern surrounding them. "You know, I wasn't sure if I should ask you . . . well, twice." His subdued laughter carried across the field. "But, Gracie, I'd love to court ya . . . if you'll have me."

Her heart, which had sunk earlier, was beating fine again as her fear began to subside. Yet it was impossible not to recall Henry going out of his way to talk with Yonnie back in the barn.

Still, Yonnie was asking her to be his girl — again!

She pondered his question. They would be a couple, and — fond as she was of him — wouldn't that be a wonderful-*gut* thing?

As if sensing her uncertainty, he said, "If you're wonderin' . . . Henry says you were right to break things off with him. He holds no ill will toward you, Gracie."

She wanted to cry right there. Her former beau had essentially given his blessing.

Yonnie reached for her hand. "I'm ready to win your heart."

Tears coursed down her face as Grace looked into his smiling eyes and laced her fingers through his. “Oh, Yonnie . . . you already have.”

Prologue

The September afternoon was not only brisk in temperature but golden in color, and I was missing Heather. Taking a short break from making apple dumplings and apple pies — with my favorite herbal ingredient, rosemary — I sat down at the kitchen table to write her a letter. The enticing smells of cinnamon and brown sugar lingered in the kitchen as I shared my dearest secret with my new sister.

In the months since we learned the truth, Mamma and I've been blessed to receive oodles of letters from Heather, as well. She sounds relieved to be finishing up her master's thesis soon, all the while preparing the Virginia house to sell . . . having left Bird-in-Hand the Tuesday after Mamma's confession. That house was just recently put up for sale, since Heather's most recent blood tests were quite encouraging. *Thank the dear Lord!*

Earlier, Heather had told me she'd received a promising report on her *first* round of blood work, six weeks after leaving the Wellness Lodge. Her original doctor is still rather guarded, if not skeptical. *Though I hope to make him a believer in naturopathy yet,* Heather wrote. Time will determine that, along with her long-term prognosis. She'll have follow-up appointments with Dr. Marshall here, once Heather returns in November, the beginning of Amish wedding season.

As for the much-awaited letters from the adoption registry, both Mamma and Heather received word back from Ohio within just a short time. Each made a copy of her letter to send the other, to document what they already knew. Not a soul could ever begin to persuade our mother that finding Heather in such a unique way was anything but our heavenly Father's doing. And, too, finding Mamma has brought such peace to Heather! Truly, she's a delightful addition to our entire family. I expect Samuel Graber will be just as pleased to welcome her into *his* family come Christmas, when Heather hopes to contact him. I daresay Heather is quite courageous!

Hurrying out to the mailbox now, I breathed in the pungent scent of woodsmoke and slipped my special letter inside. I really wish I could see Heather's face when she receives it, because it won't be too much longer until Yonnie and I will be published, following the second Preaching service in November. Reserved as he is, Dat will stand before the membership after the final prayer and invite everyone who is courting age and older to my parents' house on Tuesday, November twenty-fifth. Ach, but Dat and Mamma will be so pleased when they know for certain that Yonnie and I are, indeed, a match. To think I'll be the bride of an assistant buggy-maker — almost laughable, since Yonnie was always eager to go on foot nearly everywhere!

Then, just two days after our wedding, my new husband and I — and my family, including Dawdi Jakob and Mammi Adah — will visit with Heather and her father again. She and Jim "Wannalive" Lang are coming to Roan Nelson's new house for Thanksgiving. A mighty healthy feast is planned, with many locally grown vegetables and one exceptionally large, free-range organic turkey. Even Dr. LaVyrle Marshall is invited — perhaps to help with the meal preparations. Seems she and Heather's father have been seeing each other quite a lot lately, what Heather calls a most interesting "side effect" of her treatment here.

Raising the wooden flag on the mailbox, I glanced up the road, toward the phone shanty, wanting to sometime give Heather a call — *surprise her.* But today there were more pies to bake for the roadside stand. Oh, the amount of fruit preserves we've sold, too, with wonderful-*gut* herbs mixed in — peaches with thyme and stewed tomatoes with basil. We've also sold lots of pumpkins cut straight from the vine, thanks to Adam's hauling the largest ones to the stand in Dat's old wooden wheelbarrow. A big help!

I turned toward the house, still soaking up God's vivid handiwork — the yellow, orange, and crimson trees that marked the flow of Mill Creek. The sugar maples were altogether fiery red, alive with color.

Mamma spotted me coming and waved as I walked past the kitchen window. She's more settled than I've ever known her. *Forgiven by God and the People,* Dat said months ago.

I'd say she's forgiven herself, too.

Before Heather left in June, Mamma gathered up the remaining poetry books from Samuel Graber and gave them to Heather, who was mighty glad for them. *"This is all I have of my birth father,"* she said, even though Mammi Adah insisted she also has some of his facial features. I have a hunch Samuel's twin sister, Sarah, just might come to Bird-in-Hand once she learns of Heather's identity. And she will, too. You just can't keep something like that a secret — once it's known.

"We're comin' full circle, ain't?" Mamma said to me with a knowing smile not long ago.

"Like the tide." I thought back to my day trip to Cape May, New Jersey, in early August. Yonnie lined up Martin Puckett to drive us, and surely it was the best surprise of my life . . . other than stumbling accidentally into my half sister over at Eli's Natural Foods last spring!

Yonnie and I searched for more of those Cape May diamonds, but we didn't find a single one that bright and happy afternoon. We *did* walk for hours along the shoreline, though, amidst the shrieks of seabirds and the roar of waves, breathing the salty air and eating more than our share of cotton candy before returning home that night. It was there we held hands and promised to share our hearts for always — nary a secret! And we pledged our dearest love . . . not just to each other, but to our gracious Lord. For all the days of our lives.

ACKNOWLEDGMENTS

These are the incredible people God has handpicked to make my writing world go round, and for whom I am particularly grateful:

Hank and Ruth Hershberger, who helped with details regarding Lettie's kneeling confession.

The good folk at the Lancaster Mennonite Historical Society, who specialize in historical accuracy and are most helpful.

Barbara Birch, my dear sister, who generously shared her journal account of her naturopathic battle plan for fighting her cancer, nearly six years ago.

David Lewis, my husband and first editor, who lives and breathes fiction just as I do. And who makes very green, very healthy breakfast drinks for me!

My industrious and cheerful consultants, who double- and triple-check Amish-related facts and review and proofread entire manuscripts.

My friends and colleagues at Bethany House Publishers — Jim and Ann Parrish, who continue to believe in my work and cheer me on with their prayers. Dave Horton, who schedules my writing deadlines with an eye for practicality and helps develop my best book ideas. And Steve Oates, who has a remarkable way of getting my books into the hands of multitudes of readers and who plans the fastest-paced book tours known to man . . . or woman.

Julie Klassen and Rochelle Glöege, my incredible editors, whose ingenious creativity and expert edits advance my writing, making the journey truly joyful and fun. Thanks also to Helen Motter, my wonderful copy editor.

Debra Larsen, Jim Hart, and Noelle Buss, my publicists, whose marketing and promotional expertise are second to none.

Paul Higdon and Dan Thornberg, whose imaginative way with cover design and illustration prompts me to send thank-you emails in an enormous font when I first lay eyes on mock-ups. You guys keep me smiling-happy!

Virginia Campbell, for the delightful piecrust-making anecdote, straight from the "life pages" of her own childhood.

Mary Jane Hoober, for superb and prompt research about Indiana Amish culture.

Judith Lovold, who kindly shared information on ailing old mares, such as dear Willow.

Martha Nelson, whose wise and encouraging words lift my spirits when I'm on deadline . . . and before and afterward, too.

Lee and Carol Birch, whose expert knowledge of lambing is greatly appreciated.

Susan Pelham, who quite humorously combined the words *FaceTube* and said I could use it in this book.

Mona Paulson, for specific help with all things Deitsch!

My faithful partners in prayer, whose time spent before the throne of grace helps keep my eyes ever focused on heaven's calling. To God be the glory!

ABOUT THE AUTHOR

Beverly Lewis, born in the heart of Pennsylvania Dutch country, is *The New York Times* bestselling author of more than eighty books. Her stories have been published in ten languages worldwide. A keen interest in her mother's Plain heritage has inspired Beverly to write many Amish-related novels, beginning with *The Shunning,* which has sold more than one million copies. *The Brethren* was honored with a 2007 Christy Award.

Beverly lives with her husband, David, in Colorado.

The employees of Thorndike Press hope you have enjoyed this Large Print book. All our Thorndike, Wheeler, and Kennebec Large Print titles are designed for easy reading, and all our books are made to last. Other Thorndike Press Large Print books are available at your library, through selected bookstores, or directly from us.

For information about titles, please call:
(800) 223-1244

or visit our Web site at:
http://gale.cengage.com/thorndike

To share your comments, please write:
Publisher
Thorndike Press
295 Kennedy Memorial Drive
Waterville, ME 04901